I0769060

Fading Blossoms

Anastasiya Serada

Trigger Warning

This book contains material that may be disturbing or triggering to some readers.

Content includes:

- Physical violence and combat
- Blood, injury and death
- Strong language
- Sexually explicit scenes
- Emotional and psychological trauma

Reader discretion is strongly advised. This book is intended for mature audiences.

For the wicked flowers

Chapter One

VESNA.

Vesna strolled toward the forest, listening with satisfaction to the crunch of snow beneath her boots. The dawn unfolded slowly, and golden rays of sun flooded the horizon, bathing the sleepy forest in hues of gentle light. The trees swayed in the gust of chilly wind, as if awakening from a profound sleep. But the air hung flavorless—not a single flower remained on Earth, leaving the world shrouded in grey.

Even though it was early May, snow still covered the ground. The natural order of the world had shifted after flowers disappeared from the Earth. Still, Vesna caught the faintest scent of awakening nature in the crisp air— or at least, what remained of it. She let down her long, creamy pink hair, and the sweet scent of magnolia filled the air with life and magic.

Centuries ago, when the Divine Blooms had covered the earth, the air had been delicately woven with the fragrances of myriad flowers. The Divine Blooms received worship as gods, and they had answered the prayers of the people. They prayed to the divine orchid for money and luck, to the divine rose for love and passion, to the divine sunflower for strength, happiness, and wealth. People with divine magic used to be born even more often than people without. But one day, the Divine Blooms had simply disappeared, and prayers went unanswered. The flowers that used to cover the earth withered, and soon there was not a single petal left on Earth. Nature became grey, mourning her lost beauty.

Time passed, and humanity developed in its own way without magic. The Divine Blooms became just a rare whisper in the night prayers of ordinary people.

Even though trees and flowers had lost their ability to bloom a long time ago, after the Divine Blooms abandoned humanity, still, from time to time, a child would be born with the magic of the divine flowers. It was the only reminder that magical flowers had once adorned the Earth. Now, only green leaves or completely bare trees remained. Nature had lost its captivating touch.

With the Divine Blooms gone, magic was slowly vanishing forever. *It's time for the Divine Blooms to finally answer my prayers,* Vesna thought, and a shiver of painful excitement ran down her spine. She didn't know what the coming blooming season would bring her, but she secretly hoped that it would bring change. Although her aunt Nina wanted her to stay here and hide forever, Vesna's heart and her magic were seething with the desire for revenge. It wasn't just desire; it was a need. Vesna was thirsty for it, and all these years, she had patiently waited for her time to fully bloom and tap into the true power of her magic: hexes and curses.

Aunt Nina thought her obsession with revenge was unhealthy. She was right, but Vesna couldn't help it. Losing her mother had changed something in her... Now and then, thoughts of normal life tried to creep in, but she always pushed them away. She never let herself wonder what came after revenge. It was as if her very existence hinged on completing this one task.

Exhaling another sigh, Vesna continued her search for herbs that might help with stress. Her aunt was getting more and more paranoid as Vesna's birthday approached. Vesna would turn twenty-five years old, the age of full bloom for people who still held the magic of the Divine Blooms. And Vesna didn't have just any magic—although nowadays, having the magic of any flower was dangerous. She held the ancient magic of the divine magnolia, the very first flower to appear on Earth —the same magic that had taken her mother's life. Vesna took a deep breath, trying not to think about the past. Sadness and nostalgia wouldn't help her in getting revenge.

She wandered through the forest, getting into the most impassable places, where even the sun's rays barely reached, but still, she couldn't find any herbs. The magic was indeed disappearing, taking with it not only the beauty and power of nature, but their food and medicinal remedies too.

Her birthday was a little less than two months away, but she still didn't have a clear plan for her revenge. So, she prayed several times a day, begging the Divine Blooms to show her the way.

She sat on a tree stump, awakening her magic. She had trained for years, practicing calling her pollen in seconds. Her mother had left a book of spells, and Vesna not only knew them by heart, but had practiced them in the deep forest for years until it became as easy as breathing.

Every cell of her skin seemed to move, releasing fairy dust. A cloud of her magical pollen covered her slender body and instantly illuminated the bleak reality. She prayed silently to the Divine Blooms to give her a chance to take revenge. Still sitting, she looked up, imagining what this forest would look like if there were still flowers in the world. She could clearly see the flowering trees in her mind's eye, petals scattered on the ground like a beautiful canvas, the enchanting scent of magical pollen in the air. It was like a fairy tale… Unfortunately, fairy tales only existed in books.

The crackling of branches caught her attention, and her head shot toward the noise. Her aunt stood beside her. Nina's gaze was heavy with indignation.

"Nina," Vesna muttered, quickly calling her magic away and waving her hands to get rid of the sweet fragrance of magnolia that filled the tasteless air.

"Stop waving your hands. I could smell magnolia as soon as I entered the forest," her aunt scolded.

"It's not like there's anyone in this forsaken place anyway," Vesna said, tamping down the guilt she felt. "I'm tired of hiding. The only way we'll be safe is if I go after Boris myself."

Nina sighed heavily. "You don't know what you're talking about."

"Of course I don't, because you barely tell me anything about my mother!" Vesna snapped and stood up abruptly, hurrying away into the dense forest. She knew her aunt feared that she would suffer the same fate as her mother, but Vesna had no intention of hiding in these woods forever. She wanted revenge—to make sure the man who had killed her mother got what he deserved.

"Vesna! I'm just trying to protect you! The rafflesia would kill you if they knew you existed!" her aunt shouted after her, but Vesna just quickened her pace, disappearing between the trees.

She walked aimlessly, thinking about the rafflesia. They were the reason her mother was dead. The rafflesia-born were parasites, a threat to all magic. When the Divine Blooms had still covered the earth, the giant reddish-brown rafflesia flower attached itself to them, blooming with a stench of rotten flesh and draining their magic away. This flower and people who wielded its magic had no magic of their own; they stole it from others to survive. Eventually, they had caused the Divine Blooms to lock themselves away in a sacred area that the magical people called the Veiled Wilds.

Vesna shook her head, trying to come back from these useless thoughts. She shifted her gaze up; the gloomy sun was already high above the horizon. She had to go back. Even though she was cut off from the real world in this isolated place, she needed to be ready when the time for her revenge came. So, she read every day, devouring every book Nina could find on flowers and their magic, hoping that one day it would prove useful.

To her surprise, the door was open, and Vesna tensed; no one knew where they lived. She was certain that Nina had gone to work after finding her. Her aunt worked as a librarian in the nearest village. Vesna had never been there; it was too dangerous. Everyone would know immediately that she had magic. Her eyes and hair were the color of magnolia petals, creamy pink, as if the divine magnolia herself had kissed and blessed her, and her fragrance was strong, even overpowering.

She entered the house, trying not to make a sound. If someone was here, she would just hide outside. She lurked behind the door, trying to hear something.

"But Nina, it was a message from the Divine Blooms themselves," a woman's voice pleaded. "They showed me in a dream where you live, so I could deliver the message."

"She won't repeat her mother's fate," Nina snapped. "To hell with the Divine Blooms. They abandoned us, cowardly locking themselves away in the Veiled Wilds."

"They had no choice!" the woman insisted. Her voice was youthful, bright, but calm at the same time. Vesna had the feeling that she had heard it before.

"I don't trust flowers that have chosen themselves and not the people who worshiped them," Nina replied in a steely voice. "I hid Vesna for a reason, and she's not going anywhere. We don't need another night of vanished petals."

Vesna stiffened at the mention of the night the rafflesia had massacred people with magic, draining them dry, only to find Vesna's mother… *"The sacred one"* —that was what everyone called her mother. Boris, the leader of the rafflesia, had drained every drop of her mother's magic. That was the night everything had changed.

Maybe my prayers have been answered, Vesna dared to hope. Taking a fortifying breath, she opened the door and walked in to see a beautiful young woman with short golden hair and a face covered with freckles standing in the middle of their tiny room. She looked like the sun itself.

"Vesna!" The woman's face lit up, and she ran up and hugged Vesna tightly.

Vesna tensed in surprise, but didn't pull away. The woman's hair brushed her face lightly, and Vesna caught a hint of her scent, but it wasn't floral; the woman didn't have magic. She smelled of some kind of herb.

Moving away a little, Vesna said, "Do I know you?"

"You don't remember me?" The woman's grey eyes widened slightly in disappointment. "I'm Anna. We were inseparable when we were kids. I lived with my parents right next to you and your mother."

Vesna looked at Anna again, trying to remember her. The memories of her childhood in the city were vague. Too much time had passed. "Sorry, I don't."

"You called me Goldie, because of my hair and my marigold magic," Anna said with a smile, as if she were seeing the past before her eyes.

Vesna suddenly remembered the citrus scent, earthy and slightly sweet, but Anna no longer carried that scent. Vesna gasped, looking at Anna in horror. "They drained your magic?!" she said in shock, fear shooting through her body at the thought.

"No, I camouflaged it with a potion," Anna replied casually, gesturing to her face. "My golden eyes too."

Vesna's brow creased as she looked Anna over. "Your hair looks exactly like your flower, though," she said doubtfully.

"Hair isn't a problem." Anna smirked. "It's in fashion nowadays for humans to have colorful hair. They still remember the Divine Blooms."

"It's time for you to leave," Nina said flatly.

Vesna noticed Anna's body tensing. "But I've just arrived!" she pleaded, her voice trembling slightly. "And let me tell you, driving a car is not a simple task! I'm sure I have bruises on my butt. I prefer when they appear for a completely different reason," she said with a grin.

"Spare us the intimate details," Nina snorted.

Vesna giggled. Anna seemed fun to be around, and she hadn't had a friend in a long time.

"I need to talk to Vesna," Anna stated firmly.

"About what?" Vesna asked, excitement and fear taking over her like a thunderstorm over a flowering meadow.

Her enthusiasm didn't go unnoticed, because Nina sighed heavily, lowering her gaze. "Fine. Let's sit down, since you've come all this way," she grumbled.

Vesna sat in front of Anna, her gaze roaming over her face, trying to find some sign that Anna had magic, but it was impossible to notice. Her eyes, her scent, everything seemed normal. "What about your tattoo?" Vesna asked suddenly. When people with flower magic turned twenty-five and fully bloomed for the first time, a tattoo of their magical flower would appear on their face, showing the world that the magic of this Divine Bloom blessed them.

"Potion," Anna said playfully. "Marigold is bright and noticeable; the magnolia tattoo will be easier to hide."

"She doesn't see anyone; there will be no need to hide anything!" Nina said quickly.

"You can't decide for me!" Vesna snapped, immediately regretting her harsh tone.

Nina just bit her lip, saying nothing. It wasn't their first fight. Sometimes Vesna was too blunt with her aunt, who just wanted to protect her. But Vesna was always clear about her goal, and she couldn't have anyone, not even Nina, change her mind.

"Well, if Vesna stays here after what I tell her, I'll leave you alone," Anna said, looking from Nina to Vesna earnestly.

The time for revenge to bloom has finally arrived, Vesna told herself excitedly, breath catching in her chest. "Please tell me."

"My marigold magic gives me the power of prophetic dreams," Anna said. "But I can't force dreams. The divine marigold must send them to me. I can try calling them through prayer, but there's no guarantee it will work. Sometimes I feel like the divine marigold doesn't even hear me behind the doors of the Veiled Wilds." She took a deep breath, her eyes glistening slightly. "Anyway, a few nights ago, I had a dream! It was as clear and vivid as reality itself. It was truly magical!"

Vesna frowned, wondering what Anna was getting at. "Was it about me?"

"Yes, it was about you." Anna cleared her throat. "We all know the prophecy…"

Vesna became rigid. The prophecy had killed her mother. Ever since the Divine Blooms disappeared, no one had been able to find the Veiled Wilds—no one except the sacred one. According to the prophecy, a woman born in winter, blessed with the divine magic of the magnolia, could find the fern flower. Once the flower was picked, the gates to the Veiled Wilds would appear before it.

"It's just a stupid prophecy! And the fern flower is just a myth! Nadia never found it!" Nina fired off, nervously standing up and pacing from one corner of the room to another.

Anna bit her lip, glancing at Nina. She hesitated slightly before saying, "My grandmother received the original prophecy in a dream, so it must be true. Her magic was strong."

"Forgive me if I doubt the credibility of the divine marigold, but all the prophecy did was provoke an attack by the rafflesia, which eventually led to the night of the vanished petals." Nina's voice wavered.

Vesna knew from her aunt that the rafflesia were slowly dying without the ability to parasitize the Divine Blooms. The rafflesia drained people with magic, but it wasn't enough. It was nothing compared to the magic the Divine Blooms had held. The parasite needed to get inside the Veiled Wilds. And according to the prophecy, the sacred one was the key. But when Boris had captured Vesna's mother, Nadia couldn't find the fern flower, or maybe she just chose death—no one knew for sure—so Boris just drained her, gaining power so strong that it was rumored that he no longer aged.

"I understand, but let me finish," Anna pleaded. "I received the second part of the prophecy in my dream."

Vesna rolled her eyes in frustration. "Are you going to get to the point?" Anna talked a lot, but so far, she had said nothing important.

"Sorry, I get carried away sometimes." Anna shrugged. "Inside Boris's building, I saw a book woven from magnolia petals that only the sacred one can open. It holds the secret to the location of the Veiled Wilds. According to my dream, it's time for the sacred one to open the Veiled Wilds, helping the Divine Blooms to destroy the parasites!" Anna nearly shouted, practically jumping in her seat with excitement.

"The sacred one?" Vesna whispered. "But my mother is dead…"

"My dream wasn't about your mother," Anna whispered back, locking eyes with her. "It was about you."

"Nonsense!" Nina snapped, her voice shaky. "The sacred one is supposed to be born in winter, like Nadia. Vesna was born in June!"

Vesna was silent. Of course it was nonsense, but maybe Anna was her way to get into the city unnoticed.

And once Vesna turned twenty-five, she could finally go to Boris and curse him to death.

"How am I supposed to help the Divine Blooms destroy the rafflesia? And why now?" Vesna asked, voice barely audible, meeting her aunt's gaze.

Nina's face turned pale, and she was barely breathing. Vesna hated doing this to her, but she had to avenge her mother.

Anna nervously shifted from side to side in her chair, drawing Vesna's attention again. "Well, that part wasn't clear. I mean, it was … but then I forgot it," she said, lowering her eyes. "Vivid dreams are hard to remember, even for me. But I'm sure I'll remember the rest soon. It can't be a coincidence that I had this dream right before your twenty-fifth birthday, just when you'll be blossoming the strongest in your life!"

It was true; this flowering season would be the brightest in Vesna's magical life. Plus, according to books, the fern flower bloomed on the night of Ivan Kupala, a special magical night celebrated yearly for centuries. It was a night when the veil between reality and magic thinned, offering people a rare chance to find the mythical fern flower that could grant extraordinary power or even perform miracles. The night fell in late June, coinciding with the blooming season of those who wielded magnolia magic, which now lasted all summer under the new order of nature. Before, magnolias used to bloom from early spring until the first whispers of autumn.

"You will blossom on the night of Ivan Kupala. If your heart is pure, you'll be able to find the fern flower … and open the gates of the Veiled Wilds," Anna said hesitantly, probably realizing how unrealistic it all sounded.

Vesna's intentions were far from pure, and a needle of guilt prickled her heart as she looked into Anna's hopeful eyes. Anna was just a naïve believer clinging to the hope that her gods would return. And Vesna was going to use that hope to get to Boris.

"Sure," Nina muttered under her breath, clearly irritated. "And then she'll somehow have to help destroy the rafflesia too. We all know the Divine Blooms can't interfere in the human world; they can only answer our prayers. They will be useless, as always."

"I know it's not ideal, but we can't keep living like this," Anna said. "We owe this to our parents, to the Divine Blooms, who blessed us with magic. Besides, I have this feeling that I forgot something important. Like it must be done, no matter what!" She closed her eyes, clearly struggling to recall the details of her dream.

"The Divine Blooms don't care about you anymore," Nina whispered. "No one cares about magical people."

"Mother cared," Vesna muttered.

She didn't believe in some new prophecy that Anna could even barely remember. But she was willing to play along if it got her closer to Boris. "And are you sure you can make me look normal?" Vesna asked, noticing Nina paling immediately at her words.

"I'm sure," Anna said with enthusiasm in her sunny voice. "I know an herbalist who's a master of potions."

"Vesna," Nina said, worry in her non-magical grey eyes.

Vesna knew that Nina's heart was probably shattering into a million pieces right now; she'd raised and loved Vesna as her own daughter. But Vesna had always known she'd have to leave her aunt behind, perhaps forever, if she wanted to get her revenge.

Vesna bit her lip, trying to hide the tears that suddenly took over. *Stay strong, Vesna,* she scolded herself. *You can't survive in a fading reality with a gentle heart.*

Her aunt came closer and tightly hugged Vesna. "Don't let anyone wither your blossoms," she whispered.

"I won't," Vesna whispered back, no longer able to hold back the tears.

They just stood there in each other's arms for a while. Vesna let all her fear and pain flow out through her tears. She knew she might die; Boris was said to be powerful and dangerous.

When Vesna's sobs had finally begun to fade, Nina took a deep breath and glanced at Anna. "So, Anna, what's your plan?" she asked, gently wiping the tears from Vesna's face.

Vesna looked up at Nina with a gentle smile, then pulled her into a tighter hug. She was grateful to her aunt for accepting her decision, for not making it even harder.

Anna's voice was laced with hope when she spoke, as if infused with the magic of the divine marigold itself. "We must get inside Boris's building and find the ancient book that I saw in my dream," Anna detailed as Vesna frowned. It sounded dangerous, but so far, this plan worked in her favor. She needed to get inside Boris's building anyway … to kill him. "To do that, we need to get close to the rafflesia somehow. Fortunately, I work in a club where some people who work for Boris love to hang out. I can get you a job there. If we befriend at least one of them, maybe we can use him to get into Boris's building."

"You want me to work in a night club?" Vesna raised an eyebrow. She'd never done anything but live in the woods with Nina. Her days consisted of reading and wandering the forest. How was she supposed to go from that to working in a club?

"We can discuss the details later," Anna said with a nervous smile, noticing Nina's disapproving look.

"Fine, then I need to pack quickly," Vesna thought out loud. She didn't want to show her fear to Nina; her aunt was already worrying enough. She hugged her again, breathing in her scent deeply. She wished to memorize it forever, in case this really was goodbye.

VESNA PACKED her things under Anna's watchful eye. It turned out that none of Vesna's dresses were good enough for the city, much less for working at the club.

"Once we're done with the herbalist, we need to go shopping," Anna said, taking out almost all the dresses from the bag Vesna had packed. "My boss has a special dress code for female employees."

"Naked?" Vesna drawled sarcastically.

"No." Anna laughed. "But it's still a club, and you must look the part. Plus, the guys who work for Boris have their type too."

Vesna shrugged. She had obviously never known a man while she lived with Nina. Despite her determination, she admitted to herself that she was scared to return to the city that had taken her mother, scared to face Boris, and scared to even face people, for that matter. But her need for revenge was stronger than any fear. *I would rather die trying than stay here,* she decided.

Anna sat on Vesna's bed, studying the room. "What's with all these paintings?" she asked, looking at the walls.

"My mother loved to paint," Vesna told her. She

walked over to the wall and picked up a painting of the divine magnolia—a majestic ancient tree, adorned with delicate creamy-pink blossoms, that had gifted magic to the world for the very first time.

"Are you going to bring them all?" Anna asked with a hint of panic. "My place is tiny."

"No, just this one," Vesna said. It was a perfect painting to bring with her; it reminded her of what she was trying to accomplish.

"What was your mother like?" Anna asked, getting comfortable on the bed.

"I don't remember her much. I was only five years old when Nina took me away," Vesna sighed. "And my aunt refuses to talk about my mother."

"Why?" Anna blurted out, surprised.

Vesna just shrugged. She had no idea why Nina stayed silent whenever Vesna mentioned Nadia, but she didn't think it was fair to her at all. And it especially wasn't fair to her mother, whose legacy should have been honored and not forgotten.

Chapter Two

VESNA.

"You must be feeling like a flower that got picked and carried away from its meadow," Anna said softly, getting inside the car.

"This place has never been my home. My mother was my home, and she's gone forever," Vesna muttered, looking at Nina, who stood on the steps of the old house, tears streaming down her face. Nina tried to force a smile, waving to her until the car disappeared completely into the forest.

Vesna rolled down the window and sat looking at the passing trees, trying to fight the sudden sadness that had gripped her heart. After all, she liked this place. She knew every tree, every forest path, every clearing. *This wasn't your home,* she mused, saying goodbye to this place and to her old self.

Her gaze quickly shifted to Anna as the car hit some tree stump. Anna clearly wasn't a skillful driver, or maybe she just wasn't used to driving in the forest. "Are we safe?" Vesna asked nervously.

"Absolutely," Anna assured her. "I don't really need a car in the city, so this is my first time driving, but I learn quickly when it's…" She didn't finish the sentence, because they hit something else, and the car bounced. "But put this thing on, just in case." She pointed to the seat belt.

"I know what a seat belt is," Vesna muttered.

"Good to know." Anna smiled softly. She cleared her throat and turned to face Vesna, a touch of warmth in her eyes. "You must have been through a lot."

"Please watch the road!" Vesna screamed in panic as the car drove straight toward a huge tree. She didn't want to talk about her life and her feelings, and she certainly didn't want to die in a car accident. "Who even gave you a car?"

"My boss, Alex. He has the most alluring magic of the divine rose," Anna said, smiling to herself. "I told him I was going to scout for a new talent for the club," she reported, clearly pleased with herself. "By the way, what's your talent?"

"My sacred magic isn't very useful in a fight right now; it can only enhance other magic. But after I finally fully blossom, I'll be able to cast and break curses and hexes." Vesna paused. "And I can keep a lover faithful."

"The last one might come in handy." Anna grinned. "But I mean your human talent. If we're gonna get you a job, you need to be able to do something."

"I see…" Vesna muttered. She only had her magic, and she hadn't even considered that human talent might be necessary for this task. "What do you do?"

"I'm a bartender. But that's because I can't dance or sing. But the tips are good, so I'm not complaining."

Vesna frowned at that. "I thought without flowers, most alcohol was gone too."

"Well, I work with what's left. You'd be surprised how many cocktails I can make with just whiskey or rum," Anna said, winking. "I'd love to try wine, though."

Vesna shook her head firmly. "I wouldn't. I need to be in control all the time." She wasn't going to town for fun, and with an enemy like Boris, she needed to be on guard.

"Noted." Anna smirked. "So, what about your talent?"

Nina loved to listen to Vesna sing. But Vesna felt a little awkward and even scared about singing in front of Anna. Maybe her voice wasn't as good as her aunt thought. "Well, my aunt thinks I have a beautiful singing voice," she said, unconsciously lowering her eyes.

"Let's hear it."

"Now?" Vesna asked in a panic. She had just met Anna … sort of. It seemed ridiculous to sing to her right here and now.

Anna raised an eyebrow at her. "If you want to get closer to the rafflesia, you need to blend in, and definitely loosen up," she scolded gently.

"Fine," Vesna said, rolling her eyes.

She closed her eyes, steeling herself. She'd never sung in front of anyone but Nina, and she could feel a nervous flutter in her stomach. Ignoring it, she took a deep breath and sang one of her favorite songs about endless fields and distant unknown lands. Her soft, flowing voice filled the car. Anna listened without interrupting, an almost serene smile playing on her sunny face.

When Vesna finished, she finally opened her eyes, waiting for the verdict. "So, what do you think?" she asked impatiently.

Anna seemed lost in thought for a moment. "Magical," she said, her voice quieter than before. "I've always dreamed of seeing distant lands." She shook her head slightly, as if returning herself to reality. "Alex will be really pleased."

"Well, as long as Alex is pleased." Vesna smirked.

"And hopefully someone who works for Boris," Anna added, winking.

"As long as they're not rafflesia or poison," Vesna said immediately.

"Why not poison?" Anna asked, glancing at her with a raised eyebrow.

"I've read a lot about people with poisonous magic," Vesna said, "and it's clear that they bring nothing but death."

"I don't think there's much poisonous magic left in the world," Anna said. "I only know one guy. He works for Boris, actually. And he's friends with Alex."

"I'm not surprised that a poisonous one works for Boris," Vesna said. Poisonous flowers and people who wielded its magic meant only one thing: death magic. Vesna had read a lot about it and had long since decided it was bad news. "Well, if it's just one guy, I'll have no problem staying away from him."

"Got it. No poison magic for you." Anna smiled. "But I have nothing against them. I know Alex wouldn't be friends with someone unworthy."

Vesna widened her eyes. Did Anna seriously believe someone working for Boris could be worthy? "I have too many problems as it is. The last thing I need is to be near poison and die before I can do anything."

She turned to the window as they came out onto a small highway toward the city, leaving the forest behind. Vesna had forgotten how bare nature looked outside the forest; everything around seemed even more grey and lifeless. She let her hair down, filling the car with the luscious scent of magnolia.

"I don't think you realize how strong your sweet scent is," Anna said, staring at her. "I could smell it even when you were hiding behind the door. Here, at least cover your hair with my scarf."

"Right," Vesna agreed, quickly putting on the scarf. She couldn't be as open about who she was now that she was out of the forest.

I have finally stepped onto the path of revenge. A mix of fear and excitement swirled in her thoughts.

VESNA SOUNDLESSLY THANKED the divine magnolia when the car finally stopped in front of an old house without any accidents on the way. Though it had been a close call. She promised herself that she would never ride in the same car with Anna again.

"The herbalist lives here," Anna explained.

"Can we trust her?" Vesna asked, fear gripping her. She was now in rafflesia territory, and the last thing she wanted was to fall into their trap and lose her magic.

"Yes, she's been helping people with magic for many years," Anna said, clearly trying to calm Vesna down.

They stepped out of the car, and a strong wind took Vesna's breath away. The air was cold and empty, without a hint of magic. She couldn't help but stare at the tall buildings in the distance, piled on top of one another. Vesna couldn't remember what the city had looked like when she left it so many years ago. But now it seemed soulless, as if the spirit had left it along with the magic.

"Come on, someone might see you." Anna opened the gate of the small house.

Vesna followed her without saying a word. Part of her still felt like this was all a dream, and she was so afraid of letting it slip away.

Anna knocked impatiently on the door, shifting from foot to foot, obviously trying to warm up. Vesna was shivering too; her flimsy dress and jacket did nothing against the chilly wind.

Vesna heard light footsteps, and the door opened. An old woman with grey hair, wearing a wool dress with a shawl on her shoulders, stared at them with her big green eyes. She was more than just old. She looked ancient; her wrinkled face resembled a flower that had withered without water many springs ago. Her grey head bowed, and her eyes widened as her gaze fell on Vesna.

"Quickly." She grabbed Vesna's hand and practically dragged her inside, locking the door behind them.

The house was small but cozy, filled with old furniture. There were rugs everywhere, including the walls. But what caught Vesna's attention were the dried herbs hanging all over the house. Their smell made her heart beat faster.

"Where did you find all these herbs?" Vesna asked, not even thinking about formalities. She had never seen so many in her life. She hadn't even thought this many still existed.

Anna looked reproachfully at Vesna. "Sveta, this is…" she said, but it seemed Sveta didn't hear her.

"The most sacred flower in the world," Sveta whispered, her eyes watering. "Your scent…" She sniffed the air, coming in close to Vesna. "Sweet and luscious," she said, barely audible because her voice trembled. "Precious child."

How could she know for sure that I'm magnolia? Vesna thought suspiciously. There were many other flowers with creamy pink petals and a sweet fragrance.

"Good eye, Sveta," Anna said nervously. "This is Vesna. And we need your help. Vesna can't go into a town like this. We need the full package—eyes, scent, and once she blooms, also the tattoo covering."

"It's May, so you're going to bloom soon," Sveta said, her breathing uneven suddenly.

"Yes, magnolia blooms from early June…" Vesna tried to explain, but Sveta rushed to the kitchen and reached for some dried herbs above the stove.

"Your magic is so strong and pure, even stronger…" She paused. "It won't be easy to mask it," she was mumbling, grabbing one herb after another. "Vesna!" she screamed, then laughed hysterically for several seconds until her laughter turned to tears.

Vesna looked at Sveta and then at Anna in complete confusion, not understanding why the herbalist was crying.

"She's a little weird," Anna whispered, leaning toward Vesna conspiratorially.

"I heard you!" Sveta shouted from the kitchen.

"She wasn't talking about you!" Vesna shouted back, not wanting to upset her even more.

Sveta came out of the kitchen, her hands filled with various dried herbs. "Well, what do you want to smell like?" She looked at Vesna, who stared blankly at her. "Only people with money can afford to smell like herbs now. They pay a fortune for it. If someone asks, some guy presented you with perfume," Sveta explained. "I have cilantro."

Vesna sniffed the herb and frowned; the smell was too strong. "Do you have something … milder?"

"Marjoram?" Sveta suggested.

"What on earth is marjoram?" Anna raised her eyebrows.

"Come smell it." Sveta found the herb and handed it to Vesna, watching her intently.

The way Sveta was studying her made her nervous, but she brushed off the feeling. *I have a rare magic, after all.* And Anna had assured her that the herbalist was trustworthy.

Vesna took a deep breath, inhaling the scent of the herb. The aroma was slightly citrusy with sweet pine notes, warm, gentle, and comforting. It wasn't bad. Nothing like the perfection of magnolia, but she couldn't be picky.

Anna leaned closer to smell the herb too. "Why didn't you tell me you had something this nice?" She stared at Sveta. "Everyone thinks I have terrible taste in perfume! I walk around smelling like oregano!"

Vesna couldn't help but giggle. She liked Anna. She seemed independent and lively.

"Don't complain," Sveta muttered. "You could have chosen worse, like garlic." She laughed again, loud enough for the whole neighborhood to hear, looking a little possessed.

Vesna and Anna exchanged glances, and Vesna knew that Anna was thinking the same thing she was: they needed to get out of here as quickly as possible. "What about her eyes? You suggested grey for me, the most boring color," Anna complained again.

"It's difficult to cover pink eyes, but green will do," Sveta muttered, staring intently into Vesna's eyes, and she couldn't help but feel uneasy again. Her gaze seemed to want to penetrate the very depths of her being, as if trying to get to all her secrets and thoughts.

"Green is fine," Vesna blurted out, wishing to get away from this woman.

Sveta moved even closer to Vesna, whispering right in her ear. "You'll bloom even brighter than a cherry blossom in spring."

This woman is so old, she's probably seen the cherry blossoms with her own eyes. The thought ran through Vesna's mind. "Did you know the sacred one?" she asked on a hunch, holding her breath. Nina didn't ever want to talk about her mother, but Vesna would be happy to hear at least something about her.

Sveta didn't even glance at Vesna as she headed to the kitchen again. "I didn't have the pleasure," she said indifferently.

"I see," Vesna whispered sadly. She desperately wanted to know at least some details about her mother's life. Had she looked for the fern flower? Did she try to fight Boris? Clearly, the herbalist wasn't the one to answer her questions.

Anna and Vesna were sitting on the sofa, watching Sveta grind herbs into powder, measuring the amount by eye. A true herbalist through and through. Vesna had only read about them in the books Nina brought her from the library where she worked. According to the books, anyone with magic could do it, but it took a lot of practice.

"Almost ready! I don't have any vervain today, but tomorrow I'll bring you a stronger potion," Sveta reported from the kitchen.

"No! Don't risk coming all the way into the city," Anna said immediately. "Boris is looking for you. I'll come to you myself around lunchtime."

"Okay," Sveta said with a wave and shifted her gaze to Vesna. "Why are you here?"

Anna and Vesna looked at each other again. "She could be helpful," Anna whispered, making sure the herbalist didn't hear her.

Vesna tensed. Sveta might not be a threat, but she clearly wasn't in her right mind. But until Vesna bloomed, she had to play along with Anna's plan. "Ask her about the book from your dream," Vesna finally said.

Anna winked. "I think Boris has a special book. It's big and white. Do you know anything about it?"

"Boris and his books," Sveta sighed. "He has a library. The book you're looking for should be there."

"I see," Anna said, her shoulders dropping slightly. She'd clearly expected to hear something more useful.

"Try to become important to him, and he might invite you to his spring ball. It's in one month," Sveta said, her eyes briefly sparkling with life. "His spring balls are magnificent! If he finds me, I might attend too." She laughed.

"Blooms forbid," Anna said in horror. "He's been looking for you for years. Just lay low."

Vesna thought the ball might be the perfect time to find out more about Boris and how to get to him when the time for revenge came. With lots of guests, she could probably pass unnoticed. "We must go to this ball," she whispered, staring at Anna.

"Easier said than done," Anna said, and then narrowed her eyes playfully. "But possible."

A few minutes later, the potion was ready. Sveta held a simple glass in her hands, filled to the brim with a grey-green mixture that looked like swamp water.

"Do you have any alcohol? She shouldn't drink alone," Anna said.

"Not for me," Vesna muttered, a little crossly.

Sveta stared at Vesna with interest, as if trying to understand her. "I have an herbal tincture. I made it myself," she said proudly.

"Perfect!" Anna winked at Vesna. "A little pleasure never hurts."

"Do whatever you want, as long as it doesn't affect me," Vesna mumbled.

Once it was filled, Anna raised her glass. "To your new life, Vesna. May the Divine Blooms return!"

Sveta nodded once, then turned to the glass she held, quietly whispering a spell. The potion moved inside the glass, slowly turning into a green sparkling liquid. Vesna shifted her gaze to Sveta. The herbalist's pollen didn't leave her body like it should have when she used magic. *Her flower is about to fade; there's no pollen left in her veins,* Vesna mused while Sveta handed her the potion.

Vesna brought it to her lips and frowned. It smelled disgusting. Still, she drank the potion down in one gulp. The bitter-sour liquid burned her mouth terribly, and she grabbed Anna's glass from her, quickly washing the potion down with the tincture.

"What did you put in there?" Vesna asked when the fire in her mouth finally died down. "I'm going to throw up!" She stood up, but suddenly the nausea stopped, and she felt warm magic filling her veins. Her head was spinning, and everything around her became blurry. "I need to lie down," she said—just before the darkness took her.

Vesna could barely open her eyes; her eyelids felt heavy. She didn't immediately understand where she was. The bright light blinded her eyes, and noise and the smell of garbage hit her. She looked around carefully and realized that she was in the car. Anna was driving, constantly pressing the horn and shouting at the other drivers. "Move away, idiot!"

"Where are we?" Vesna whispered and tried to sit up, but her head was heavy.

"Almost home," Anna reported. Her words echoed in Vesna's mind. She doubted this city would ever be her home again. "I decided not to waste time."

"Did it work?" Vesna asked nervously.

"Like a charm," Anna assured her, smiling. "Rest. We still have some time before our arrival."

Vesna turned to the window, but she couldn't sleep. Her heart was beating so fast that she thought it would jump out of her chest. She had taken the first step, and there was no turning back. Revenge would finally be hers.

People, cars, and buildings seemed to merge into one great mass, like different magical pollen in spring. From the car, she couldn't see how tall the buildings were, but they seemed to reach up to the sky like naked giant trees. One monolithic brown building stood out from the others.

Anna followed her gaze. "Boris lives up there. He's one of the richest and most influential people in the city. He's even trying to become mayor to gain complete control."

"Do they know who he is?" Vesna asked, hatred filling her heart at the thought of the man who killed her mother.

"Yes, he doesn't even try to hide his magic. Just like

the people who work for him. They answer to no one, fear no one. They practically terrorize the city, searching for the magical ones in the hopes of draining us," Anna said, clenching her fist on the steering wheel. "Besides, he doesn't age. Thanks to your mother's magic, he's remained strong and just as young as he was years ago," she said, reaching for Vesna's hand and squeezing it. "Fuck him."

A lump came to Vesna's throat as she thought of what Boris had done to her mother. *Stop it, Vesna. You must be stronger than this,* she thought, taking a deep breath. *Delicate flowers are doomed to wither in this fading reality, and only the wildflowers can survive.*

Anna drove into the parking area of some random building and stopped right at the entrance.

"I live right next to the club in free housing that Alex provides to his employees. The apartment is tiny, but it's home." Anna smiled. She was clearly happy to be back.

She walked up to the first floor, and Vesna followed her silently. The apartment was not at all what Vesna had expected. Furniture was stuffed into the tiny space, and photographs with various inspirational phrases covered the walls. Anna wasn't lying; the place was small —like, *super* small. But it had Anna's personality; it screamed positivity.

"Do you want to see your room?" Anna broke the silence.

"Yes," Vesna said quietly.

"I've never used it, so once you earn some money, you can decorate it the way you want, or at least buy some furniture."

Anna opened the door to the small room. The bed took up most of the room … and that was all. Apart from the bed, the room was completely empty. The window was nice, though, with a large sill where Vesna could sit and look out at the city.

Vesna decided she should at least thank Anna. After all, she didn't have to help her. "It's nice, thank you," she said, entering and walking over to the bed. As soon as she sat down, the mattress shifted alarmingly beneath her, and she toppled over. The mattress was apparently water-filled.

"Oh." Anna giggled. "I bought it when waterbeds were popular, but I didn't have the money to replace it. I know it's tricky." Her face seemed to light up every time she smiled.

"I'll get used to it."

They looked at each other in silence. Vesna wanted to be alone, to think about everything. Fear—but also determination—filled her heart. But Anna still stood in the doorway, as if expecting something.

Finally, she cleared her throat. "We can hang out in the living room. I don't think you should be alone."

"I'd prefer to be left alone tonight," Vesna said. She wanted to think everything over and make a clear plan for revenge.

A hint of sadness ran across Anna's face, but a second later, she was already smiling sweetly. "With your singing voice, I'm sure Alex will hire you right away. He's an admirer of true talent. Tomorrow, I'll show you around the city."

"Thank you," Vesna said, unable to hide her excitement, and smiled wildly. She wondered what the city and life here were like.

"Don't mention it. We've all lost something," Anna's voice echoed. Vesna hadn't even thought about the fact that Anna had probably also lost her parents or other family members on the night of vanished petals. "Get some sleep. Tomorrow, a new life awaits you."

Vesna tossed in her waterbed for hours, excited and scared. Despite the fear that came with the path she'd chosen, she was determined to follow it, no matter what. Catching sight of her still-unpacked bag, she stood quickly, pulled out the painting she'd brought from home, and hung it above her bed.

I'm doing this for you, Mom, she thought, and tears filled her eyes. Sometimes, when she was all alone, she allowed herself to be weak. But only for a moment. Thoughts that she should be stronger and more determined always replaced the sadness.

Chapter Three

MIR.

Mir walked into his apartment, slamming the door, ready to kill anyone in his path. The maid who was mopping the floor looked at him from under her brows, her gaze full of fear.

"Is there anything…" she whispered, but Mir cut her off at once.

"Disappear," he said through clenched teeth.

The maid practically ran outside, and Mir went into the kitchen and poured himself a drink. The meeting he had come back from had not gone as planned. It had been a disaster.

How could I have screwed up so badly after all these years? he thought, growing even angrier.

Mir had been working for Boris since he was seventeen. His poisonous datura magic made him the perfect candidate to work for the rafflesia, especially after he had turned twenty-five years old. Mir's magic could kill, and it could cause hallucinations, both of which were useful to Boris. But Mir couldn't care less about Boris; he had his own plans. All these years, he had been the perfect rafflesia soldier, passionately waiting for the time to fulfill his painful dream: to destroy poisonous magic once and for all. As far as he was concerned, datura magic was not a gift, but a curse, and he was determined to save anyone else from suffering because of it like he had.

It was the only reason he stayed close to Boris. He had to be there if Boris ever figured out how to get to the Veiled Wilds. When the time came, and the Veiled Wilds were opened again, Mir would be there to destroy the divine datura once and for all.

Boris gave all people with magic a choice: work for him, sharing their magic little by little with the rafflesia to keep Boris's people alive, or die. Mir was different. His magic was poisonous, so the rafflesia weren't after it. Mir could work for them without sharing his magic. *No one wants poisonous magic, not even parasites.*

He walked to the window, sipping his drink as he gazed out over the city veiled in night. The darkness masked the ugly, naked reality that the rafflesia had wrought on Earth.

When Mir came to Boris, he had taken him in with no questions asked, immediately exposing him to the cruel and ugly reality the world had become. Mir became one of Boris's closest people. All the important deals went through him. And he wanted it that way.

"Dammit," Mir cursed as his thoughts returned to the failed meeting.

He needed to interrogate a human about the book that Boris was looking for. Boris believed that it contained some information about the location of the Veiled Wilds. He was obsessed with finding this hidden realm where the Divine Blooms lived. Just when Mir was about to use his hallucination power on the human, armed men had entered the building. Mir lost his temper, killing everyone.

Boris will be furious. He needs that book, Mir thought. Well, the human was dead now. Mir knew Boris might kill him; he got rid of people for even the smallest mistakes. Not that Mir liked his life all that much, but he couldn't die until he dealt with the divine datura.

A knock on the door brought Mir back to reality. "Come in," he said, knowing full well it was one of Boris's guys.

It was Ivan, Boris's right hand. He entered, adjusting his brown hair, which reached almost to his shoulders, and the apartment Boris provided Mir immediately filled with a disgusting smell of rotting flesh. Even after so many years of working with the rafflesia, Mir still hadn't gotten used to it. Ivan was a parasite, same as Boris.

Ivan narrowed his eyes, a satisfied smile spreading across his face. "The boss wants to see you," he said.

"Okay," Mir replied indifferently, sipping his drink.

Ivan's face turned purple, and he breathed angrily. He was used to everyone respecting him, even fearing him. But Mir thought Ivan was an overpaid bully and nothing else. "Do you think that an unworthy poison like you has the right to make Boris wait?"

"I'll come when I finish my drink." Mir turned away to the window.

Ivan muttered something under his breath and left, slamming the door with all his might.

After finishing his whiskey, Mir left his apartment, and while waiting for the elevator, he thought about Boris. Mir knew that the rafflesia's ruling would be absolute if Boris found the Veiled Wilds. He had gone to incredible lengths to find it—which meant lots of people had to be bribed or killed. Mir was sick of being a part of it, but he still wasn't any closer to his goal.

Boris's apartment occupied the entire top floor. When Mir entered, his boss was sitting in his throne-like chair in the center of his enormous penthouse, Ivan standing to his right. Mir held his breath, trying not to make a face at the reek of rotting flesh. It had to be the worst-smelling flower in the world, and the scent was so strong here that he couldn't think straight.

Boris glared at Mir from his throne, his brown eyes, spotted with white, clearly raging. Mir knew that the white color had appeared after Boris drained the magic of the sacred one to the last drop. He was the perfect embodiment of his flower—a parasite that lived only on other people's magic.

"My poisonous friend, come closer," Boris sang from his throne. "I learned things haven't gone according to plan with the human."

Mir took a few steps, stopping a few meters away from Boris. He didn't want to get any closer; the man's smell was unbearable. The last thing he needed was to puke in front of his boss.

"It didn't." Mir cleared his throat, looking for the right words. Boris hadn't gotten all his power by being understanding; he'd gotten it by being ruthless. But to outsiders, he appeared charming—honest, even. "The human brought armed men with him. I had no choice but to kill them all," Mir said simply, as if it had been his plan all along. Boris couldn't have known that Mir had simply lost control.

Mir saw Boris's eyes flush with anger at him, and the smell of rotten flesh grew even stronger. Obviously, he was furious. "You know I need this book. I need to open the Veiled Wilds!"

Mir held his breath, afraid Boris might teach him a lesson. He couldn't drain his magic, but his roots could rip through his bones, or even his heart. It hurt like hell.

"Why don't we look for another way to find the Veiled Wilds?" Mir dared to suggest.

"Watch your tongue," snapped Ivan, who had been silent until now.

Boris raised his hand. "It's okay, Ivan," he said. "We can, but you have been looking for the herbalist for years and still have not brought her to me!" His eyes flashed with a dangerous glint. Yes, Boris had enough sacred magic in his veins, but who knew how long it would last?

Why does he think the herbalist can help find the Veiled Wilds? A suspicious thought ran through Mir's mind. "I'm working on it," he said. "The herbalist is powerful, using charms and spells to mislead us."

"I needed her here yesterday!" Boris shouted, rising from his throne. Even Ivan tensed up. But the next second, Boris took a deep breath and sat down again. He rarely lost his temper. "If it weren't for your unique ability, my dear poisonous friend, you would be dead already. But I can't sacrifice such a valuable man," he said, though his words sounded like a threat. Mir knew Boris would kill him if he made another mistake, no matter his ability. "From now on, Ivan will watch you."

"Yes, Boss," Mir immediately agreed, trying not to reveal his true feelings. Ivan was loyal, and he would most definitely make Mir's life even harder.

"Now, the politician we need to … *convince*." Boris emphasized the last word, which implied that Mir would need to use his hallucination magic. "He'll be in Alex's club tomorrow night. I don't really care about being mayor, but people are starting to complain. They're calling us the mafia, and I don't want my men getting in trouble while we're looking for the Veiled Wilds."

Fuck, Mir cursed internally. He hated dragging Alex into this mess. Boris had only spared Alex and his gracious rose magic because he was useful. Maybe Boris was a parasite, but he was a clever one. He could let his men drain Alex, or he could use him and his club for his own gain.

"Go there, take some girls. Don't draw attention to yourself," Boris said, touching his brown beard. "You know how it's done."

Mir knew very well how it was done. He would be twenty-eight this flowering season, and he had become as ruthless as Boris during all these years of working for the rafflesia. Mir told himself his own fight was more important than all the destruction he had caused while working for Boris. Some part of him thought he would even the score of being a monster once all the poisonous magic left this world forever.

"Will do, Boss," Mir said, meeting Boris's gaze. He was tired of being his errand boy, but the time had not yet come. *Be patient,* he told himself. *The Veiled Wilds cannot be locked away forever.*

THE NEXT DAY was no different from other days. Mir searched the city for magical ones, hoping they would lead him to the herbalist. But it seemed the magic people had learned their lesson with the rafflesia. After all, they were the tender bloom, and the parasite was the plague.

Mir walked home through a park that had once

bloomed. Now all the trees and plants looked like they were rotting from the inside. Sometimes it felt as if the rafflesia were the only real magic left in the world. Mir sat under a dying tree, looking up at the sky. The world was a mess, a disaster, all thanks to the parasite that slithered like a shadow into the flowering meadow. The humans suffered, food was scarce, but they had lost something more than food; they had lost hope, along with their gods.

Mir noticed a small herb growing lonely under the tree. He reached out to it in surprise. It was almost impossible to find any herbs these days. Even Boris didn't know how the herbalist found them for potions. *Or maybe he does,* Mir wondered, realizing Boris knew the herbalist was a woman, and he was almost as obsessed with her as he was with finding the Veiled Wilds.

Mir picked the herb, and inhaling the scent, froze in surprise. It was marjoram, his mother's favorite herb. When she could find it, she used it in every dish she cooked for him. Even after all these years, Mir hadn't forgotten the smile on her face, her warm embrace. Sad thoughts took hold of him and carried him away into memories, like flower petals carried away by a strong wind.

His parents were human, and though they could tell Mir had magic when he was born, they didn't know what flower blessed him. Until Mir turned six years old, his life had been paradise. But as he grew, his magic began to manifest. Mir still remembered the look on his parents' faces when they realized his magic was poisonous. His touch made people go numb, weakening their heartbeat. And instead of looking at him with love, like they'd always done before, his parents began to look at him with fear. He remembered the day they abandoned him at the orphanage, how he begged them not to leave him, told them he loved them … but they didn't listen. At first, Mir prayed to the divine datura, asking for mercy, asking it to take away his magic and return his parents to him. But his divine flower never answered his prayers, and one day, Mir stopped praying altogether.

The rest was a painful story that left an eternal, scorching thorn in his heart. From that moment on, Mir was determined not to let anyone into his life—other than Alex, who was more like a brother to him than anything else after growing up together in the orphanage. But Mir knew Alex was the exception. Most people wanted nothing to do with poison. And if they did, eventually they would abandon him, just like his parents had.

Lesson learned. Mir took a deep breath; it was just silly memories brought back by the familiar scent. *Fuck that,* he cursed, shaking his head and tossing away the herb.

MIR WAS on his way to the club, following Boris's orders. It was a neutral zone of sorts, where magic met ordinary people. Everyone knew Alex didn't choose a side. He was just trying to survive in a fading reality. Alex was a year younger than Mir, and when Mir started working for the rafflesia, he had saved up money and helped Alex open his own club. Alex was an artist at heart, and Mir had to get involved to make sure the club was profitable. Boris agreed to leave Alex alone if he would let the rafflesia do its own thing at the club when necessary.

The guard, Anton, stood in front of the door, directly beneath the club's sign: FADING BLOSSOMS.

"Still working for that parasite?" he asked, letting Mir in.

"Not everyone can afford to be idealistic." Mir smirked.

When Mir had investigated Anton to see if he had magic, he realized Anton was a worshiper of the Divine Blooms, despite being just human. Apparently, he was a part of some organization that planned to oppose the rafflesia. Mir reported nothing to Boris. Humans weren't part of his job.

Mir slowly walked in, scanning the club. He often came here to forget himself and enjoy the company of someone new. Women usually wanted to get to know him, but one night was all that Mir could offer them. He was afraid of being rejected if they saw what his magic could do.

Alex saw him right away and headed over. Alex didn't question Mir's decision to work for Boris. He questioned none of his decisions, for that matter.

Tonight, Alex wore a rose-patterned suit, his red eyes mirroring the rose-petal-colored paintings on the ceiling and walls. He was proud of his magic, and Mir knew that Alex still prayed to the sacred rose in times of need. But Mir also knew that his prayers went unanswered.

"You're early tonight," Alex sang, hugging his friend.

"No rest for poison." Mir grinned.

"Are you working?" Alex asked, walking to the bar.

"I am, dammit," Mir muttered, and Alex looked at him in surprise. He knew Mir well, and Mir never complained or shared anything about his work.

"Come on, let's have a drink," Alex said, sitting down on a barstool in the center of the bar, inviting Mir to sit next to him. Anna was working behind the bar and nodded to Mir. "Anna, darling, whiskey, please." Alex smiled at her. She didn't answer, but quickly grabbed the bottle from the wall.

Alex turned to Mir. "Spill it."

"I need to find the herbalist," Mir said, and Alex frowned. Mir knew his friend liked to remain as neutral as possible. And Mir hated putting Alex in this position, but he was desperate. "Someone obviously knows something. I need your connections."

"Even if I knew someone, you know I don't work for Boris," Alex muttered, sipping his drink.

"This is for me," Mir said. "I need the herbalist. Boris is sure she knows something about the Veiled Wilds."

"Dammit," Alex said, his voice suddenly breaking. He knew about Mir's obsession with destroying the divine datura. "I'll ask around."

"Thank you." Mir paused, noticing that Anna had stopped by the wall of bottles, probably listening to their conversation. At first, Mir considered teaching her a lesson, but he decided against it. Alex was a friend—his only friend, for that matter. He didn't want to make a scene in his club.

"And tonight?" Alex asked, clinking glasses with Mir.

"You've got some politician coming to the club. I want a table right next to him. And send some girls to our tables."

"Whatever you need. After all, this place wouldn't be here if it wasn't for you."

"Thanks, man," Mir said simply and patted Alex on the shoulder.

"By the way, I have a new singer! She's as beautiful as the first flower in spring," Alex reported enthusiastically. He admired genuine talent, often helping broken artists survive.

"It's about time you brought in some fresh faces. Where did you find her?" Mir asked. He was glad to talk about something meaningless, something that would take his mind off his problems.

"She's Anna's friend." Alex nodded, looking at her. "Anna, where is your friend from?"

Anna clearly didn't want to talk, or maybe she didn't want to get closer to Mir. She spoke without looking at him and continued mixing the cocktail. "She grew up in a village not too far away. I offered to help her settle in the big city."

"How do you know her?" Mir asked, noticing how tense Anna was and wondering why.

"Is this an interrogation?" Anna said, crossing her arms.

"This one doesn't mince words," Alex said, laughing. "Come on, I'll show you to your table."

THE HOURS SLIPPED BY. The band was playing loud music, and drunk people were dancing on the dance floor, trying to forget about reality for at least one night. The two girls Alex sent over were already drinking and dancing playfully next to Mir, attempting to gain his attention. Mir ignored them, watching the politician at the next table. These girls weren't his type, plus he hated when they were drunk. Alcohol intoxication reminded Mir of the effects of poison, and he hated everything that was associated with his divine flower.

One girl sat beside him, gently placing a hand on his shoulder. "I'm Olga. Pleasure to meet you, poisonous one."

Mir looked at her with irritation. *What a stupid nick-*

name, he thought, removing her hand. He glared at her, hoping to scare her with the poison that filled his eyes.

"Wow! So much magic," she said, draping herself on him again. "Why don't you show me what you can do in private?"

Mir was bored. He could have had some fun, but Olga was clearly too drunk for his taste. He was deciding how to get rid of her when the lights went out, and a red spotlight shot onto the stage. A girl, clad in a delicate but seductive beige dress with red flowers printed on it, slowly walked onto the stage. Her creamy pink hair was long and shiny, as if woven from gentle tulip petals. Her eyes shone like a green meadow in the midday sun. She approached the microphone and parted her full lips.

Mir couldn't look away.

And then she started singing.

The sound of her voice was fucking *everything*, tender and erotic. Mir was blinded; he no longer saw anyone around him but her. The song itself was beautiful, if a bit outdated and naïve for his taste. She moved slowly to the beat of the music, and there was something real, something raw in her voice. Mir had a feeling she didn't belong here, like a blooming flower caught in a hungry shadow.

As she was finishing the song, Mir noticed that all the men were staring at her, their gazes hungry. It was no secret that some dancers and singers who worked at the club were up for some extra fun. Mir had to get to her first to make sure no one would steal this enchanted flower before he got to her.

She hadn't finished the song yet, but Mir already was walking toward his friend. Alex sat at the bar, sipping his drink and listening to the song with his eyes closed, moving his hands to the beat of the music as if he were conducting.

"Tell her to join me at my table," Mir said firmly, and Alex's eyes shot open.

He frowned at Mir. "Leave Vesna alone. She's too innocent." Alex paused. "She might be afraid of…"

"My poisonous magic?" Mir finished. He shook his head. This girl was too perfect to let slip away, and he wanted to have a good time. She looked exactly like someone who could take his mind off work and the rafflesia. "I promise to behave. Bring her… Vesna." He liked the taste of her name on his lips.

"You know, sometimes I regret that we're friends," Alex said, exhaling loudly. But he stood up and walked to the stage as Vesna finished the song.

Mir returned to his table, a little nervous. He couldn't remember the last time his cold, poisonous heart had risen because of a woman. He sipped his drink, ignoring Olga, who was saying something to him. Mir was staring at the stage instead. Vesna frowned when Alex spoke to her. Then she took a deep breath, her perfect chest rising. Mir saw how she pursed her full, rosy lips before following Alex.

This will be interesting, Mir thought, licking his lips. He continued to sit, looking hungrily at Vesna as she followed Alex to the table. Mir's gaze shamelessly slid from her perfect hips to her slender waist, to her chest, to the pale, almost marble skin of her neck, to her petal-soft lips.

Finally, she approached, and their eyes met. He didn't see fear, but rather irritation with a small spark of curiosity. They just looked at each other, and Mir was pleasantly surprised that she didn't break into a fake charming smile the other girls always did.

"Vesna, meet my friend Mir. Mir, this is my new singer, Vesna," Alex said, clearly not enjoying this at all.

Mir still hadn't gotten up. He studied Vesna, tilting his head. She looked normal, but he could almost swear he saw something else behind her green eyes. Mir held his breath in surprise as her fragrance reached him. It was sweet and all too familiar: marjoram. Of all the perfumes in the world, she had to choose the one that evoked memories of when he was still a happy, innocent child. Behind the sweet aroma, there were other notes that were barely noticeable, but Mir couldn't make them out.

Mesmerizing, the thought flashed through his mind. "Please, sit at my table." Mir moved aside slightly, making room for Vesna to sit next to him.

She opened her perfect mouth to say something, but then quickly closed it and turned to Alex instead. "Is this part of my job?" she asked bluntly, her bright voice like forest streams of melted snow.

"Well, no," Alex replied, shrugging his shoulders.

Mir narrowed his eyes; something was telling him this girl was a wicked flower.

She leaned slightly toward Mir and whispered, "I will let you poison someone else." She glanced at the datura tattoo on his cheek.

Her words echoed painfully in his heart, and he cleared his throat, trying not to show his feelings. He laughed a little unnaturally before speaking. "That's not what I was planning to do with you," he sang suggestively.

Her pale face turned pink, and she pursed her lips. "What a relief," she said sarcastically.

Mir finally stood up, afraid she would leave, and leaned toward her ear. "I'm happy to show you what actual relief is." He enjoyed this little game. She wasn't just gorgeous; she sparked a curiosity in him.

"As tempting as that sounds, I think I'll pass," Vesna whispered back. "Enjoy your evening." She turned around, and Mir watched as she hurried toward the bar.

But the night was still young, and he would not give up that easily.

Chapter Four

VESNA.

As directed, Vesna followed Alex to the far table after her song finished. As they approached, her heart literally stopped. A muscular man dressed in black was sitting on the couch. She dared to meet his gaze, diving into eyes she would never forget. They were like a night-blooming flower that reflected the full moon, cool and majestic. He looked at her shamelessly, studying her body like a hunter studied his prey. Her gaze slid quickly over his face, where the tattoo of a datura flower glowed.

His eyes are white as snow, but his heart is probably darker than a black dahlia, she thought, and a shiver ran down her spine.

When he moved closer, she couldn't help but inhale his tart fragrance with hints of almonds and honey. His scent reminded her of a tender night, exotic and intoxicating, and somehow peaceful.

Vesna heard her own heartbeat, and she pinched herself, trying to fight his effect on her. He smirked, tilting his head, and licked his lips. Vesna blushed; his intentions were obvious. He didn't even care that he had invited her to his table when there were other girls with him.

Run, Vesna, she commanded herself. *People like him carry death in every glance, in every movement of their lips, in every beat of their heart.*

After their brief interaction, she strolled to the bar without looking back and sat down in front of Anna.

"He's handsome, right?" Anna winked, looking at Mir still sitting at his table.

"Nothing special," Vesna muttered, and grabbed her water, wishing to change the subject.

"Well, he's the poisonous one I was talking about."

Vesna's eyes widened. "He works for Boris?" she asked, horrified. She had never been so close to anything or anyone connected to Boris, and suddenly, it was hard to breathe. Revenge seemed easier in her head than in real life. These people were powerful, and she could easily get caught.

Vesna froze as she caught the sweet scent of magnolia in the air. She could swear her magic was slowly returning, even though today Anna had brought her an even stronger potion Sveta had made that morning.

"Are you okay?" Anna asked, narrowing her eyes. She had probably noticed that Vesna could barely breathe.

"Are my eyes green?" Vesna whispered, her voice trembling, afraid her magic was coming back.

Anna stared into her eyes, studying them, before whispering back. "Yes, they're normal. You're just stressed." She quickly stepped around the bar and stood beside Vesna. "Come with me."

They entered the dressing room, and Anna locked the door behind them. She whispered a spell, and golden pollen drifted from her body, slowly approaching Vesna. For a moment, Anna's eyes shifted to the shade of her divine flower. Vesna had never seen such beautiful magic. The pollen shimmered like sunlight, illuminating the entire room. A strong citrusy, spicy scent with lingering notes transported Vesna into a blooming reality. The pollen touched her pale skin, covering it, trying to seep in. No pollen had ever touched her before, and she was glad it was Anna's magic.

Suddenly, she felt a foreign power overtaking her own, and it felt solemn. Her heartbeat slowed in seconds. "Thank you for everything," Vesna said gratefully, looking at Anna.

"Don't mention it." Anna smiled. "You can stay here before your next song. I have to go back to the bar."

When Anna left, Vesna sat at the dressing table, staring at her reflection. For years, she had lived in a false reality that shielded her from the dangers of the real world. She couldn't imagine what Anna or any magical person had gone through.

VESNA STOOD BEHIND THE STAGE, waiting for her cue. As a slow tune began, she walked to the microphone. Even though the lights were dimmed, she saw snowy eyes staring at her from a far table.

Mir's gaze burned into her. Vesna might not have lived a real life, but she wasn't totally naïve. He was probably undressing her in his mind, and her magic surged in protest. She skipped a few lines of the song to calm her pollen, trying not to give herself away.

When the song ended, she rushed to the bar, hoping to avoid Mir. Yes, he was close to Boris, but she was hoping to find someone else who would help her reach Boris without poisoning her along the way.

"Are you feeling better?" Anna asked gently.

Vesna nodded. "Yes, all good," she said, though she still felt Mir's gaze. She turned toward his table.

He was talking to Alex. She had to admit that Mir was handsome; he stood out in this club. His body was strong, and magic swirled in his eyes.

"Alex is coming over," Anna said, her eyes sparkling as he approached. From her expression, Vesna realized Anna might like him as more than just a boss.

"Anna, my darling," Alex sang. "You've been working all night. Why don't you and Vesna join us at the table?"

Before Vesna could object, Anna was already at his side. "We'd love to," she said with a charming smile.

Vesna sighed. "I'm better off here," she said dryly.

Alex leaned in, and Vesna inhaled his scent deeply. It was floral and sweet, with a hint of honey. "Mir promised to behave."

Vesna doubted anyone connected to Boris ever kept a promise. But Anna wasn't going to miss her chance with Alex. She tugged Vesna's hand and led her toward Mir's table.

Vesna didn't look at Mir. She sat across from him, eyes scanning the room, making it clear that she didn't want to be here.

Grabbing his drink, Mir got up and sat down on the table right in front of her. "Having fun?"

"Not at all," she said, finally meeting his gaze.

He dove into her eyes in return. "If you're only working here for money, I'll gladly take you under my wing," he sang suggestively.

"You do charity work? How kind of you," she said

sarcastically, though she felt how her cheeks blushed at his words.

Mir laughed, surprising her. His face softened, and small dimples appeared near his mouth. "So, what do you say?"

"I'll pass," she retorted. She had no intentions of getting cozy with him. She turned her head to look away, but he moved faster, touching her chin. His touch was gentle, and goose bumps ran down her spine.

"Your eyes should only be on me," he said seriously.

She stared at him, caught off guard. "And what should I do when you're not around? Close my eyes?"

Mir licked his lips. "That would work."

"Like I said, find someone else to poison."

"Do you have something against magic, wicked flower?" Mir asked, narrowing his eyes.

Before Vesna could respond, the stench of rotting flesh hit her. She turned to the entrance. A tall man with long brown hair walked toward Mir's table. As he approached, his gaze slid over the girls, then landed on Vesna. His smell overwhelmed her, corrupting everything inside. She thought of running away, but quickly reminded herself that this was the path she had chosen.

The man smiled slyly. "Is this poison boring you?" he asked, moving closer to Vesna. He reeked of alcohol. "I'm Ivan."

She held her breath, feeling her pale face become whiter than snow on a frosty winter day. Time dragged, but she couldn't say a word, hatred and fear tightening her chest.

Mir stood up, placing a hand on Ivan's shoulder. Vesna noticed how his deadly magic swirled inside his eyes. "Get lost," he growled through clenched teeth. She had a feeling he didn't like Ivan, which was odd, since Mir was working for the rafflesia.

Ivan looked at Mir with hatred. "The lady is clearly not into you," he retorted. "Rightfully so; no one sane would want to be near the poison you're filled with," he seethed.

"I won't repeat myself," Mir warned him, clenching his fist.

Vesna rose swiftly, standing beside Mir. She didn't want to draw attention to herself, and she couldn't stay near Ivan and his scent another moment. "Want to dance?" she asked Mir, her eyes pleading. *Please, let's dance,* she begged silently.

Chapter Five

MIR.

Wicked flower, Mir thought, hiding a smile. "Disappear, Ivan," he said before leading Vesna to the dance floor.

Mir hated dancing, but for this wicked flower, he would make an exception. He took her hand. It was so gentle, as if he were touching the petals of a flower. For some strange reason, he felt his magic swirl with a new vigor, as if her very touch could empower him. *She's just another girl. Don't you dare fall for her,* he scolded himself, pushing away this strange feeling.

Mir placed his hand around her slender waist, shamelessly pulling her closer. Slow music was playing, and he could hear her deep breathing. For the first time in his life, he didn't know what to say.

Mir finally broke the silence. "Where do you live?"

"We don't have to talk," she said with an unnatural smile, probably noticing that Ivan was still watching them.

"Come on, wicked flower. *You* asked me to dance," Mir teased.

"I was just trying to avoid trouble. I don't want

attention, especially on my first night here," she explained. "And stop calling me 'wicked flower.' I have nothing to do with the magical world."

"I can't. You seem like a wicked flower to me," Mir said, twirling her a little faster. "So, where do you live?" He looked deep into her eyes, waiting for the answer.

She took a deep breath, as if giving in. "I live with Anna. I just moved here from a neighboring village." She paused. "Temporarily, until my birthday."

"When is it?" Mir asked.

"I'll turn twenty-five in June," she muttered, her gaze clouding over, as if she were thinking about something else.

"I'd be happy to show you around."

"Anna will show me around," she answered immediately.

"Not the places I know," Mir sang. This girl clearly required a different approach, and he didn't mind putting in a little more effort than usual. "How about tomorrow?"

He felt her body tense in his arms. "I need to practice some songs."

"We can practice different songs." He leaned toward her ear. "Songs of moans and deep breaths."

She blushed, and her eyes sparkled. "I'd rather sing a solo," she said archly and removed her hands from his shoulders, showing that the dance was over.

The moment her touch left him, he felt a strange emptiness, but he pushed it away. This wicked flower seemed like too much trouble for just one night. He was better off finding someone else.

Before Mir could respond, shouts caught their attention, and they both turned to see what was going on. Stupid Ivan had taken the task Boris had assigned to

Mir into his own hands. He was at the politician's table, holding him by the throat.

"Fucking parasite," Mir cursed, then looked at Vesna briefly. "Enjoy your solo. Excuse me."

She said nothing, because there was clearly nothing to say. They were from two different worlds, completely wrong for each other. Mir knew they would probably never speak again. He hastened over to the table, leaving Vesna on the dance floor, but the irritation of her rejection washed over him.

Mir whispered a spell, and datura pollen left his body, plunging everything around him into white mist. It quickly reached Ivan, clinging to his skin. He didn't even have time to react and release his roots.

Boris shared lots of magic with Ivan, but tonight Ivan was drunk, so it was easier for Mir's pollen to affect him. Ivan froze, unable to move, looking at Mir with an angry gaze. People around them screamed, and in a matter of seconds, the club was almost empty. The politician sat on the couch in horror, watching Mir approaching him.

"Hello," Mir said, standing over him like a rock. "Tomorrow, in an anonymous vote, you will vote for Boris," he said in a tone that left no room for debate. "If not, we will replace you with someone who is more cooperative. Understood?"

When the politician didn't answer, Mir decided to push even harder. He whispered the spell again, and more magic left his body, this time almost touching the politician. "First you will feel your mouth go dry, but you won't be able to drink water, no matter how hard you try. Then your pupils will dilate, your vision will go blurry, and your heart will beat so fast that you won't be able to breathe.

Then comes my favorite part: the hallucinations. Don't worry, I'll make sure they're pleasant. At the end, a lovely part follows—seizures, coma, and death." Mir moved his hand a little, and his magical pollen stopped just before it touched the politician's face. "So, should I cast a spell?"

The man looked terrified, his face red and sweaty. "I will vote for Boris," he whispered. His body remained still, only his eyes moving, watching the pollen drifting near his face.

"Smart decision." Mir grinned, calling his magic away from him. "Go."

The politician immediately ran outside, constantly looking back. Mir was used to people reacting to his magic like that. He was a deadly flower, after all.

"Take your disgusting magic off me!" Ivan said through clenched teeth, still unable to move.

"Boris gave *me* this task." Mir turned to him, his eyes burning with hatred.

"He doesn't trust you anymore! And for good reason. You were so busy with that girl, you'd forgotten to do your job!" Ivan fired.

Mir had completely forgotten that Vesna was there. Even though he had decided to leave her alone, he turned around to see if she had seen him using his magic. Vesna was still standing on the dance floor. Her face was pale, and her eyes… They were full of horror. She looked at him like he was a monster. *Technically, she isn't wrong,* Mir thought, and his heart ached. He was doomed for rejection and loneliness because of his power. Maybe it was her eyes or the familiar scent of marjoram that brought back old memories, but Mir clearly remembered his mother looking at him the same way—with disappointment and fear.

Anna ran up to Vesna and quickly pulled her backstage, as if she were in danger just by looking at Mir.

Fuck this, Mir cursed, calling his magic back from Ivan and rushing to the exit.

"Mir, wait!" Alex shouted after him, but Mir only quickened his pace.

If you get closer to people, they will always hurt you, he thought as he got into the car.

MIR DIDN'T WANT to see Boris; he just wanted to go to his apartment and sleep. Ivan would definitely try to turn Boris against Mir even more. What he had done tonight was dangerous. Boris preferred hallucinations to threats. He wanted a clean job, and tonight had been a mess.

As soon as Mir arrived, Boris sent for him. His boss wasn't alone. He was lying on a bed with several girls, sucking on their magic with parasitic roots that crawled out of his hands and attached themselves to the girls. Mir hated seeing this part. He could feel the divine magic leaving the girls' bodies, seeping into Boris's veins and turning into something ugly. The girls didn't realize that one day, Boris would drain them completely. They wouldn't just become normal humans; they would die. But they didn't seem to care. Mir had to admit that Boris was resourceful and charming when he needed to be. If someone told Mir that these girls were in love with Boris and willingly gave him their magic, he wouldn't even be surprised.

"Let's finish later, ladies," Boris said, calling his roots back.

Ivan ran inside just as the girls were leaving the

room. Mir took a deep breath; he needed to remain calm and act as if he had done nothing wrong. So, he kept quiet. It was better to let Ivan hysterically tell everything, then explain himself.

"Boss," Ivan said, lowering his eyes. "Mir made a mess of it. And he paralyzed me with his poisonous pollen! He is completely unmanageable!" he fired off, out of breath.

Mir watched Boris curiously, wondering how he would react. But Boris was silent, not a muscle moving in his face. He had been in power long enough to learn how to remain calm and turn any situation to his advantage.

"He focused on some stupid girl, completely forgetting about your task. So, I took matters into my own hands."

Protective instincts Mir didn't even know he had rose up inside him as he listened to Ivan speak. *She's not stupid,* Mir raged.

"Mir?" Boris locked eyes with him.

Tamping down his anger, Mir met Boris's gaze head-on. "I did what needed to be done," he lied. "I waited for the politician to get drunk, so no one would wonder where he'd disappeared to. Alex sent him girls to make sure everything went according to the plan." Mir paused, thinking that explaining too much would raise suspicions. "Then Ivan came and screwed everything up."

Boris touched his beard, clearly mulling that over. "Will he vote for me?"

"Without a doubt," Mir replied, hiding the smirk he wanted to throw at Ivan.

Boris walked over to him and Ivan. "I don't need my people fighting each other. We have too many enemies as it is. And Mir, from now on, focus only on the herbalist. You have two months to find her before Ivan Kupala Night, or get ready to see eternal hell."

"Understood, Boss," Mir said calmly. If Boris was sure the herbalist could help find the Veiled Wilds, then Mir should find her no matter the cost to magical people. He decided to see Alex first thing in the morning. Every year, as Ivan Kupala Night approached, Mir waited for the Veiled Wilds to open. He didn't just wait; he hoped. But his hopes were dashed every year. Mir was no closer to destroying his cruel divine flower. *Alex should ask around about the herbalist. Maybe this year will be different,* he thought hopefully.

As Mir and Ivan were about to leave, Boris stopped them. "Ivan, you will starve for a week for your interference," he said indifferently.

"Yes, Boss," Ivan muttered, trying to keep a straight face.

Mir practically ran to the elevator, wanting to get away from the stench of rotten flesh as quickly as possible. But Ivan caught up with him.

"I would watch your back from now on," Ivan said through his teeth, his eyes seething with malice.

But Mir paid little attention to Ivan's threats. He went to his apartment to sleep, but tossed and turned in his bed, thinking that he should accept Alex's old offer to live in one of his employees' apartments rather than in Boris's building. Mir needed a place where he could be alone sometimes, and where the smell of rotten flesh didn't penetrate even through the thick walls.

To his surprise, his thoughts drifted to Vesna. She was intriguing, and his magic swirled next to her. He remembered every detail of her face and body. Every thought about her was perfumed with lust, and he instantly became hard. "Fuck me," Mir cursed, frustrated with his reaction to this wicked flower. She clearly wanted nothing to do with poisonous magic, even for one night, and he knew better than to go after someone who rejected him so overtly—just like his parents had. He decided to forget about her altogether and not go to the club on the nights she performed.

MIR KNOCKED on Alex's door for quite a while before Alex finally opened it. He was wearing a robe embroidered with roses, a cup of coffee in his hand.

"Mir, it's Sunday," Alex complained, opening the door wider and walking over to the couch. "Have mercy on me. Rose is a delicate flower."

"I couldn't wait. Besides, it's almost noon," Mir reasoned. "We need to find the herbalist."

"I asked a few people yesterday. But everyone knows I'm under the rafflesia's protection. They don't trust me."

"They trust you more than they trust me," Mir said, and paused abruptly when he saw a girl coming out of the bedroom, a book in her hands. He didn't like the idea of her hearing about the herbalist.

Alex followed Mir's gaze, then shook his head. "Please don't poison Julia," he scolded.

Rolling his eyes at his friend, Mir then turned to Julia, putting steel in his voice. "You heard nothing, got it?" He wanted to remind her of who she was dealing with.

"Yes, I don't want any trouble," Julia said, freezing in place as she met Mir's gaze. She was clearly afraid of him. "I was just leaving." She cleared her throat. "So,

Alex … do you want to visit this place with me?" she asked quietly, looking down at the book in her hands.

"Too depressing for me. Put the book back," Alex said, without even looking up. "Bye, Julia."

As soon as she left, Mir stood up and paced the room, thinking out loud. "Where can the herbalist be hiding?"

"How would I know?" Alex shrugged.

"Give yourself more credit. Charm someone with your magic, for flower's sake, if you need to…" A knock on the door interrupted him. "Oh, what, did Julia forget to kiss you goodbye?"

"Shut up." Alex rolled his eyes and walked to the door.

To Mir's surprise, Anna was standing there, nervously biting her lip.

"Rise and bloom, neighbor!" she sang unnaturally. "I saw a girl leaving your place and thought you were already awake." Her voice sounded a little on edge.

"What do you want?" Alex asked, clearly unhappy that everyone had decided to ruin his Sunday.

"Your best employee needs to borrow your car again." Anna placed her hands together in a prayer.

Crossing his arms, Alex frowned at her. "What for? You never borrowed my car before Vesna showed up," he said. "Is she already going back to her village?"

Mir tensed at the possibility that she might leave because of him. "I may have scared her yesterday," he said, clearing his throat. "But going back to the village because of me is drastic. Tell her I will leave her alone."

Anna's eyes widened as she looked past Alex to Mir; she clearly hadn't expected to see him here. "Mir, hi! No, she's not going back to the village," she said, a little put off. "So, can I borrow the car, Alex?"

Alex sighed. "Okay, but no scratches this time."

"I promise on the divine pink roses!" Anna sang.

"I didn't know you worship the Divine Blooms. So many people just gave up on their gods," Alex said, checking his coat for the keys.

When he finally found them and handed them to her, Anna sighed in relief. "Thanks."

Mir watched her practically run off, and alarm bells started ringing in his mind. There was something suspicious in how Anna was acting. He immediately stood up, grabbing Alex's coat. "Let's go." He gave his friend a little push.

"I'm still in my robe!" Alex protested. "I need time to get ready."

"You look stylish." Mir smirked, walking out of the apartment.

"I don't take style advice from a man who wears nothing but black," Alex fired, but grabbed his coat from Mir, put it on, and followed him.

Anna didn't know Mir's car, so following them wouldn't be difficult. Perhaps he was wasting his time, but some instinct told him that Anna was hiding something. And after years of working for Boris, Mir had become very good at reading people.

They sat in the car and waited for Vesna and Anna to show up. Alex kept complaining about his ruined Sunday. "I'm only coming along to see your expression when they stop at some restaurant to have fun."

"There they are," Mir interrupted him.

Vesna was wearing sunglasses, although it was cloudy outside. Her body was covered with what seemed like millions of layers of cloth. Yet she waved the fan in her hand without stopping, which was more than strange. Spring was late this year, and the air was still frosty.

"What the fuck is Vesna wearing?" Alex said, sitting up straight.

"Exactly my thoughts," Mir said, stepping on the gas.

They drove for quite a while, entering the outskirts of the city. Alex watched in horror as Anna seemed to hit every object on the road in his car. "This is the last time I give her my baby! She's a terrible driver!"

The car turned onto an empty street lined with old houses. They looked abandoned, and Mir became even more suspicious. Yesterday, he had sensed something else trying to overpower Vesna's scent from within.

But it couldn't be… If she were a flower… Mir didn't even want to finish the thought, a sinking feeling settling in the pit of his stomach.

Chapter Six

VESNA.

Sveta was in the middle of preparing a potion in the kitchen when Anna and Vesna practically barged in without even knocking on the door. Startled, Sveta spun around, and her eyes widened in mute horror when she saw Vesna.

Vesna had woken up to the magical scent of magnolia enveloping the entire room. At first, it had been like a warm hug, until she remembered where she was. She'd rushed to the mirror and found that the potion Sveta had prepared for her was clearly too weak to contain her magic. Her eyes had regained their natural color, and her scent was even more overpowering than before.

"I didn't realize how strong your magic is," Sveta whispered mostly to herself. "I'm going to need you both to strengthen the potion with your magic when it's ready. My spells alone aren't enough." She was already grinding the herbs into powder.

"No problem," Anna agreed, settling herself on the couch. "So much for a nice Sunday. I was planning to show Vesna the Graffiti Grove."

"The grove can wait," Vesna said.

"We will discuss it later," Anna insisted.

"There is nothing to discuss!" Vesna snapped. "I'm a disaster right now!"

"We will definitely discuss it," Anna whispered, winking.

Vesna looked at Sveta pleadingly. "See? She's never serious!"

Sveta just laughed, looking into Vesna's glowing eyes. Her gaze was warm, and her eyes slightly watered, as if she could feel the burden Vesna carried in her heart.

"What are you really doing in the city?" Sveta asked, but both Vesna and Anna remained silent. "I can't help you if I don't know what you're looking for."

Anna was staring at Vesna, clearly waiting for permission to speak. Vesna needed Sveta; it probably wouldn't be the last time she needed her help. Besides, she didn't have to tell the truth. She could share Anna's version instead.

"I'm the sacred one," she said, without flinching.

Sveta froze with the herbs in her hands. For a moment, she didn't even seem to breathe. "Cruel gods," she muttered to herself.

"Didn't you hear her?" Anna asked, springing to her feet, too excited to sit still. "She's the sacred one! The Divine Blooms will return!"

"Lower your voice," Sveta said, shooting her an angry look. "I need to work."

Vesna looked at Sveta, surprised. She had expected someone who helped magical people hide their powers to be overjoyed at the sacred one's return. But Sveta looked more shaken than hopeful. She ground the herbs into powder, muttering under her breath. Even Anna fell quiet as Sveta worked.

Vesna barely noticed how her thoughts kept drifting to Mir's bewitching eyes last night, shining like stars she would never dare to reach. She had to admit that her heart beat faster when he had wrapped his arms around her waist as they danced. *It's only because he's the first man who has ever touched me,* she decided. *It has nothing to do with anything else. He's nothing but trouble.*

She ambled around the house, inhaling the scent of dried herbs, imagining what the world had smelled like when the Divine Blooms had lived among people, before they had locked themselves away in the Veiled Wilds. Vesna longed to experience that time when sincere prayer always received an answer. She knew what her wish would be… She wanted to spend at least one more day with her mother, to hear her voice again, to feel her gentle hand on her hair. When Nina had taken Vesna away from the city, Vesna was only five years old. She could only recall scattered moments of time spent with her mother.

Vesna inhaled the scent of dried basil on the windowsill, wondering where Sveta had managed to gather so many herbs. She was old and had little magic, yet so many people were alive because of her.

"How did a woman with little magic become the herbalist that Boris himself is looking for?" Vesna dared to ask.

Sveta cleared her throat. "I was lucky to find a special map. That's how I discovered places where herbs still grow."

"Where did you find it?" Vesna asked. She had never heard of such a map.

Sveta bit her lip. "Someone gave it to me."

Some movement outside the window caught Vesna's eye. She pressed her forehead to the glass, trying to see if anyone was there. Panic threatened to overtake her as she wondered if Boris already knew about her somehow. "We need to check outside," she said, but couldn't make herself move.

Anna jumped up from the couch immediately. "It's too dangerous for you to go out now. Your scent can reach people in other houses, maybe even in passing cars."

"It's also dangerous for you," Vesna tried to argue, but Anna had already left.

Vesna nervously looked out the window while Anna walked around the house.

"Don't worry," Sveta muttered, not taking her eyes off the potion she was making. "Anna has been through a lot; she knows how to stand up for herself."

"What happened to her?" Vesna had never asked Anna about her life or her family, but the more time she spent with her, the more she wondered how Anna had become who she was now.

"I don't know all the details, but I know that after the rafflesia attacked her parents, there was very little magic left in their veins. But it was just enough to survive. Anna took care of them for years, but no matter what she did, they became weaker and weaker," Sveta reported. "People who are born with magic can't survive without it."

Vesna felt a lump in her throat. Anna had been through something terrible, yet she stayed true to herself even now.

The door swung open, and Anna stepped inside. Her face lit up with a smile, as always. "Did you miss me?"

"Yes!" Vesna sighed with relief, surprising herself at how much she'd worried while Anna was outside.

Anna's eyes widened; she clearly hadn't expected such a warm welcome. "No one is there. You're just nervous," she said in a gentle, caring voice.

"It's ready," Sveta finally reported, rubbing her hands with satisfaction. "Now it's your turn, Vesna."

Vesna nodded. She had never used her magic openly. Nina hadn't wanted her to have anything to do with the magical world. Still, Vesna had practiced in the forest when Nina wasn't home. The memory of her aunt throbbed painfully in her heart. *I'll see Nina again,* she tried to convince herself.

Vesna took the potion in her hand, watching the green liquid shimmer. A creamy pollen erupted from her body as she whispered a spell. Her magic seemed thicker than she remembered. Perhaps it was changing as the blooming season was approaching. She noticed Anna and Sveta looking at her magic with admiration.

The scent of magnolia filled the room, and it felt like spring had come early, filling hearts with hope. Her pollen was slowly mixing with the green potion.

"I forgot how beautiful magnolia magic is," Sveta muttered, tears welling up in her eyes.

Vesna looked at her, confused. "I thought you had never met the sacred one."

"I haven't," Sveta said quickly. "I meant in theory." She cleared her throat. "Your turn Anna. Maybe your magic will give Vesna a prophetic dream."

"As they say, no pressure." Anna had to put in her two cents. Her fingers curled around the glass as she whispered a spell. Glowing pollen illuminated everything around her, filling the room with a citrusy and spicy scent. She also prayed, asking the divine marigold to send a message through Vesna's dreams.

The moment Anna was done, Vesna grabbed the glass and raised it to her lips. She didn't want to wait. The sooner she hid her magic, the better.

"Drink it on the couch. You'll fall asleep, like the last time," Sveta suggested.

"Right," Vesna agreed. She sat down and drank half the glass at once. This time, the potion wasn't so bad; the flower magic masked the unpleasant taste. Her eyelids became heavy as soon as she finished the potion. She didn't even notice how she fell asleep…

VESNA FOUND herself in a vivid dream. A blooming fern flower in the middle of tall grass immediately caught her attention. She froze, unable to breathe with the amount of magic the flower held.

I hope this dream will come true. The thought echoed in her head. The flower was blossoming with every color imaginable, enchanting her. *Where am I?* She forced herself to tear her gaze away from the flower and looked around, trying to figure out what this place was.

It was some ancient, abandoned forest. Withered trees grew everywhere, and their petals covered the ground. The rustling of the trees sounded more like muffled voices. Vesna stood still, her eyes closed, listening to the whispers in the air. Somehow, she knew this was important. This place was whispering some secret to her, but no matter how hard she tried, she couldn't make out the words.

"Follow the poison," the voice whispered clearly, and

before Vesna could hear anything else, she opened her eyes.

SHE WAS STILL LYING on the couch. Anna was sitting at her feet, drinking coffee. "She's awake!" Anna cried.

It took a while for Vesna to come back to reality; her dream had been so vivid. She could still see the glow of the fern flower in front of her eyes. *I hope it's real,* she thought, sitting up slowly.

Anna snuggled up to Vesna, and unable to contain her joy, she hugged her. "You're back to normal!" she reported with relief.

Vesna didn't answer, looking at a point in the distance, still hearing the silent pull of the fern flower.

"Did you see anything?" Anna asked, staring at Vesna. Her voice wavered slightly.

Vesna realized how important it was to Anna. She believed Vesna was the sacred one, that the very existence of magic depended on her. And yet Vesna had to admit that all she could think about was her mother and getting revenge. That thought crept into her mind, a thought that made her shudder. She knew that if she had to choose between destroying the rafflesia or simply killing Boris, she would choose revenge, no matter the consequences for everyone else.

"So?" Anna stared at her, waiting for an answer.

Vesna frowned, trying to remember everything. The details of the vivid dream were quickly fading from her memory. She opened her mouth to speak, but suddenly couldn't remember where she had been in the dream. "I saw the fern flower, but then…" She frowned, trying to focus. "I can't remember."

Anna smiled sadly, clearly trying to mask her disappointment. "It's normal. Vivid dreams are hard to remember, especially for someone who doesn't have marigold magic."

"Follow the poison," Vesna whispered, as the words came to her out of nowhere. "I was told to follow the poison."

"Dammit," Anna cursed and stared at Vesna. "So, he really is the way."

Vesna knew what Anna was thinking. It could be no coincidence that she had met Mir on her first night at the club. The Divine Blooms knew better, and they had made it clear that she should stick with him. But inside Vesna, everything protested. And not only because she wanted to avoid poisonous magic, but because Mir held such a seductive allure. And at such an important moment, her thoughts shouldn't linger on his snow-white eyes and muscular body.

"I don't know if I can do it." Vesna shook her head.

"Vesna, think about it." Anna dove into her eyes, trying to reason with her. "He's close to Boris himself. He has access to the building." She paused. "And he obviously likes you."

Even though Vesna and Anna were after different things, Mir had to be the way forward. Anna was right: Mir did seem interested in her, at least from what she had seen yesterday. And judging by his interaction with Ivan, he must be close to Boris. If she played it smart, he could be her ticket to the spring ball, and maybe even to Boris himself.

"Who are we talking about?" Sveta asked, breaking the silence.

"Mir," Anna whispered.

Sveta's eyes clouded over. "I know that name. He's

looking for me on Boris's behalf," she muttered and then laughed quietly.

Vesna looked at Sveta, at her old, tired face, and saw a hint of madness in her eyes.

With a sigh, Vesna said, "And the Divine Blooms couldn't have given me the message yesterday, before I told him to leave me alone?"

"He'll survive." Anna smirked. "Just be more charming with him tonight."

"What if he doesn't come to the club? I practically told him to never talk to me again," Vesna said.

"Oh, you know nothing about men, Vesna. Mir will be there," Anna assured her.

I know nothing about men. The thought bloomed painfully in her mind. She wasn't sure what she was so afraid of. Of course, she was afraid of being discovered and killed by the rafflesia, but there was something else too… A seed of worry had sprouted in her soul that getting close to Mir might distract her from her plan.

Vesna checked her eyes maybe a million times before leaving for the club. To her surprise, Alex came to her dressing room as she was about to go on stage.

"Alex?" she asked, looking into his rose-kissed eyes. His scent was even more enticing in the small room, away from other people. Vesna liked roses, and Alex couldn't have been a more accurate representation of his flower. He was handsome, playful, and friendly, but kept to himself, just like his flower. And Vesna was sure he could use his thorns if he needed to. "Do you need something?" she asked, a little lost as Alex looked at her silently, as if he were seeing her for the first time.

"Not really, just came to check on you." He cleared his throat, as if waking from his thoughts. "Nice dress."

"It's in honor of your flower," she said timidly, smoothing her dress. It was bright red, studded with green gems that represented the leaves of the rose, the same temporary eye color as Vesna's. "So, do you need something?"

"No," Alex murmured, his voice uncertain. Something was clearly wrong with him today. "I asked the band to pick out some modern songs for you tonight. I hope that's okay with you."

"It's okay." Vesna smiled slightly. She would sing anything to get closer to Boris.

"After the performance, sit at the bar for a while; the guests like to chat with the singers and dancers."

"Fine, if they really just want to chat." Vesna raised an eyebrow meaningfully.

"Well, if you've already dealt with Ivan and Mir, the rest will be a piece of cake for you." Alex smiled.

The mere mention of Mir's name made Vesna tense up. "Will Mir come tonight?" she asked, trying to sound as casual as possible.

"I'm not sure. His boss has a grudge against him, so Mir might work tonight." Alex shrugged.

Vesna nodded, feeling a strange mix of disappointment, dread, and anticipation. She needed Mir to follow through with her, if her dream was true. But she was afraid of letting such poison close to her.

When she walked onto the stage, she realized the club was even more crowded than yesterday. She tried to see if Mir was there, tried to catch his enchanting, intoxicating scent in the air. But as far as she could tell, he hadn't come. Disappointment filled her being. Her entire plan depended on Mir. *What if he isn't really inter-*

ested in me? If he wasn't, she had no idea how to get his attention. The thought worried her.

Alex had prepared an entire show. While Vesna was singing, girls in short red dresses were dancing in the background. And the musicians were whistling to the beat of the music, warming up the crowd. But tonight, the song left her lips mechanically, without any feelings. She desperately wanted to finish the performance as soon as possible and check if Mir was here.

She glanced around the room as the last beat of the music faded and the projector lights went out. *He didn't come,* she thought disappointedly and headed for the bar.

Several men approached her, complimenting her voice, asking her meaningless questions. Vesna was polite and even smiled a few times, since Alex had asked her to entertain the guests. But out of the corner of her eye, she kept glancing at the entrance, hoping that Mir would walk in, blinding everyone around with his poisonous gaze.

"He didn't come," Vesna whispered to Anna, who was working behind the bar.

"If not tonight, then tomorrow. Be patient. Even flowers need time to flourish, and our plan certainly won't work overnight," Anna assured her. "Oh, you have company."

The smell of alcohol smothered Vesna as soon as the man approached, grabbing her hand even before he spoke.

"Get your filthy hand off me!" Vesna demanded.

"Or what?" He laughed, squeezing her hand even tighter.

Vesna shoved away from him, but his grip was relentless. "Leave me alone, pervert!"

He smirked. "Isn't it your job to entertain customers?"

"Entertain yourself somewhere else!" Anna said, leaning over the bar.

But before Anna even moved, Mir appeared next to Vesna. His eyes flashed with death as he looked at the man's hand gripping hers. White pollen appeared in the air, and Mir effortlessly removed the man's hand from Vesna and pointed it straight into the mist.

"He *poisoned* me!" the man screamed in horror.

"No one touches her, got it?" Mir said through gritted teeth, his voice sharp as a blade. "Get lost, or I will kill you," he warned, his voice deadly low, and Vesna knew he wasn't lying.

He came! The thought ran through her mind, and she couldn't help but smile with relief. So far, everything was going according to her plan. "Thank you," she said, glancing at Mir.

He held her gaze shamelessly. His snow-white eyes looked even brighter against the black clothes, like shining stars in the dark sky. She felt his honeyed scent seep into every cell of her body, and she was afraid that she would start hallucinating from it.

"Did he hurt you?" Mir dove into Vesna's eyes, and to her surprise, she saw genuine concern.

"No," she answered quietly, hiding the mark left by the man's grip on her hand.

Mir's gaze darted to the reddened skin. "Bastard! I must chop off his hand!" he declared, ready to leave.

"No!" Vesna screamed in horror, grabbing Mir with both hands. "I'm sure he learned his lesson," she said almost pleadingly.

"You care about a dirty human?" Mir raised an eyebrow.

"I'm human too," she breathed.

"Right," Mir muttered, looking at her with a frown. "I'll tell you what. I will let him live, *if* you come with me." He smiled, and Vesna frowned. Even if she had planned to get close to him, she still didn't trust him. Who knew what the poisonous flower was up to? "I promise to be good. We got off on the wrong foot yesterday."

Vesna froze for a second; it felt a lot like an actual date. But she decided she was just following the plan. "Fine, but this isn't a date. And keep your hands to yourself," she said, standing up.

"I'm not that desperate." Mir smirked. "But when the datura blooms, stay away from me."

"Why?" Vesna asked, though she knew the answer. Apart from amplifying magical powers, the blooming season intensified every emotion in magical people as they blossomed. Love, hate, or desire—everything was heightened to its peak. These were raw, uncontrollable feelings.

"The blooming season amplifies all my desires—and you, wicked flower, are one of them," he said bluntly, staring at her.

"Noted," Vesna muttered, a shiver running down her spine from his sinful gaze.

Chapter Seven

MIR.

WHAT MIR AND ALEX SAW THROUGH THE WINDOW LEFT them both speechless. This was obviously the herbalist's house. Boris was right: it was a woman. But that wasn't the most shocking thing. Even the revelation of the fact that Anna had magic wasn't that shocking. But the thought that Vesna wielded magic—and not just any magic, but the magic of the first sacred divine flower on earth—left Mir stunned.

He couldn't hear anything after Anna went to check outside and they had to hide farther away, but he'd heard enough before that. The moment he had been waiting for so many years had finally arrived. The sacred one was here. He would have a real chance to put an end to the poisonous magic and finally leave Boris and all the rafflesia behind.

Mir knew full well that the path of the sacred one would be difficult, most likely even tragic. If Boris learned that the new sacred one had appeared, he would stop at nothing until he claimed her. Mir had to protect Vesna, no matter the cost. She was the key to opening the Veiled Wilds. He couldn't let Boris have her. Even though Boris also wanted to find the Veiled Wilds, he was still a parasite. He had completely drained the last sacred one, and there was no guarantee he would be able to control himself once he found Vesna. Mir didn't know what exactly she was doing here, but it was obvious that she was up to something, given she was in the city with just enough time before Ivan Kupala Night.

He couldn't help but hold his breath in awe when he saw Vesna's eyes sparkling with ancient magic. It was mesmerizing—holy, even. Her true eyes were creamy with a hint of pink, like magnolia petals themselves. And her smell… It was so perfectly sweet, overwhelming, and enchanting. He could smell it even from the outside. The traitorous thought of how divine it would be to inhale that scent in a moment of bliss, when she would bloom under his sinful touch, drove him crazy.

Cut it off, Mir, he commanded himself. *You only need her to get to the divine datura.*

"What the fuck?" Alex interrupted Mir's thoughts. "You can't trust anyone these days!" he fired, watching Vesna's magic leave her body. "Do you see her eyes?" he asked quietly.

"Yes," Mir muttered. "Sacred magnolia."

Alex froze, looking at Mir with fear. "You can't take them to Boris," he said suddenly. "I know you're loyal, but—"

Mir hadn't let him finish, sensing Alex's uneasiness. Anna was his friend, and Alex had never wanted to be involved with the rafflesia in the first place. "I won't. Not yet, anyway," Mir assured him.

Vesna was no ordinary girl. Her magic was ancient, alluring, and unknown. Mir knew little about the divine magic of magnolia. He had to learn everything about it, if he was going to use her.

Unfortunately, Mir and Alex couldn't hear everything. They had just watched, patiently waiting for Vesna and Anna to leave the herbalist's. For a moment, Mir considered going inside. Boris would leave him alone if he brought him the herbalist, and Mir would be able to focus on Vesna. But it wasn't about Boris anymore... Only Vesna mattered now. She could find the Veiled Wilds. Mir had to think. He was closer than he'd ever been to getting what he wanted.

"Let's go back," Mir muttered to Alex.

Alex's red eyes sparkled. "Will you let the herbalist be?"

"First, I need a plan—and you need to help me."

"Anything you need, man," Alex said, and Mir felt grateful to him for the millionth time. He could always count on Alex.

Mir had driven back deep in his thoughts, but Alex seemed too excited to remain silent. "So, the time has come! Hopefully, it won't be the night of vanished petals all over again," he muttered.

"The sacred one will have us this time," Mir said, surprising even himself.

Alex's eyebrows shot to his forehead in surprise, and hope shone like a moon in his eyes. "Are you going against Boris?!"

"Boris is just a parasite. I only work for him because I thought he would find the sacred one. But apparently, I was wrong. I don't need him."

"You can stay in the apartment in my building. Let's go get your things!" Alex practically shouted, his voice full of happiness, even relief. "You don't belong there; you're not a parasite."

Mir laughed. "Not so fast. I need to be next to Boris now more than ever. If Vesna is in danger, I'll be the first to know." He paused. "But I'll take you up on your offer anyway, to be as close to Vesna as I can."

"You're right, but I just want the rafflesia gone," Alex said, quickly adding, "Don't tell your boss."

"Your secret is safe with me." Mir smirked. "We still don't know what Vesna is planning. If she's appeared in the city, then something has changed in the divine plans." He paused. "She must be here for something. That's the only reason a sacred one would put herself at such risk by coming into Boris's territory."

"He could drain her like the last sacred one," Alex muttered.

An ugly image immediately flashed before Mir's eyes. "I won't let that happen. I need to get to the Veiled Wilds, and not even Boris can stop me when I'm this close."

"You still want to destroy your divine flower…"

The look Alex gave him had Mir looking away in discomfort. They'd had this conversation countless times, but nothing Alex could say would change his mind.

"Don't leave me, man," Alex whispered.

"Don't tell anyone about what you saw today," Mir said, needing to change the subject. He couldn't take the sound of Alex's heart breaking. "And act normal around Anna, and especially around Vesna."

"But they have magic!" Alex said, clearly still in shock. "They are one of us!"

"Alex, don't ruin it. Do you understand?" Mir asked, his voice steely. "We still have time before Ivan Kupala. I need to be next to her, to be sure she opens the Veiled Wilds for me."

"Fine," Alex muttered, rolling down the window and letting in the cool air.

Mir caught a warm note on the breeze. Flowering season was coming, and he knew that magnolia was the first bloomer. Vesna had mentioned she'd soon turn twenty-five. It would be hard for her to hide once she came into full bloom.

"I'm with you, no matter what. But don't you dare disappear from my life," Alex said, so quietly, as if he were talking to himself.

Mir knew that Alex probably suspected that destroying the divine datura could mean the destruction of everyone who wielded its magic. It meant that Mir could die… *Maybe I'll finally feel the peace that datura flower is supposed to bring at the very end. Maybe this will be my way of atoning for all my sins,* he thought.

MIR SPENT the rest of the day in the public library, looking for information on the divine magnolia. Boris had most of the books on the Divine Blooms in his private collection, but he didn't allow anyone to set foot in there. Luckily, humans still had books on flower magic.

The librarian brought out a huge encyclopedia, eyeing Mir suspiciously. Mir wore sunglasses to hide his white eyes, but people could still smell him. In truth, he didn't care. People knew that divine magic still existed, or at least they gossiped about it.

He quickly flipped through the pages, looking for a picture of a magnolia flower. It was one of the first drawings. Mir read the caption underneath the picture.

From what Mir had seen, Anna's own magic sparkled like the golden rays of the sunset. After reading about several flowers that matched this description, Mir concluded that Anna had the magic of the divine marigold flower. This flower gave the magic of prophetic and vivid dreams, as well as the ability to enter the dreams of others. It could speed up healing. He still couldn't believe that all these years, she had been right under his nose, and he hadn't even suspected she was a magic wielder.

He sat in the library, not even realizing that it was already dark outside. It wasn't until the librarian approached him, nervously clearing his throat, that Mir finally left. He had no intention of staying home tonight —or any future nights, for that matter. Vesna was too important to leave alone. Even if she wanted nothing to do with him, he had to find a way to be next to her.

Mir quickly got ready, afraid of being late. He had waited too long for this moment to go wrong. Before he left, he noticed a stack of invitations to the upcoming spring ball and cursed. The last thing he needed was to worry about Boris's stupid ball. Mir had been tasked with delivering invitations to all the important human families and politicians—even those who were against the rafflesia. Boris used the ball as a way to get information out of people, hoping to learn something about the Veiled Wilds. And with Mir's magic, they wouldn't even remember attending.

When Mir walked into Fading Blossoms, he saw Vesna immediately. He was late, and she had already performed. Now she was sitting at the bar, talking to Anna. Vesna looked like a delicate rose in her red silk dress. Mir had to admit she was breathtaking. His heartbeat quickened, and he licked his lips, watching her perfect body from behind. The interest and attraction he had tried to suppress yesterday sprouted again at the mere sight of this wicked flower.

Just as Mir was deciding how to approach her, a drunk guy approached Vesna first. He gripped her hand, and that was enough to drive Mir to the brink of madness. He felt his magic spiraling inside his veins, and his vision blurred slightly from the amount of poison that was demanding to get out.

"No one touches her, got it?!" Mir snapped, stalking over to them both and towering over the man. He wouldn't let anyone touch this wicked flower, and not just because she was sacred, but because *he* wanted to be the one to touch her. Mir wanted to poison the drunk right there, but quickly changed his mind. He remembered how Vesna had reacted to his magic yesterday. He didn't want to scare her away again.

To Mir's satisfaction, Vesna agreed to leave with him. As she stood up, Mir couldn't help but stare at her bright red dress, which hugged every curve of her body perfectly. The urge to take it off and taste her, inhaling her actual scent and feeling the flowers blooming on her skin was too strong. But she wasn't just any girl. Mir cleared his throat instead, trying to suppress the desire to possess this flower.

They got into his car, and Mir smirked as he noticed that Vesna had put her seat belt on. No girl that sat in his car had ever done that; it was impossible to kiss or anything else with the seat belt on. *Tonight will be different,* he thought, feeling disappointed. He couldn't deny that he was drawn to her. It would be perfect to taste this flower right now. But his plan was more important.

Still, Mir stole glances at her as he drove. She didn't speak to him, looking out the window instead. He would have given anything to know what she was thinking. But he knew for sure that she didn't think of him the way he thought of her, and he couldn't blame her.

"So, where are you taking me?" Vesna finally asked, turning her head to meet his gaze.

"It's a surprise," Mir replied with a honeyed voice.

"I hope you're not some kind of maniac who kills girls at night to practice his magic?" she asked seriously.

Mir laughed. "No, I wield poison magic, but that doesn't mean I'm a maniac."

"Just checking." Vesna raised an eyebrow. Her eyes glittered slightly, as if she were enjoying the moment. And Mir smiled to himself. It was nice to see her forget about his poisonous magic for a moment and see *him* instead.

"So, if I'm not your type, and this drunk guy clearly isn't your type either, then who is?" Mir dove into her eyes. "Don't tell me it's Alex."

"He's not bad, and I like roses," Vesna drawled, as if considering the possibility. Mir squeezed the steering wheel, somehow feeling jealous. "But no." She shifted in her seat, trying to get comfortable.

"Roses have too many thorns, but datura has none," Mir said suggestively.

"I'm pretty sure I read that datura has thorns on its seed capsules. That's why they called datura the devil's trumpet." Vesna bit her lip immediately, as if realizing she'd said too much.

Of course you did, Mir thought, but he wasn't going to draw attention to it. Vesna shifted again, trying to straighten her legs. "Let me move the seat back, so you have more room," Mir sang, reaching his hand across her body.

His cheek was almost touching hers, and he could feel her warm breath on his skin, a tremor running through his body. He froze, clenching his fist and fighting the overwhelming desire to feel her soft lips against his. Her closeness was mind-blowing. He was sure he could bloom before his season even began, just from her touch.

"We're going to crash into something," she whispered huskily.

The way she looked at him, her eyes wide and her cheeks slightly pink, made his magic stir. Mir licked his lips and slowly backed away. "Has Anna shown you Graffiti Grove?" he asked, clearing his throat, still feeling the warmth of her sacred body.

"No, but she threatened to take me there under duress, because—"

Vesna didn't finish because Mir started laughing. She looked at him with surprise.

"Under duress?" Mir asked, still laughing.

"I'm serious." Vesna pouted.

Mir couldn't help but stare at her. She was so different, so beckoning. "This is one of my favorite places in the city. We're almost there," he said, stepping on the gas, afraid he would try to kiss her if they stayed in the car any longer. But he had a goal only she could help him with, and it was bigger than just the desire to taste her.

Mir opened the door for Vesna, his hand lingering on the handle, unsure of how to act around her. She was the sacred one, but he still saw the wicked flower that had intrigued him at first sight. He extended his hand, helping her out of the car. To his satisfaction, she didn't argue, and her gentle touch burned him with some kind of tenderness. He felt his magic flare up, like the last time he had touched her.

"I didn't think you were a gentleman." She dove into his eyes. Her gaze penetrated deeper into his soul than the roots of any flower could.

If this world were fair, we wouldn't be growing on different sides of the meadow, he thought sadly. "You don't know me, but I hope that will change soon." He cleared his throat and shifted his gaze away from her, reminding himself that he was just using her. "Graffiti Grove is this way," he said, heading into the dark alley.

Vesna followed him closely, as if afraid of the place. Mir stopped when the colorful graffiti began. He had loved this place since he was a teenager. It was his escape from reality.

Mir watched Vesna as she stopped next to the first graffiti. It seemed she didn't even remember anymore that he was there. He studied her eagerly, her full lips parted slightly, her eyes shining as she looked at the image of the first sacred flower on earth—her flower. The graffiti depicted the first bloom of the divine magnolia, when sacred magic flowed, permeating and enchanting everything around. It was a hundred million years ago, and for a long time, there was only one sacred flower. People prayed to it, and some children were born with sacred magic, their eyes different from the eyes of ordinary human babies, and their scent could enchant everyone around.

"This is my favorite flower," Vesna whispered, moving to the next graffiti.

Mir remained silent, sensing that she was oblivious to her surroundings, as if the past had somehow overtaken her. The second generation of Divine Blooms was portrayed on the next wall.

"Since you don't wield magic, you probably don't know these flowers," Mir said, walking up to the wall and pointing at the flowers one by one. "Lavender, sunflower, rose, datura, foxglove, hibiscus…"

Her mesmerizing eyes darted to his before she spoke. "Your sacred flower is pretty."

"Maybe to others," Mir muttered before adding, "but to me, it's ugly."

Vesna's eyes widened, as if she could sense his pain and anger for his divine flower. Mir hadn't planned for her to know what he thought of his magic, but for some reason, he couldn't pretend around her. He decided he'd have to be careful from now on. "I must admit, I don't know all of them myself," he said, quickly changing the subject. "Like these." He stopped next to the image of small purple flowers.

"This is the divine forget-me-not flower," Vesna whispered, smiling to herself. "It symbolizes the lasting memories of the people you've cherished."

"Hmm, I see," Mir said curiously. Of course Vesna knew all about flowers and their magic. He wondered if she had read about it, or if the divine magnolia had somehow given the knowledge to her together with the sacred magic. She was a mystery that he wasn't destined to solve. "Well, it's no wonder I don't know its name. It's not my kind of flower at all."

Vesna turned to him, her eyes wide in surprise. "You don't have anyone you would like to remember forever?"

"No," he replied simply. "Well, actually, I do: I have Alex. And you?"

Vesna took a deep breath before answering. "My mother."

"You're lucky," Mir said, then quickly hurried to the next wall. He didn't want to talk about his parents.

Vesna followed him, and Mir narrowed his eyes. The other night, Ivan had clearly frightened Vesna. But Mir wanted to see her reaction to the graffiti of the rafflesia flower, wanted to see how much she hated it.

Vesna gritted her teeth as soon as she looked at the huge reddish-brown parasite. Mir noticed she took a deep breath, as if trying to calm herself down. He immediately realized that she hated the rafflesia and everything associated with it. *Why are you here, then, so close to your enemy?* Mir wondered.

The next wall had no graffiti, only the words: *The Veiled Wilds.* "Why is this wall empty?" Vesna turned to Mir.

Mir had to hide his smirk. Vesna was an excellent actress. She acted as if she really knew nothing about the Veiled Wilds. Yet Mir wasn't mad at all; she was doing what she had to. "The Divine Blooms abandoned people, locking themselves away in some unknown place. We call it the Veiled Wilds," he explained patiently.

The next graffiti was simply unbearable, even for Mir: the night of vanished petals, when rafflesia had brutally drained all the magic wielders.

"How did you survive?" Vesna asked quietly.

"Rafflesia spared the children, so that they would

have someone to parasitize," Mir explained. "Besides, no one would want to drink poison, not even parasites."

Her eyes locked on him in silence, when suddenly the sound of heavy footsteps approached quickly. Mir turned toward the noise, stepping in from of Vesna to shield her. "Don't say a word," he muttered.

Ivan appeared in the alley, dispelling the gentle atmosphere with his nasty smell. Several of his men followed him. "How's the date going?" he asked with a smirk. "I was waiting for you near the club, but you made my task easier by coming to this deserted place."

"Ivan, get lost, for your own sake," Mir warned him through clenched teeth.

"I told you, I forget nothing. I'll not starve because of you. It's time to get rid of the poison," Ivan said with a crooked smile on his face. He pulled out a knife, and his men followed his example.

"Let the girl go," Mir demanded, still shielding Vesna.

"It's a shame to get rid of such a beauty, but I don't need witnesses." Ivan grinned and quickly moved toward Mir. His men did the same.

"Run. This won't be pretty," Mir said, turning to Vesna for a second. This fleeting glance was enough to see the fear inside her bottomless eyes. "I'll find you. Go!"

She stared at him with a look full of regret, as if she didn't want to leave him, but the next second, she dashed into the depths of the alley.

"Catch up with her!" Ivan ordered one of his men.

Mir had no time to waste; he had to finish Ivan and save Vesna. He immediately released his pollen, while Ivan and his men put out their parasitic roots. Depending on how much magic they absorbed, the roots were either weaker or stronger. Ivan seemed to be the only one whose roots would be difficult to cut.

Mir's pollen quickly moved toward the parasites. He had never summoned so much magic before, but the thought of Vesna being in danger seemed to strengthen his powers. His poison spread across the parasites. Ivan's men, affected immediately, began to experience all the stages of datura's poison. They fell to the ground, barely able to move, begging for water. Soon the hallucinations came, and they screamed so loudly that Mir got a headache. The next second, the alley was silent as they froze lifeless on the ground.

But Ivan remained unaffected. *The parasite came prepared,* Mir thought with hatred. Ivan had probably found a magic wielder and drained him just before arriving, so Mir's magic couldn't seep into his veins so easily. Now, Mir's only option was to fight. If he managed to cut him, his poison would enter his bloodstream that very second.

Ivan was the best fighter among Boris's men. He wasn't easy to defeat. Mir dodged his attacks, but Ivan dodged just as skillfully. With a swift movement, Ivan's blade slashed Mir's hand, and a crimson stream of blood gushed out. At the same moment, one of Ivan's roots dug into Mir's shoulder.

Hatred flared in Mir's eyes. *It's time to finish you,* he thought angrily.

He raised his hand, growling in pain, and cut off the root embedded in his shoulder with his blade. Then he advanced toward Ivan again, moving his knife quickly.

Just then, a distant scream full of pain and hopelessness filled the alley, and Mir's heart stopped for a second. It was the gentle and magical voice of Vesna... He was too late.

Like a madman, he attacked Ivan again and again, not even really seeing the man in front of him; only Vesna's face stood before his eyes. Mir cut Ivan's chest deeply, and he screamed in pain. Mir whispered a spell immediately, and his magic finally squeezed into Ivan's cut, instantly sending him into a coma. Turning swiftly, Mir ran with all his might.

The time was melting away into a painful eternity. Vesna had escaped quite far, and Mir ran for a while, peering into the darkness for anything that resembled a human silhouette. Suddenly he stopped, and his magical blood froze in his veins like a flower freezing in winter.

Vesna lay on the ground, holding her hand to her stomach as blood flowed from her wound like a red river. Mir felt nothing for a second, as if his heart had left him. Then for the first time in his adult life, he felt a fear of losing someone. He had no time to explore this feeling further.

Mir looked at the man standing over Vesna, a bloody knife in his hand. Something snapped inside him, and for the first time, Mir called upon magic he didn't think he possessed. The datura flower had another name; people called it the devil's trumpet—and Mir was ready to play it. His pollen swirled in the air, and from its depths, snow-white petals of datura, covered in knife-sharp thorns, wove their way out. They rushed toward the man and pierced his body. Within seconds, he fell lifeless to the ground.

Mir ran up to Vesna just as she lost consciousness. Her pale face was even whiter than the petals of his divine flower. He took her in his arms, holding his breath. She was so small and fragile, and he tried not to squeeze her too tightly.

"Don't you dare die on me, wicked flower. Not like

this." Mir knew she couldn't hear him. But somehow, by talking to her, he felt she was not lost yet.

As if in a nightmare, Mir went to the street. Night was still covering the city. He walked to his car, noticing that the tires were all flat. *Fucking parasite, I will get even with you,* he cursed with hatred.

Mir had to hurry. Vesna's wound was too deep… The only thing that could save her now was magic. Luckily, Alex's club was nearby. Mir walked as fast as he could, carrying the precious flower in his hands. Vesna was unconscious the whole time, and he listened to her barely audible breathing with bated breath.

"Don't leave," Mir muttered to her—the same words he'd said to his parents the day they'd brought him to the orphanage. *Pull yourself together,* he thought, angry at how weak he was when it came to old wounds. *She can't die. I'm so close…* But his heart stopped as he looked at her almost lifeless face. He growled, stopping the thought that there could be more to it—the thought that when this wicked flower had entered his poisonous life, his magic had surged through his veins again, as if he'd come back to life.

Mir didn't even think about using the back entrance of the club. Anton, the security guard, looked at him in shock. "Move," Mir commanded, his voice full of determination.

Anton immediately stepped back, opening the door. "Smells like rafflesia had a hand in this."

The club was already closing, so almost everyone had left. Only two drunk customers were sitting at the bar, talking to Anna. Mir looked around the room, and his eyes flickered when he saw his friend coming out from behind the curtain.

"Fuck!" Alex said loudly, and everyone stared at the entrance.

Anna immediately left the bar. "We're closed!" she shouted to Anton.

Mir went to one table and carefully laid Vesna on the couch. *Still breathing,* he thought hopefully, lowering his head to her lips.

"What happened?!" Anna asked, her voice trembling. She leaned over, checking Vesna's pulse.

"She lost a lot of blood." Mir's eyes shot to Alex. "Rose magic controls blood flow. Come on!"

Mir glanced at Anna too; marigold magic could speed up healing. But Mir knew Anna wouldn't risk using it in front of him. She stood there, completely lost, her eyes fixed on her dying friend. Alex also just stared at Vesna, as if paralyzed.

"Alex, use your fucking magic, for flower's sake!" Mir yelled angrily.

Alex jumped, but thankfully acted immediately. He whispered a spell, and the red pollen slowly grew, sending a pleasant, fruity, and slightly mossy scent through the room. It slowly touched Vesna, completely enveloping her body. Mir could barely breathe—maybe because of the overpowering scent of roses, or maybe because his heart ached when he looked at Vesna's pale face again.

"What next?" Alex whispered, as if afraid to break the silence.

"Send more magic," Mir insisted. "Then let's find something to clean the cut with," he said and saw Anna's face relax a little. Of course she would use her magic as soon as they left. At least, he hoped she would.

Mir felt like shit; he shouldn't have brought Vesna to the grove. It was dangerous. *He* was dangerous. He and his magic had brought nothing good to this world. It was stupid to think that Ivan wouldn't try to attack him after Boris had sided with Mir yesterday.

Mir watched as Alex's gracious magic once again entered Vesna's wound, and Mir felt hatred for the divine datura again—it was poisonous, dark, and completely useless right now.

"I'll keep an eye on her," Anna said as soon as Alex finished.

Mir practically dragged Alex backstage.

"What the hell happened?!" Alex demanded, hastily grabbing some alcohol and clean towels.

"Ivan." Mir fell silent, his heart filling with guilt. "He wanted to get rid of me."

Alex's brows slammed together, and he whirled on Mir. "And you put *the sacred one* at risk like that?!"

Mir hadn't expected such fury. He knew Alex was a believer, but looking at his friend now, Mir realized Alex worshiped the Divine Blooms with all his faith.

"We need scissors," Mir muttered, trying to tamp down the guilt he felt.

"Yes." Alex's voice was empty. "Let's go."

"Wait." Mir reached a hand out, stopping his friend. "Anna wields the magic of marigold; it can speed up healing."

"Do you think she'll use it right in front of us?" Alex asked doubtfully.

"I hope so. But let's wait until she finishes."

They stood behind the curtain, watching the golden pollen cover Vesna. Anna whispered one spell after another, and Mir realized that her magic was not only strong, but she knew how to use it. The scent of marigold filled the club. They waited a little longer, even after Anna finished; he didn't want Anna to suspect that they knew about her.

When they finally returned, Mir sat next to Vesna. She looked like a dying flower, torn from its magic. Alex set water, towels, alcohol, and scissors on the table, intending to tend to Vesna's wound.

"Give it to me. I'm not sure you know how to clean wounds. If she…" Mir cleared his throat. "When she wakes up, we don't want a fever." He grabbed a towel and soaked it in water. Then he carefully cut Vesna's dress with the scissors and began cleaning the wound of blood.

"Who attacked her?" Anna demanded.

"It had nothing to do with Vesna. Ivan and his men came for me. Vesna…" Mir fell silent. "She was in the wrong place at the wrong time."

"You asshole!" Anna snapped, her gaze cutting into him. "You put her in danger! Poison will always be poison."

Anna wasn't saying anything he didn't already think, but her words squeezed into his soul and pierced him with pain all the same.

Alex opened a bottle of whiskey and poured himself a full glass, then turned to Anna. "Want some?"

"Please." She sat down next to him and rested her head on his shoulder. "My nerves are on edge."

"Tell me about it." Alex smirked sadly, brushing away a few strands of hair that had fallen over her face.

"Did you at least kill them?" Anna faced Mir.

"Some. But Ivan will come out of his coma in a few days," Mir answered, now wiping the wound with alcohol. He tilted his head, listening to Vesna's heartbeat. He sighed with relief. "Her heartbeat is getting stronger; all we can do is wait."

"Good." Alex clapped his hands, then stared at Mir's blood-stained shirt. "You know I hate the sight of blood. Let me get you some of my clothes."

"I'm not dressing up in your flowers," Mir protested, staring at his cuts. He had completely forgotten that he was wounded too.

"Too bad." Alex cut him off, already heading backstage.

"Where did you take her?" Anna asked, and Mir narrowed his eyes at her.

Obviously, Vesna staying with Anna wasn't a coincidence. She didn't just know what Vesna was looking for; she was helping her. Mir knew little about Anna. He hadn't thought she had magic, so he never focused on her. In truth, he didn't focus on anyone unless it was part of his job. Alex had been his only companion ever since they were kids. He had to admit it felt strange, sitting here together with them, helping Vesna, making sure she would survive. But he also had to admit it wasn't that bad.

"I showed her Graffiti Grove," Mir muttered.

"Why the fuck did you take her there at *night*?" Anna snapped, crossing her arms and glaring at him.

"It was a mistake," Mir said guiltily.

Her hardened gaze widened with surprise. "I'm glad your poisonous heart can admit it when you're wrong," she snorted.

Alex returned with a red shirt decorated with a pattern of rose petals and handed it to Mir. "Here, change into this."

Mir immediately shook his head. "Seriously, you—"

"No, not a word," Alex said firmly.

Mir put on the shirt, muttering under his breath. "I look like a clown," he said helplessly.

"The color red makes your eyes pop," Alex said, a hint of sarcasm in his voice.

"Shut up." Mir rolled his eyes just as Vesna made a barely audible sound. He tensed, unable to hide the hope he felt. He moved closer to her, sitting on the edge of the couch, trying not to move her body.

"Vesna," he whispered, and his voice sounded too nervous.

"My name sounds beautiful on your lips," she whispered back, clearly still in a daze.

Anna loudly cleared her throat. "She's hallucinating or something."

"Obviously," Mir said, but a faint smile touched his lips.

"Where am I?" Vesna looked around and tried to sit up, but then she growled, her face contorted in pain. She put her hand on the wound, trying to see it.

"You're at the club. Alex helped heal your wound." Mir said the first thing that came to his mind. He wanted to say so much more. He wanted to apologize for putting her at risk.

"How bad is it?" Vesna turned her head to Anna.

"It's not that bad," Anna said, much calmer than Mir had. "But you will need to rest for a few days."

"Are you going to fire me, Boss?" Vesna tried to smile, looking at Alex.

"You wish," Alex teased, happiness shining in his eyes.

"How did I get here?" Vesna squeezed out the words, grimacing in pain.

"Too many questions, wicked flower," Mir said, adjusting her pillow. He felt relieved and even happy. Not only because he still had a chance to reach the divine datura, but also because he would be close to this wicked flower.

Mir thought about taking Vesna to his place, to be close in case her condition worsened. But it wasn't safe; he couldn't risk bringing Vesna under the same roof where Boris lived. *I need to move into their building.* The desire to leave the rafflesia forever and live his own life suddenly overwhelmed him. But he quickly dismissed the thought. He would be a fool to believe that his color-less and poisonous life could ever truly blossom.

Chapter Eight

VESNA.

VESNA TRIED TO RESIST THE FEELING THAT FILLED HER heart. But looking at Mir, Anna, and Alex next to her, she felt grateful and even happy that the divine magnolia had sent friends to her. Well, maybe calling Alex and Mir friends was a stretch, but that was how she felt at that moment.

She remembered nothing after the attack. But she remembered everything that had happened before. Mostly the way Mir studied her face when she looked at the graffiti. It was as if he wanted to read her mind, to see as deeply as her soul. And the worst thing was that part of her wanted to let him in. This city was changing her, and she was afraid of what those changes might bring.

When Ivan showed up, she hadn't known what to do. If she was powerful, it certainly didn't look like it back there. She simply ran, leaving Mir alone. She could have sent her magic to empower Mir and help him win the fight, but the stakes were too high. She couldn't risk her need for revenge just to help this poisonous man. But a small part of her soul was whining even more than her wound. She didn't owe him anything; on the contrary, he was practically an enemy. After all, he worked for Boris. Still, she couldn't help but feel like a traitor for leaving him there alone.

You don't owe him anything, Vesna.

"As much as I love my club, I think we should take Vesna home," Alex suggested, yawning.

"Yes, I feel a lot better now," Vesna agreed, trying to stand up. Her stomach was burning, and she groaned in pain. Mir quickly walked over to her, intending to carry her. "I don't need your help," Vesna protested, holding her hand out to stop him. He waited, his arms crossed, watching her with a knowing look she wanted to smack off his face.

With an annoyed huff, she ignored him and tried to stand up again, but it felt like all the strength left her body. She looked at Anna pleadingly.

"Don't look at me. You're tiny, but I'm not carrying you." Anna folded her arms.

"Roses are too delicate to lift heavy things," Alex said, though no one had even asked him to help.

"Don't call her heavy," Mir protested, and Vesna blushed. Against her better judgment, she liked his attention. "May I, wicked flower?" Mir sang, holding out his hands.

"Fine," Vesna muttered, giving up.

His arms wrapped gently around her body, and he lifted Vesna up with no effort. Somehow, it felt so peaceful to be in his arms—and it had been quite a while since she had felt any peace in her heart. She was constantly fighting with life, with unfair circumstances, even with herself. She felt tired, and giving up, she laid her head on Mir's shoulder. Her face was right next to his, and she inhaled his almond-honey scent.

She studied him secretly. Mir always wore dark clothes; he looked completely different in a bright red shirt covered in roses.

"I like the new style," Vesna whispered playfully.

"Are you trying to piss me off?" Mir muttered, but a faint smile touched his face.

"I think it suits you," she teased.

"Totally agree," Alex sang behind them. "From now on, I can be your stylist. Time for you to let some color into your life."

"Shut up." Mir rolled his eyes.

He crossed the street, holding Vesna tightly, and she couldn't help but feel his tense muscles against her skin. She shivered from the wave of heat that suddenly bloomed inside her. Vesna looked up to meet his eyes. "Anna will take care of me; you don't need to come with us." Her voice trembled a little, and she hoped Mir hadn't noticed how her magic rushed, empowered by his closeness.

"They attacked you because of me," Mir insisted, diving into her eyes and gently brushing aside a stand of her hair that had fallen over her face. "I need to make sure you'll be okay."

His gesture was so gentle that she felt a little embarrassed, lowering her flushed face. Maybe there was something noble in Mir's poisonous heart. *Stop it, Vesna. He works for Boris,* she reminded herself. "Fine," she agreed, trying to appear indifferent.

Mir held her tightly, and Vesna wished he would walk faster. His closeness was affecting her, and she couldn't let that happen.

"Where is your room?" Mir asked when they entered the apartment, the warmth of his words tickling her skin. Vesna didn't answer right away, trying to fight the urge to feel the heat of his tempting lips. Her mind traitorously wondered what a poisonous kiss would taste like.

When the pause dragged on, Vesna finally cleared her throat, literally squeezing out words. "The room on the left," she whispered, still feeling herself under his spell.

Mir slowly entered her room, looking around the tiny space. A glint of curiosity flashed in his eyes as he glanced at the painting of the divine magnolia on the wall.

"I didn't know you're a believer," Mir said, walking over to the bed.

"I'm not, it's just a pretty painting," Vesna lied, shrugging. *Just leave, already,* she begged internally.

Mir carefully sat down on the bed, holding Vesna in his arms. The waterbed quaked beneath them, throwing Mir off balance. He collapsed onto the mattress just as Vesna landed on top of him. She quickly held out her hands, her face hovering mere millimeters from his lips, her hair falling over him like a cascade of petals. He froze, breathing hard and staring into her eyes. His gaze made her forget the pain that seized her stomach. Her magic seemed to melt into a honeyed nectar under his intense gaze, and everything inside ached from a strange languor. *This is dangerous territory I should never explore,* she told herself, the guilt of feeling so alive around him covering her like snow covering fallen leaves. For a second, she thought he might have used some kind of glamor spell on her, and she quickly remembered everything she had read about the divine datura flower. But she soon realized that Mir had no such charms. His magic was silent, lonely, and cold, like death itself. It had nothing to do with attraction.

"What the hell?" Mir cursed. "Who still uses waterbeds?"

"Anna," Vesna muttered.

He stood up with difficulty, carrying her again. The situation was absurd, and looking at his confused face, she couldn't help but laugh sincerely, even though her wound ached again. First Mir stared at her in surprise, but then a barely noticeable smile touched his face too.

"Wicked flower," he whispered, as if casting a spell. "You can't sleep here. It's bad for the wound," he decided and headed for the living room.

Anna and Alex were sitting in the kitchen, drinking coffee. "What now?" Alex rolled his eyes, looking at Mir.

"She can't stay here. Let's go to your place." Mir made his way to the door. "I hope you don't use waterbeds?"

"What?" Alex asked, a frown creasing his forehead, but he followed Mir without question.

Vesna watched them curiously. They acted more like friends, even brothers, than anything else. *I wonder how they met.* "Anna, are you coming?" she asked, not wanting to be alone with Mir.

"Yes," Anna said behind them.

Alex apparently lived on the top floor, and Vesna noticed that with each floor they passed, Mir's breathing became heavier and heavier. "This building could use an elevator," he said, taking a deep breath.

"I can try walking on my own," Vesna suggested. "Or maybe Alex can carry me a bit after all."

"Wicked flower, get this into your head; no one but me will touch you, got it?" Mir said seriously and hugged her body tighter.

Vesna wanted to object, so that he wouldn't get the false impression that she had suddenly become obedient.

But she had no strength. The wound ached again, and her whole body was burning.

"Good flower." Mir smirked and looked at her. Her face must have been red, because she noticed his white eyes suddenly clouding over. "You're burning up," he whispered, his voice tense with worry. He quickened his pace, almost running. Alex pulled out the key to open the door, but Mir seemed to have gone a little mad. He kicked the door, and the lock broke.

"Are you crazy?! I just spent a fortune on that door! It was custom-made!" Alex shouted.

"Sorry, I'll replace it," Mir said, quickly entering and carefully lowering Vesna onto the couch.

He lowered his face to Vesna, as if silently begging her to hold on, but Vesna could barely focus on him. She felt like she was on fire, and she was trying so hard not to pass out again. She dove into his eyes, seeing nothing around her except his poisonous, mesmerizing gaze. "I'm fading…"

"Stay with me," he whispered to her, touching her forehead with his hand. "Alex, I need something to break the fever! Licorice fern, bay laurel, anything!"

"Let me check." Alex hurried into the kitchen. "Herbs are so hard to find these days. I paid a fortune for them."

"I might have some herbs too," Anna admitted and ran back to her apartment.

"Alex, bring me some cold water and towels too!" Mir ordered.

Vesna could no longer tell if this was reality or a hallucination from the high fever. "I'm burning," she whispered with great effort, the energy and magic slowly leaving her body.

"Stay with me, wicked flower," Mir almost begged, applying a damp towel to her forehead.

Vesna tried her best to fight off sleep, clinging to his voice, afraid she might never wake up if she gave in. "Keep talking," she whispered helplessly. "Tell me something about you."

Mir spoke loudly, obviously on purpose, trying to keep her awake. "I got into a fight at the orphanage once. A boy with sunflower magic kept picking on me because I had datura magic—evil and poisonous, in his opinion, even though I was born that way and couldn't choose what magic I wanted. At that time, I hadn't yet accepted that the boy was right about my magic." Mir smirked, pain in his voice. "Alex and I weren't friends yet, but he stood by me when he saw that the fight was ten to one. Of course, he was beaten so hard that he couldn't open one eye for a week..." he said, and Vesna could picture everything as vividly as if she had been there when he was a child. She had never really thought of him as someone with a childhood, who had his own fights.

Even poisonous flowers have a story, she thought, closing her eyes helplessly, unable to fight any longer, and she fell asleep.

Vesna had nightmares all night. She saw ridiculous things... First, she saw her mother sitting next to Boris on some kind of throne. Behind them was a giant rafflesia flower next to a tall, beautiful magnolia tree covered in flowers, which willingly gave its magic to the parasite. Vesna felt hot sweat covering her entire body, but she didn't have the strength to even open her eyes. As if in a delirium, she felt a cold wet cloth constantly touching her face and body, and it was like an evening of relief after a hot day. She smelled the scent of roses and marigolds several times during the night, but again, she wasn't sure whether it was just a dream or reality.

WHEN VESNA WOKE UP, it took her a few minutes for the events of the previous night to come back to her. She touched her wound, and to her surprise, realized that it no longer burned. Her gaze wandered around; the room was large and bright, with vast windows decorated with curtains patterned with roses. It felt as if she had woken up in a rose garden. There was no one here, but she could hear the sound of running water. Vesna examined her wound again, noticing that someone had changed her into a nightgown. Her face flushed at the thought that it might have been Mir. She sat up carefully, and her head spun for a few minutes.

I need to go to Anna's, she decided.

Taking the first step, she frowned. The wound sent a sharp pain to her back, and Vesna immediately leaned on the couch, afraid of falling.

The bathroom door swung open, and Mir stepped out, catching her off guard. The steam was still dancing around his damp skin, and a towel hung low on his hips. Drops of water from his hair trickled down his powerful chest, outlining a muscular body.

Vesna held her breath as she drank him in. *Why does he have to look so hot?*

Mir's bright eyes darted to her, and she bit her lip. In truth, he looked like a perfect sin, like sex itself. She had to admit it would be nice to feel his body against hers. *I have more important things to focus on,* she scolded herself, shifting her gaze to the window.

"Don't be so shy, wicked flower," Mir sang, clearly pleased with her reaction.

Vesna pouted her lips, wishing she could run away right now. The further she was from him, the safer. But her wound still hurt, and she just stood there, leaning against the couch. "Nothing I haven't seen before," she lied.

Mir's eyes flashed like lightning in the sky. He quickly approached her, stopping only inches away. "Such a stubborn flower," he breathed out, and bending slightly, picked her up in his arms.

"Put me down!" she protested as Mir headed for the window.

"It's my fault you're injured, and I intend to take care of you until you're fully healed," he said, setting her on the sill. "You can't even stand."

"I'm fine!" she snapped.

"Wicked flower, you're not fine. Trust me, I know what it's like to be stabbed," he said simply, and Vesna couldn't help but look down to see a huge old scar running across his lower abdomen. From the way it looked, she knew it was probably deeper than hers.

Not sure what had come over her, she touched the scar gently with her fingers. "Who did this to you?" she whispered.

Mir didn't answer, as if frozen by her touch. After a moment, he moved even closer, leaning over her like a cloud over a lonely flower in a clearing. "Careful," he whispered, brushing her ear with his words.

She shivered as his breath whispered across her skin, burning her hotter than she'd felt the night before. It was torture. "You're too close," she said, her voice shaking.

Mir froze in place and sighed heavily, as if weighing his words before speaking. "What is your end game?"

"No end game," she said, though her heart stopped as she realized he might suspect something. She held her breath again, looking into his eyes. "I'm just trying to make a new life for myself," she insisted.

Mir moved closer to her face, his lips almost touching hers. "You'd better not be fucking with me."

"I am not," Vesna whispered, finally finding the strength to pull away from him. Staying close to Mir was dangerous, both literally and figuratively. The more time she spent near him, the more chances he had to learn about her magic. Plus, this attraction to Mir was dangerous too. She needed to focus on her revenge.

"Sorry to interrupt your foreplay," Anna said, standing in the doorway. "Alex is at my place. We're having breakfast. Wanna join?"

"Yes," Vesna answered quickly and looked at Mir, waiting for him to let her go.

"You can't walk," he muttered. Vesna was about to move anyway, but Mir looked at her reproachfully. "You have to take it slow," he insisted. "Anna, watch this stubborn flower while I get dressed."

"Understood," Anna agreed immediately, and Vesna threw her an angry look.

Mir left for the bathroom, closing the door behind him.

"Help me down," Vesna begged, staring at Anna.

"No, you've heard Mir." Anna made a stern face.

"Unbelievable!" Vesna raged.

Anna put her finger to her lips, and quickly approaching Vesna, whispered almost silently. "This is the perfect opportunity to get close to him. If you don't remember, you need him."

Anna paused, and Vesna nodded. She wasn't likely to forget her dream. *Follow the poison.* But somehow, following him felt like jumping into the unknown—thrilling, but terrifying.

"Besides, I think you should give him more credit. Mir saved you yesterday. He carried you in his arms all the way to the club."

"Did you use your magic?" Vesna whispered, making sure Mir couldn't hear them from the bathroom. She clearly remembered smelling the scent of marigold last night.

"Yes," Anna said. "But I assure you, they didn't see me use it."

"Thank you," Vesna murmured. She hugged this beautiful golden flower. Anna had risked her own safety for her.

"You're welcome. But it was a team effort," Anna said timidly. "You should know that Mir tried to save you as if you were the most important person in the world. Last night, he didn't let me or Alex touch you. He fought your fever himself," she reported.

"I'm afraid he suspects something," Vesna confessed. "Why else would he save me?"

"Seriously?" Anna raised an eyebrow. "Maybe because he *likes* you—and when I see the way you look at him, something tells me you might like him too."

"Nonsense. He's working for Boris," Vesna said firmly. "Besides, I don't trust poisonous magic."

Anna took a deep breath. "I heard his story about the orphanage yesterday." She paused. "He was born with poison; he didn't ask for it."

Just then, the bathroom door creaked, and Mir came out. "Ready?" he asked without waiting for an answer, quickly approaching Vesna and picking her up.

"You've got one determined nurse." Anna giggled, following Mir to the door.

"Shut up." Vesna rolled her eyes.

Mir exited Alex's apartment, carefully holding Vesna in his arms. "I have to leave after I take you to Anna's, but I will be back later." He cleared his throat. "What happened to you is my fault. I just need to see what's going on back with the rafflesia. But don't worry, it won't take long."

Vesna didn't answer. Anna was right: it was a perfect chance to get closer to Mir. But somehow, a feeling of being trapped overcame her.

"She'll be home. Count on me, Mir," Anna said.

"It's hardly a home," Mir muttered. "Her room is empty, just the stupid waterbed."

What should you care? Vesna protested internally. "It's not stupid! I actually like it. It's comfortable," she lied.

"Right." Mir smirked, raising an eyebrow.

"We need to furnish your room," Anna said, looking at Vesna.

Vesna pouted her lips. "Fine, let's decorate it."

Anna smiled, shifting her gaze to Mir. "Will you come with us to buy furniture?"

"I live to shop," Mir said sarcastically. "But Vesna needs to rest for at least a week. Her wound is deep," he added more seriously.

Vesna didn't plan to rest for the whole week. She planned to see Boris's building, at least from the outside. To learn his routine, to count how many men he had.

When they entered Anna's apartment, Alex sat in the kitchen with his feet up on the table, as if he were at home. "Anna! I want to eat breakfast here every morning! It's delicious," he sang, shoving an enormous piece of bacon into his mouth.

"Sure, but I'm gonna charge you for it," Anna teased, sitting down on the chair next to him.

Mir gently lowered Vesna onto the couch. "Be a good girl." He winked, and before she could respond, he turned toward the kitchen. "She shouldn't move. I will be right back."

"Don't you want breakfast?" Alex called after Mir.

"Next time," Mir said, walking out of the apartment.

Anna put more bacon on Alex's plate, smiling to herself. It wasn't the first time that Vesna had noticed that Anna was even more cheerful than usual when she was with Alex. But Alex seemed like a man who didn't let anyone get close to him. *Apart from Mir,* Vesna thought.

"Can I ask you something?" Vesna looked at Alex.

"Sure," he said simply.

"When did you meet Mir?" she asked, a little put off. She felt like she was overstepping some boundaries, but she wanted to know if Mir was telling the truth yesterday about him and Alex when they were kids.

"Well, it's no secret, anyway," Alex said, settling more comfortably in his chair. "My parents died when I was eight, and I ended up in an orphanage. Mir was already there." He paused, clearing his throat. "His parents were humans, and as Mir got older, they finally realized that his magic wasn't bright and pretty; it was poisonous. So, they just left him. Long story short, we became friends. We're two lonely flowers, helping each other survive," Alex finished and grabbed the last piece of bacon. "Do you have more?"

"But of course, anything for my dear boss." Anna laughed.

Vesna wasn't listening to them. Her thoughts had

drifted to Mir. He'd had a hard life, and now she understood why in the Graffiti Grove he had said that his
divine flower was ugly. He probably blamed it for taking
his parents away. Still, he worked for Boris, and there
was no way to justify that.

"But I helped him as well, mostly with girls," Alex
said playfully, looking at Vesna. "As you can see, I'm very
charming."

"I just saw Mir half naked, and somehow I doubt he
needs help with women," Anna teased.

"Are you saying he's better-looking than me?" Alex
asked, standing up. "Here, check out these muscles." He
quickly started unbuttoning his shirt.

"For flower's sake, put it back on." Anna laughed.

Vesna giggled. Her wound ached, but somehow, she
felt happy. It all seemed so natural and normal, and for a
moment, she forgot all the burdens.

Chapter Nine

MIR.

Mir walked down an empty, sleepy street, lost in his thoughts. His attraction to this wicked flower was strong. And it wasn't just her sacred magic, or even her body. *Well, her body is perfect,* he thought, and a shiver of lust ran through him. But it wasn't just that. She was wild and tender at the same time. *A perfect mix.* Mir remembered how heavenly it had been to feel her touch on his skin, like the whisper of a spring wind touching withered petals.

When he was around Vesna, he somehow became another version of himself—a version he had buried long ago. He wanted to be brave, to be fair. But this was dangerous territory. If Mir wasn't careful, all his effort and sacrifice in working for the rafflesia could go down the drain.

He quickened his pace, unsure of what awaited him at home. Approaching the rafflesia building, he ran into Boris, who was already sitting inside his car.

"Mir," Boris called after him, rolling down the window. "Ivan is recovering."

Mir clenched his fist. "I can't say that I wish him a speedy recovery."

"I need to leave town to look for the book. Ivan was supposed to help me, because…" Boris trailed off, clearly deciding not to let Mir in on his business. "I will punish you when I get back." He snorted. "Driver, let's go!"

Mir stood there, watching the car move away. Boris rarely left his building, let alone the city. The book he was looking for was important. But right now, Mir sighed with relief. This was the perfect opportunity to be closer to Vesna and make sure she began to trust him. If she didn't plan to open the Veiled Wilds, he would force her to. Once Boris found the book, Mir would be able to learn the location of the Veiled Wilds and take Vesna there under false pretenses.

It's time to take Alex up on his offer, Mir decided.

LESS THAN AN HOUR LATER, he was at the club with a small suitcase in his hands. Fading Blossoms always felt so different during the day. Only the night could hide the sad reality, casting an illusion on people when they crossed the threshold of this place.

Alex sat on a chair near the stage and listened to the band rehearsing new songs. "It's a disaster! Imagine that your instrument is a fragile female body, and not a sack of potatoes!"

Mir laughed, and his friend turned to look at the entrance. Alex's gaze quickly shifted to the suitcase. "Mir!"

"Is the apartment still available?" Mir asked, and his voice sounded unusually happy even to himself.

"Of course, man!" Alex said. "But even if it wasn't, I would just evict these talentless musicians," he said playfully, looking at the stage.

"Leave them alone." Mir laughed again.

"Come on, I'll show you the place." Alex tapped him on the shoulder. "I can't believe you're finally here."

Alex's building was much smaller than the one Boris owned, but Mir couldn't help but think how good it felt to be here, like he was a flower that had been growing in a cave for years and had finally got out into the open.

"This apartment is right below my place," Alex reported, opening the door with the key. "It's not big, but you get light throughout the day."

"Thanks, man," Mir said, walking inside.

"You get settled in while I work. But tonight, we will celebrate!" Alex said, walking toward the door. "Welcome to the Fading Blossoms!"

Mir quickly unpacked his things and went straight over to check on Vesna. Although he tried to convince himself he was just following the plan, he couldn't help but feel guilty for what he'd put her through.

Anna opened the door and smiled sincerely. "Mir! You're just in time. I have some errands to run."

"Is she okay?" Mir asked as he walked in.

"Stubborn as ever, but she's fine," Anna reported. "I just helped her shower."

"I hope you haven't given her any solids?!" Mir asked in a panic. He'd completely forgotten to mention that earlier.

"No, she hasn't eaten yet," Anna said, grabbing her coat. "I'm leaving."

The door to Vesna's room was slightly open. She was sitting on the waterbed, and her face contorted in pain as she raised her hand, trying to comb her hair. Mir quickly entered. Watching her suffer because of him was painful.

"Let me help," he said, carefully sitting next to her, making sure the stupid mattress didn't move.

"I'm not a child," she said, clutching the comb in her hand.

"You're hurt." Mir touched her hand gently. "I promise to leave you alone as soon as you recover."

Vesna stared into his eyes soundlessly. "Fine." She cleared her throat and handed Mir the comb.

His heart was racing. All his interactions with women never went beyond sex. And now taking care of her seemed like he was losing his usual self. Tenderness overcame him as he touched her damp, tangled hair. It felt like creamy petals, wet with summer rain. Mir wanted to inhale its scent, but he didn't dare, afraid to startle her. He combed it out carefully, strand by strand, as the silence stretched out.

"Does it hurt?"

"No," Vesna whispered. "When my aunt combed my hair when I was little, it only took her a minute, and half my hair would stay in the comb."

Mir smiled. "She sounds determined."

"Well, stubborn, mostly." Vesna smirked, then smiled.

"Are you two close?" he dared to ask. He knew nothing of Vesna's life.

"Yes," Vesna said, and her voice suddenly trembled. "She raised me."

He wondered what had happened to her parents, but decided it was too soon to ask. "Well, you're lucky to have her. Life without a family is a lonely garden," he muttered, thinking about his parents.

"Do you have any siblings?" she asked quietly.

"I have Alex," Mir said and decided to change the subject. He never spoke about his family with anyone; it was too painful and completely unnecessary. "You need to eat something."

"Seriously, I'm fine." She made a stern face. "Don't you have some evil things to do for Boris?"

"No." Mir laughed. He liked how straightforward Vesna was with him. "I'm on vacation. Come on, let's go to the kitchen. I'm going to make you some soup."

Vesna rolled her eyes helplessly. "I hope you're not planning on watching me at night too?"

"Gladly, just say the words," Mir teased.

"No!" Vesna blurted out. And he noticed that her face blushed.

He scooped her in his arms effortlessly as if she were dandelion fluff and weighed nothing at all. She laced her hands around his neck, and his heart was racing from her closeness, from her wet hair touching his skin. Mir suppressed a growl and quietly carried her to the living room. It felt so simple, but intimate. He sat her gently on the sofa, placing a pillow under her back, before turning toward the kitchen.

As he cooked, he glanced over his shoulder, catching Vesna watching him the whole time. "Are you enjoying the view?" He smirked.

"Just making sure you know what you're doing," Vesna said, blushing.

"Don't worry, I'm not planning on poisoning the soup." He raised an eyebrow.

"Where did you learn how to cook?" she asked, her voice curious.

Mir knew that opening up to her might help him get closer to his goal, but he was afraid to let Vesna in, because he knew all too well what would happen when he did. She would hurt him, just like everyone else. And yet, his dream of destroying the divine datura was stronger than any fear.

"I lived in the orphanage since I was six. You learn a lot when you have to grow up on your own," he said, forcing a smile, trying to seem indifferent. He didn't want her to feel sorry for him. "What about you? What made you move to the city?" He held his breath, hoping to learn something useful.

"I need to see someone," she said quietly, but her eyes seemed to glitter dangerously.

"A man?" Mir raised an eyebrow.

"Yes," Vesna said, her voice distant. "After this, I want to leave this city."

It wasn't much information, but it was a good start. "Well, I can keep you company while you're here."

"Let' see how it goes," she said with a smile.

His poisonous magic didn't seem to bother her anymore, and Mir wondered why she had changed her mind so suddenly. He decided that perhaps his openness with her had worked, and he was slowly winning her trust. "The soup is almost ready."

Now Vesna was sitting on the windowsill, golden dusk reflecting on her serene face, while Mir was skimming over the books on the shelf. "I can read you a book," he suggested.

"I doubt Anna has anything good." Vesna turned her gaze to the shelf.

"Let's see," Mir said, quickly looking through the books. "'Kiss Me Like Fire,'" he read aloud. "Sounds intense."

"I bet," Vesna said, and he noticed the way her cheeks flushed, soft and sudden.

"It's better than nothing." He came back to the couch, handing her the book.

"Mir!" Alex barged in without even knocking. He narrowed his merlot eyes on his friend. "Oh, now I see why you moved in!"

Vesna widened her eyes. "You moved *in*?"

"Temporarily," Mir muttered.

"Let's go to the club and celebrate!" Alex sang.

Mir noticed how Vesna's eyes dimmed slightly. She was barely moving because of him, and the idea of hanging out at the club while she sat here alone seemed wrong to him. "I have to finish unpacking."

Alex intercepted Mir's gaze. "Sure," he agreed immediately.

"You should go. I'll sleep on the couch tonight," Vesna said, without even looking at Mir.

Mir felt empty inside. He didn't want to leave her alone—and that feeling scared him. *Don't let her in,* he warned himself and rushed to the door. "Great! Good night," he muttered before leaving the apartment.

Alex followed him up the steps, trying to catch up with him. "Why did you run away like that?" He narrowed his eyes at Mir.

Because I don't want her to touch my soul, Mir thought. "It's late." He brushed his friend off.

"Mir, everything is different now. You don't have to follow through on the plan you made ages ago. You can let someone in finally," Alex dared to suggest, hope in his voice.

"Alex, I'm not naïve," Mir said, trying to hide the pain that slipped into his heart. "Do you really think the sacred one can care for poison?"

"Well…" Alex drawled the word.

Mir clenched his fists. "Exactly. I'm following the original plan. Nothing has changed."

MIR DIDN'T PLAN to just sit and do nothing. He needed her to recover—not just for the night of Ivan Kupala, but to quiet the guilt that crept through his soul at the thought that she was hurt because of him. Anna was with Vesna during the morning, so Mir decided he could try to find some herbs to speed up her healing. He and Alex walked down the street, breathing in the cool morning air.

"When we get there, don't talk," Alex said. "Everyone knows you work for Boris."

"Don't worry," Mir muttered. "I just hope they have something useful."

"Herbs are so hard to find these days," Alex thought out loud. "But if the vendor has something, be prepared to pay a fortune."

"Okay," Mir muttered, thinking about the herbalist. He couldn't help but wonder how she could have so many herbs. She didn't seem rich.

The merchant they were seeking did business outside the city, near the port. There was a vast river there, connecting the city with distant lands. Alex and Mir were standing near a small barn, waiting for someone to show up. To their surprise, Anton came out, almost blocking the door with his body.

"What a surprise!" Anton narrowed his eyes on Mir. "Came to fix what the rafflesia did to the new singer?"

"So, you're still trying to resist Boris?" Mir asked,

but without irritation. Humans had a right to want magic back too.

Anton smirked. "People aren't as useless as you think."

Alex glanced between the two of them and quickly said, "Do you have anything to speed up the healing?" He paused. "The wound is deep."

"Come inside," Anton said, looking around to make sure no one was there.

Inside, the barn looked clean and organized. More men were sitting in the corner, holding knives. Mir cast a suspicious glance at the metal door they were guarding. "Quite some security you have for just herbs."

Anton caught his eye. "You keep underestimating humans," he muttered. "How is Boris's vacation going?"

Mir stared at him in surprise, wondering how he knew Boris was gone. Was he keeping tabs on the man? If Boris found out, there would be hell to pay. "Anton, a friendly warning: stay away from Boris."

"He's right," Alex said.

"Don't worry about me." Anton cleared his throat. "I can only offer you horsetail. It's good for healing, plus it restores the skin."

"I guess it's better than nothing." Alex looked at Mir questioningly.

"Okay, we'll take that," Mir said with a sigh, hoping Anna had gotten something more useful from the herbalist. "But you're behind your competition. The herbalist makes complex potions, and you only have a few herbs."

"Well, she has an advantage," Anton said with an eyebrow raise.

"What do you mean?" Alex asked, clearly anticipating Mir's question.

Anton looked Mir up and down, obviously deciding whether to tell him what he knew. "Some old texts talk about a secret map, with the locations where herbs can still be found. It completely disappeared from the radar when Boris came into power."

Mir nodded. It made sense if the herbalist had such a map. He wondered if she had stolen it from Boris. Maybe that was how he knew the herbalist was a woman.

"How the hell do you know that?" Alex couldn't help but wonder.

"My parents were members of a resistance group. There was still hope in their time," he said. "The sacred one could have changed everything."

The silence stretched on. Everyone, even the humans, was losing hope after so many years. After all, no one knew that the sacred one had appeared again. *And it needs to stay that way,* Mir decided. He couldn't risk Boris finding out about Vesna and ruining his plan if he drained her like he had the last sacred one. Mir cleared his throat, breaking the silence. "How much for the horsetail?"

"I'll give you a discount," Anton said, a smile touching his face. "You need to stitch up the wound with it, like thread."

THE SUN, setting behind the tall buildings, was even more amber than usual today. Anna had left just as Mir showed up, and Vesna was hiding in her room. He thought about knocking on the door, but decided to wait a bit. Anyway, the horsetail needed to be boiled before he could stitch Vesna's wound with it.

He put the herb in boiling water and decided not to waste any time. With everything going on, he didn't have time to exercise, and he needed to stay in shape, given his line of work. Mir took off his shirt and started doing push-ups right in the middle of the living room. Anna's apartment was so small that it was the only free space.

Eighty, eighty-one… he counted to himself.

At that moment, he noticed Vesna slowly opening the door, leaning against it; she was still weak.

Their eyes locked for a second before her gaze moved to his body, focusing on his arms. "What is that smell?" She cleared her throat and shifted her gaze to the kitchen.

Mir stood up, hiding his smile. He liked the way she looked at him. "There you are! I thought you would avoid me the whole time," he sang, moving to her. "Come. We need to stitch your wound."

He picked her up, and her ringing voice sounded right in his ear. "Is that horsetail?" Her eyes widened at the boiling water.

This wicked flower knows everything, Mir thought with admiration. "Yes."

"This will hurt," Vesna whispered.

"I promise to be gentle," he breathed, lowering her onto the couch.

"If you're going to play doctor, at least put on a shirt," she muttered, avoiding his gaze.

Mir laughed softly, but put on his shirt. He carefully pulled out the herb; it had become much more elastic. Anna had left a box of needles on the counter, and he quickly looked through them. He didn't want to use a large needle, afraid that it would be too painful. Instead, he chose the smallest needle through which the horsetail could pass.

Vesna took a deep breath. "Let's do this as quickly as possible," she said, her voice full of determination.

He looked at her in surprise. She was brave and fearless, even though her magnolia magic was soft and harmonious. "I'll be gentle," he assured her again, slowly touching her skin.

At the first piercing, she bit her lip in pain, and a low growl escaped her mouth. It echoed painfully in Mir's mind.

He carefully pulled the herb under her skin, and Vesna screamed in pain. "Aaaah!"

Mir stopped abruptly. She would need many stitches to close the wound, but at this rate, she could pass out from the pain.

What if I numb her skin? the thought occurred to him. He had never used his magic for anything useful, and at first, he dismissed the idea. But when tears filled Vesna's eyes with the next stitch, he dared to suggest it. "I could numb your skin a little," he whispered hesitantly.

Vesna looked at him in mute shock, and he immediately regretted his words. She was obviously afraid of him. She probably didn't want something so evil to touch her sacred magic.

"Never mind. It was a bad idea," Mir nervously broke the silence. *What an idiot you are.* He was angry with himself for even suggesting he could use poison to help her.

"Do it," she whispered.

Mir's eyes shot to her in surprise, and he looked at her a long moment. "Are you sure? I'd have to use my poison."

"But it'd help me," she said, taking a deep breath.

A small smile touched his face at the word—*help*. He had to admit, it was nice to think that his magic could be used for more than just death and suffering. "It won't enter your veins. I'll make sure the poison only touches your skin."

He took a deep breath, and whispering the spell, watched as his pollen slowly covered her soft skin.

"Cold," Vesna said, but she didn't pull away.

"Just a few more seconds to make sure your skin is numb," Mir said, trying to calm her and himself. He'd had never used his poison for this purpose before, and he was afraid he might use too much. "I think that's enough." He called his magic back and picked up the needle.

When he pierced Vesna's skin again, she made no sound. "It worked!" she said excitedly, her face glowing with an inner light, and this sight was mesmerizing.

Mir smiled back at her, and her eyes lit up his with grateful warmth for a moment. But she seemed to come to her senses quickly. Her smile turned into a serious expression.

"Let's get this over with quickly." She cleared her throat. "I'd rather be alone tonight."

The warmth that had just filled him left just as quickly, leaving behind an icy cold in his heart. *You're a naïve idiot*, Mir scolded himself for how easily he was ready to fall under her spell.

Chapter Ten
VESNA.

Yesterday, Vesna had completely dissolved in Mir's eyes, forgetting everything for a moment. Forgetting he worked for Boris. Forgetting even her revenge. And that terrified her. She had sent him away without so much as a thank you for stitching up her wound.

She was tired of sitting at home doing nothing, as if she'd come to the city for a vacation. She had rested enough. It was time to start watching Boris.

Anna entered Vesna's room with potion in her hand, just as Vesna was about to get dressed.

"Lie down. You'll fall asleep after the potion," Anna said, handing her the glass.

Vesna took it, but her lips stayed closed. She had to go. But she was sure Anna would try to stop her. Vesna decided she had to tell her the truth, or at least half of it.

"Not now. I'm going to gather information about Boris," she said firmly.

Anna's eyes widened. "But you're still in pain! And Mir said you needed at least a week."

"And Mir is the sacred one here to decide that?" Vesna said, feeling heat rise to her cheeks. She didn't like to lie to Anna or use her belief that she was the sacred one. But she had no other choice.

Anna nodded reluctantly. "Okay. But I'm coming with you."

They walked slowly. Vesna's wound still hurt, and she tried not to let it show. Even from a distance, she could see the tall rafflesia building. The closer they got, the faster her heart pounded. Her mother was gone, and Boris was living his best life, untouchable.

As they almost approached the building, Anna grabbed Vesna's hand. "Let's sit on this bench. If we get too close, his guards will notice us."

Vesna glanced at the two men stationed by the entrance. Their eyes were the same brown as the rafflesia flower.

They sat for hours. Vesna barely even blinked as she observed. Boris seemed to have around fifty men, or at least that was how many she counted. The guards rotated every two hours, but the building was never left unguarded. Still, she hoped that once she bloomed, her magic would be enough to deal with them. Though she knew it would be wiser to use Mir to get inside, saving her magic for Boris alone.

"If Mir invites you to the ball, we won't have to worry about all these guards," Anna said simply, but her voice was tinged with worry. "Come on. We've seen enough." She stood and held out her hands to help Vesna up.

Vesna looked at the horizon. The sun was about to set. "Fine," she said, standing and barely holding back a growl as a sharp pain ran from her stomach down to her feet.

"This place is dangerous," Anna muttered, glancing one last time at Boris's building. "I pray every night to remember the rest of the prophecy, but the divine marigold doesn't answer me." She sighed.

Vesna didn't answer, deep in thought. If something went wrong when she attacked Boris, she'd need a way to escape. She hoped to study his building during the ball, but that might not be enough.

Sharp pain shot through her body with every step, and she felt helpless. *I'll find the plans of Boris's building as soon as I can walk again,* she promised herself.

When they arrived home, Anna left for work almost immediately. Vesna tried to walk again, but barely made it to the windowsill. She pulled herself onto it on the third try, breathing heavily and cursing her wound.

She heard someone open the door with the key, and a few moments later, Mir entered her room.

"How did you get in?" Vesna asked.

"Anna gave me a spare key," Mir said, tilting his head. "Is your wound better?"

"Still hurts." Vesna pouted her lips.

"May I check it?" he asked.

"Okay," she muttered and held her breath.

He slowly lifted her shirt, and she winced as he touched her skin.

"Don't move," he said, and probably without even realizing it, he put his other hand on her waist, holding her still. Goose bumps ran across her body in an instant. She hated the way her body responded to his closeness. "The inflammation is going down, but you shouldn't tense up. The stitches might come apart." His fingers tickled the skin pleasantly, and she blushed.

I'm tense right now, she thought helplessly, and turned her head to the window.

Tall skyscrapers stretched into the sky and even blocked out the sun on its way down. She didn't like these buildings. Somehow, they reminded her of parasites that killed nature. She noticed a small part of the city that stood out among the skyscrapers. The buildings there seemed shorter and made of some other material.

"What's there?" She pointed.

"Where?" Mir asked, almost pressing his face to hers and squinting. "Oh, that's the old part of town. All the buildings there are wooden and decorated with a flower theme. It's a beautiful area."

"And how is Boris's building?" she dared to ask. "Is it beautiful?"

"It's the ugliest of them all," Mir muttered.

The tone of his voice was full of sadness, maybe even hatred. *Why did you choose to live there, then?* she thought, confused. "I want to see it during the spring ball," she dared to say. "Someone told me it's beautifully decorated for the occasion."

Mir's eyes narrowed, and for some reason, his magic seemed to cloud his eyes like a mist. "There's nothing to see there." He paused. "But I'll try to get you an invitation."

THE DAYS TURNED INTO A WEEK, and at first, Vesna couldn't help but feel uncomfortable around Mir. The constant presence of a man she barely knew seemed strange. But slowly, almost imperceptibly, the discomfort began to fade. Without her even realizing it, the rhythm of her new life began to feel natural.

Mir carried her around the house, and she didn't resist his help. She ate everything he cooked for her with a growing appetite. Every time she caught herself looking at him or laughing at something insignificant, she reminded herself that it was all part of the plan. *I'm just a great actress. That's all,* she tried to convince herself. But deep down, she knew he was getting to her.

Even though there was more to him than she'd thought, she still knew little about him. Part of her wanted to understand him, but another part was glad he didn't try to open up to her. It was safer that way.

Her wound was healing well. She grew stronger every day, and now she could walk on her own. The sharp pain that used to ripple down her spine with every movement was gone. And she was starting to feel like herself again.

But one thing still bothered her: Mir hadn't mentioned the ball or the invitation he had promised to get her.

"Mir!" Vesna screamed in panic as Mir entered her room.

She had just taken a shower and was sitting on the windowsill, still covered only by a towel. He cast a burning glance at her almost naked body and growled.

"Didn't they teach you to knock?" Vesna fired, feeling like prey under his gaze.

"No," he said, coming close to her. "How did you get there?" he asked reproachfully.

"By myself," she whispered, lowering her eyes.

"You always sit on the windowsill. Do you have honey smeared there?" He smirked. "You need to take it easy. You're just getting better," he added softly, and with one finger, he caught a drop of water that had fallen from her wet hair and was running down her neck.

She looked up at him and bit her lip unconsciously. It was as if invisible nectar were flowing from him, drawing her into the depths of his eyes every time their gazes met.

"How fucking perfect that you bite your lip," he sang, and smoothly touched her leg with his tenacious fingers.

Vesna didn't dare to move, or say anything, for that matter. His touch was too perfect, too sinful. He dragged his fingers along her leg, their touch leaving behind a burning trail. When they reached her thigh, she barely held back a moan. She didn't know what was happening to her, but it felt like a storm was brewing inside her, and Mir was the only one who could cause it to break.

She swallowed against the sensation, noticing that Mir's mouth was slightly parted, his eyes hot on where he touched her skin. His whole body was tense, like an animal ready to pounce. She wanted to wrap her legs around him and feel his muscular body against hers, and the thought made her entire core heat up.

"Stop." Her whisper trembled.

"I promise that one day you will bloom under my poisonous touch," he sang in her ear, sending shivers down her spine.

"I don't bloom," she lied.

"We'll see about that." He shamelessly spread her legs, and in one swift movement, pulled her slender body against him. "Wrap your legs around me."

Her breath caught as she felt him tighten against her body. It was everything she'd expected, and more. But it was also too much. Too close. Too reckless. She just had to stay strong until her blooming season. And after that, she would disappear and never see Mir again.

"No," she whispered, her voice trembling from the ache in her lower abdomen. She bit her lip hard, trying to pull herself together. But Mir didn't let go. Instead, he pulled her close, his arms strong and gripping.

"Wrap your legs around me, Vesna," he said again,

softer this time. "I need to carry you to the kitchen." He cleared his throat. "Anna is making lunch."

"In my towel?" She raised an eyebrow.

"Ooh…" He seemed to come back to his senses.

"I can walk on my own." She pushed him away and jumped down, heading for the bathroom to put some clothes on.

Anna was cooking, making a real mess, and the smell of burnt food filled the entire apartment. Vesna didn't even notice. She couldn't take her eyes off Mir, who sat down at the table, reading a newspaper.

So, this is how the poison gets into the veins, she thought. She finally admitted that she no longer saw him as just a means to an end—and she hated herself for feeling this way. Every time they were alone, she tried to be distant inside, and every time, she failed. She found him attractive—like, *extremely* attractive. *You've lost focus, Vesna,* she thought, getting angry.

"Mir! I think Alex wanted to see you," she lied.

He raised his eyes at her. "Seriously?"

"Yes, Anna told me earlier, but I completely forgot to mention it."

Mir shifted his gaze to Anna, and she nodded, playing along. "He did," she muttered.

"Fine," Mir said, getting up. "Then I'll see you in the evening."

Vesna nodded immediately. "Okay."

"Anna, don't let her walk too much," he said before leaving.

As soon as the door closed behind him, Vesna stood up and put on her shoes. "Let's go!"

"Do you want to have lunch outside?" Anna asked excitedly. "Anyway, I ruined the food." She lifted the frying pan off the stove and threw the burnt food straight into the trash can.

Vesna rolled her eyes. "Are you serious? We're going to the library. If we're lucky, we can find some plans for Boris's building. Even if we get the book, we'll still need to escape," Vesna said, lying to Anna again. She didn't care about the book. But she cared about Anna. She felt like a terrible person for using her friend like this, and guilt settled heavily in her chest.

"Fine, but I want lunch after that," Anna insisted.

VESNA STUDIED the vast library with admiration. Even if the Divine Blooms had abandoned people, still their culture was constantly reminding them of extraordinary magic and beauty that used to blossom in the air and their hearts. The library was in the old part of the city, the building was wooden, and the walls and ceilings were hand-painted with a rainbow of colorful flowers.

"It's an old building. Humans don't make them like this anymore. They even used to put a secret door in each room back then," Anna said, raising her head to the ceiling and studying the paintings with her mouth slightly open.

The librarian's lips pursed as she looked at Anna. "Lower your voice."

Anna smiled, squinting at the librarian's name tag. "Hi, Lisa. Do you have a section with building plans?"

"Which building are you looking for?"

Vesna and Anna exchanged glances, not sure if it was safe to ask for the plans of the rafflesia's building openly. *She's just a librarian,* Vesna decided. "Yes, the tall brown building at the main square."

"Ooh." Lisa looked them up and down. "Please follow me to the reading room. I will bring what we have."

They followed the librarian, and Vesna suddenly felt as if everyone were watching them. Anna squeezed her hand without saying a word. It was a simple gesture, but it helped Vesna to relax. She had to admit Anna was a blessing that the Divine Blooms had sent to illuminate her passage.

"I'll be right back," Lisa said, looking around and hurrying away.

"She looks suspicious," Anna whispered.

Vesna thought the same, but she didn't want to alarm Anna. "I think we're just paranoid," she muttered, mostly trying to convince herself. She shifted her gaze, trying to distract herself by studying a painting of cherry blossoms on the wall.

Lisa came back a few minutes later empty-handed. "The plans are too big. I can take you upstairs to where we keep them."

Anna and Vesna looked at each other again. "Thank you," Vesna mumbled.

"Be on guard," Anna whispered as they followed Lisa to a small, dusty room on the highest floor.

"I'll leave you to it," Lisa said, closing the door behind her.

"She's creepy. Let's find the plans and get out of here," Anna decided.

Dust filled the room as they moved papers that obviously no one had touched for a very long time.

"Found it!" Anna jumped up in excitement.

"Let me see." Vesna ran up to her. She grabbed the faded plan of Boris's building. It seemed ordinary, but what caught her attention was the space underneath it.

It looked like a labyrinth of many rooms, and at the end of this labyrinth was a gigantic round space, with a tunnel to the surface. If Vesna had to escape after attacking Boris, she could get underground and leave through this tunnel.

Anna leaned in beside her, studying the plans too. "It looks like a tunnel, but——"

She didn't finish her sentence, because they heard the door being locked. They looked at each other in panic. Anna ran to the door, trying to open it. "Lisa, we're locked in," she called, trying to sound calm.

"I am required to report if someone is interested in anything related to the rafflesia," Lisa said through the door. "I called them as soon as you arrived."

Vesna froze, feeling like she had just walked straight into a trap. Her heart thundered in her chest, and for a few seconds, she struggled to take a breath.

"Fuck!" Anna cursed, pulling at the door hysterically.

Trying not to freak out, Vesna walked to the door, pushing Anna lightly aside. She couldn't let the rafflesia find out who they were. Not yet. "Lisa," she called, trying to calculate how far the librarian was from her.

"I'm just doing my job. If you're two regular girls, you have nothing to worry about," Lisa said, and Vesna realized she was standing right on the other side of the door.

Perfect, she thought, and then whispered to Anna, "Put her to sleep."

Anna looked at her in surprise, but then her eyes shone with hope. The golden pollen left Anna's body and slowly seeped through all the cracks around the door. "Sleep. Sleep until autumn comes," she said, her voice shaking, laced with worry.

After a few minutes had passed, Lisa was now silent. But even if she was sleeping, the door was still locked.

Anna seemed to come to her senses first. "There has to be a secret door!"

"I hope so," Vesna said, pushing the huge cabinet stuffed with books away from the wall. Anna did the same. Vesna's wound whined from the effort, but she didn't care right now.

Anna managed to slightly move the largest cabinet in the room and screamed, "Here!" She pointed at part of an old door that become visible. Vesna rushed over and helped her to move the cabinet completely.

Vesna pulled at the door with all her might, but it wouldn't budge. "It's locked from the outside," she hissed.

"Let me help," Anna said, stepping up beside her. Together, they pulled again.

"There has to be something!" Vesna blurted out, scanning the room.

"Fire extinguisher!" Anna said, narrowing her eyes at the case mounted on the wall. She grabbed the biggest book she could find, smashed the glass, and pulled out the extinguisher.

"Let me do it," Vesna said, extending her hands.

"Are you crazy? This thing weighs a ton! Your wound will open again," Anna protested. Raising her hands a little higher, she hit the door with all her might, sending pieces of wood flying in all directions.

After a few moments of her pounding the door, Vesna noticed Anna's hands were shaking, and the amplitude of her blows was slackening.

"Stop being so stubborn," Vesna snorted. She snatched the fire extinguisher from Anna's hands and brought it down on the door. Sharp pain shot up her body from her wound, and Vesna bit her lip to keep from crying out. She couldn't be weak now.

Boris won't have me like this, she thought, finally noticing a small hole in the door that had appeared near the handle. She stuck her hand through. The wood scraped her skin, but she didn't even blink. Finding the handle on the other side, she pressed it, and the old door creaked open.

"Finally!" Anna exhaled happily.

They entered a narrow corridor, and Vesna could hear her own heartbeat echoing in her ears. They walked for only a few minutes, but to her it felt like eternity. When they reached the door at the end, Vesna pressed the handle and sighed with relief. It wasn't locked.

They found themselves back in the main corridor again. At the far end, Vesna saw Lisa slumped on the floor, presumably in a deep sleep.

Anna rushed to the nearby window, jerked it open, and stuck her head out.

Vesna pulled her back immediately. "Are you completely crazy? It's the top floor. We can't jump!"

"There's a fire escape from the first floor that leads to the roof," Anna said quickly.

They climbed out onto the old fire escape and rushed up, the wind blowing around them, as if helping them to move faster. They were on the roof in less than a minute.

"This smell…" Anna whispered, sniffing the air.

"Rotten flesh," Vesna said. She stopped at the edge, looked down, and realized the rafflesia's brown cars had surrounded the building already.

"We need to jump to the next rooftop," Anna

decided, looking at the next building, which was tanta-
lizingly close. "After that, the houses get closer to each
other."

Vesna held her hand to her aching wound, but it
didn't matter if it opened again. She needed to get away
from the rafflesia. That was the most important thing
right now. "Let's do it."

They ran back a little to give them space to gain
momentum. Vesna wasn't sure she could make it, and
she soundlessly prayed to the divine magnolia to give her
strength. She also prayed for Anna, realizing she was the
first person who had entered her prayers apart from her
mother and Nina.

"Now!" Anna screamed and ran to the edge.

Vesna followed her, leaping with everything she had.
They were so high up, she didn't dare to look down.
Anna was just ahead of her, and Vesna watched her as if
in slow motion. For a second, she felt like a petal floating
in the wind.

She landed hard on the next rooftop and winced in
pain. Anna was already getting to her feet. Vesna tried
to stand too, but the pain was sharp. Her wound had
reopened.

"You're bleeding!" Anna said in horror, reaching
toward her.

"It's nothing." Vesna stopped her. "Let's get out of
here," she growled, standing up.

Anna didn't move, her eyes darting rapidly, as if
reading an invisible book.

"Anna! Let's move!" Vesna grabbed her shoulders
and shook her.

Anna's gaze slowly shifted to her. "I remember the
rest of my dream," she said, her voice trembling. Vesna

stared at her, forgetting the rafflesia, forgetting even her revenge for a moment. "The Divine Blooms have blessed a new sacred one," Anna whispered, "because the previous one was unworthy. If the gates to the Veiled Wilds are not opened this summer, they will remain closed … forever. And Boris is immortal; he would rule the world."

By the time they arrived home, Vesna could barely walk. Anna used her magic, and the pain subsided a little. But Vesna couldn't ameliorate the pain that filled her heart as she was looking at Anna sitting next to her. Her eyes were fixed on one point.

"The gods will be gone forever," Anna muttered clearly to herself. She raised her eyes at Vesna. "We can't let that happen."

Vesna couldn't bring herself to lie to Anna again. "Anna," she whispered, her throat dry, her voice shaking, "I only followed you to the city because I've been planning to kill Boris the night I blossom."

Anna stared at her, her face turning pale in an instant. "Even now?" she asked, barely audible, clearly fighting back tears. "When you know for sure that you are the sacred one, and all the Divine Blooms will leave this world forever?" Tears streamed down her face.

"All I want is revenge," Vesna said, feeling empty inside. She had waited her entire life for her blossoming, only to realize she wasn't strong enough to kill Boris. He was immortal.

Anna shook her head. "No!" She stood up, wiping away her tears. Her eyes shone with a golden glow. "You can still take revenge if you follow the prophecy."

A million thoughts flashed through Vesna's mind. Anna was right; even if Boris was immortal, the fern flower could perform any miracle. Maybe its power would help Vesna kill him. She looked back at Anna. "And you're not mad at me?"

"For what?" Anna asked. "You didn't do anything that went against our plan."

"But even if I somehow find the fern flower, I can't promise what would happen after," she said, looking down. She wasn't going to give up on her revenge, even if the Divine Blooms said her mother was unworthy. Boris had killed her, and that was all that mattered.

"Don't worry about that now. Let's find the fern flower first," Anna said, taking her hand. "I believe the Divine Blooms have a plan for everything."

Vesna sighed in relief and hugged Anna tightly. She didn't deserve such a friend.

Her wound burned again, and she tensed up. It didn't go unnoticed by Anna. "You need to rest," she said, adjusting the pillow behind Vesna's back. "Should I tell Mir not to come tonight?"

"Yes, it's better if he doesn't see me like this."

Right on cue, Vesna fell silent abruptly as Mir came in.

"Sorry I'm late," he said, taking off his shoes. He probably noticed that Vesna was pale, because his eyes widened in worry. "What's wrong?"

"Vesna's wound is hurting again," Anna said guiltily.

"Did you let her go outside?" Mir asked, his gaze cutting to Anna with a glare.

"But she was so much better! We only went..." Anna paused, her eyes flicking to Vesna. "We went for a walk."

"Let me examine it," Mir said, hurrying to Vesna.

"I'll try to finish early," Anna said and walked toward the door, stopping at the threshold. "Take care of her."

Mir's gaze froze on Vesna's scratched hand, but she didn't have the energy to lie, or to even talk, for that matter, so she just stayed silent.

"Let me see." He carefully lifted her shirt, exposing the wound. He winced. "I need to clean it."

When Mir applied alcohol to her wound, Vesna jumped from the burn and grabbed his hand. They looked at each other, and she saw pain in his bottomless eyes.

Is he really worried that much about me? "It burns," she whispered.

"I'm sorry," he whispered back. "It's my fault you're like this."

"Let's not talk about that." Vesna cleared her throat. She didn't blame him. "You never talk about yourself," she said, staring at him. "Did your parents wield the poisonous magic too?"

Mir took a deep breath, quiet for a full minute. "My parents were humans. They knew from the moment I was born that I had magic, but when my magic began manifesting, poisoning everything around me..." He went silent, his voice shaking so much, he could barely speak. His memories clearly hurt him to this day. "They left me at the orphanage. That's where I met Alex. At least Alex doesn't see me as a poisonous monster."

The pain of what he had been through as a child drowned out all her thoughts. Vesna didn't care anymore that she should stay away from him. Tenderly touching his face, she traced the datura flower tattoo. "I don't think you're a monster," she whispered.

Staring at Mir, she realized that they were similar in some way—both lonely, both lost. *He's not a monster. He's just someone whose life has been hard.*

With this thought, she fell into a deep sleep.

Chapter Eleven

MIR.

Mir knew it was time to go back to the rafflesia. *Time to wake up from the dream,* he thought sadly, leaving his apartment at Fading Blossoms. He wondered if Ivan was awake or still in a coma.

That question was answered as soon as Mir entered the building. Ivan stood in the lobby, white as death, but smiling smugly at the same time. *Here we go again,* Mir thought, stopping next to him.

"You're in trouble," Ivan sang, victory in his tired voice.

"I'm glad the coma has had such a positive effect on your mood," Mir said sarcastically as he headed for the elevator. The finish line was so close that he knew he could endure everything. Although the worry that Boris might kill him before then settled in his heart, and he took a deep breath, hoping that Ivan wouldn't notice. Before Vesna had entered his life, he had been living in a nightmare that seemed to never end. But now, that nightmare would finally end on Ivan Kupala Night.

"Boris is underground," Ivan said. "You know what that means."

I can handle it. Mir took a deep breath again, steeling himself. Few people were permitted underground. Boris used the dark space beneath the building for torture. There, he also buried the bodies of magical people he had drained to death. Still, there was a part of it that not even Mir was permitted to enter.

Mir stepped out of the elevator after Ivan and shrugged as they walked down the stairs, distant screams making the air underground even thicker. Boris stood in the middle of one room of the labyrinth, his eyes blazing more than usual, a sign that he was angry.

"Do you have any explanations before I kill you?" Boris asked with pure disappointment in his voice.

"I don't think I'm the one who needs to explain myself." Mir glanced at Ivan and then back at Boris. "I was on a date, minding my own business, when Ivan attacked me. His man also stabbed the girl I was with," Mir said, pausing as his voice broke. He realized he sounded too emotional when he talked about Vesna. But he couldn't help it, anger washing over him again at the thought of what she had gone through because of him.

"Which girl?" Boris asked immediately.

Mir cursed himself for letting his feelings show. Nothing escaped Boris.

Bastard, Mir thought, trying not to give himself away. "She's a singer, an ordinary human girl," he added calmly, although inside, everything was raging. The mere thought of this parasite getting his hands on Vesna sent his magic into chaos.

"Introduce me to her at the ball," Boris commanded, slowly approaching. Mir held his breath. "My dear poisonous friend, I hope you understand my people come first."

Mir didn't move, watching as Boris released his

roots. They were slowly approaching him. It wasn't the first time that Boris had punished him this way, and Mir knew it would hurt like hell. *This will be the last time I let you torture me*, he promised himself.

The roots were closing in on Mir. Boris couldn't absorb his magic; datura was poisonous even to the rafflesia. But his roots could still enter Mir's body, breaking his bones and even his heart if the root was strong enough to reach it. Mir stood still as the roots dug into him. Everything inside him exploded, and he felt himself being torn apart from the inside. But he didn't even scream. Enduring the pain, clenching his fists and teeth, he thought instead of Vesna and the night of Ivan Kupala.

The finish line is close. This thought gave him strength.

Ivan watched in silence and satisfaction as Boris punished Mir. "Sweet," he said, barely audible, but he made sure that Mir heard him.

Boris finally called away his roots, and Mir growled from pain as they exited his body. His vision was blurry, and he could barely stand. The next second, he collapsed to the floor.

Boris just glanced at Mir and then turned to Ivan. "Ivan, bring the man."

Mir frowned, wondering who Boris was talking about. He narrowed his eyes, staring into the darkness until he saw Ivan literally dragging an enormous man into the room. Only when the man was almost next to him did Mir recognize Anton. Their eyes met, but both remained silent.

"You know him, right, Mir?" Boris asked, though Mir knew he already knew the answer.

"Yes." Mir could hardly speak. His mouth was dry, and he barely had the strength to move his lips.

"But I bet you didn't know he's in the human resistance group against the rafflesia?" Boris touched his beard.

"You took our gods from us!" Anton spat on the floor.

"It was the choice of the Divine Blooms to leave humanity. I'm afraid your insignificant resistance group is defeated. The book is now in my possession. You should be ashamed of yourself. Keeping something so important in a dirty barn is a disgrace." Boris laughed. "Had I known you had it, I wouldn't have wasted my time searching outside the city. But I admit, it was a smart move to give me the wrong lead."

"Parasite!" Anton screamed with pure hatred.

So, this is what his men were guarding in the barn, Mir realized, and his heart exploded. Boris believed this book mentioned the location of the Veiled Wilds. Mir had to steal it, or somehow find out what was written in it.

"That's enough," Boris snapped irritably.

He directed his roots at Anton. But Mir could barely see him, though he clearly heard his agony. It was torture listening to his screams, seeing his strong body being pierced by the ugly roots.

I'm sorry, Mir said silently to Anton. He didn't know him well, but he knew he didn't deserve to die like this. A lump rose in Mir's dry throat.

Suddenly, the screams stopped, and Anton's lifeless body fell to the floor.

Pure hatred filled Mir's soul. He hated Ivan, and he hated Boris even more. Mir didn't belong here. He just lay there, unable to move. He couldn't give up when he was so close to getting what he'd always wanted. He clenched his fists, fighting the urge to poison Boris and Ivan right then and there.

"Ivan, get rid of the body," Boris commanded. "I didn't think people cared anymore about the Divine Blooms, let alone were willing to die for them."

Mir watched as Ivan dragged Anton's body away.

"My poisonous friend, I'm going to be generous again. If you want to save your life, I expect you to deliver the herbalist to me before the spring ball," Boris said, looking straight at Mir.

Mir had neither the strength nor the desire to say anything. When Boris left, Mir managed to get up, growling in pain. He trudged weakly toward the exit, heading back to his old apartment.

He collapsed on the bed, almost lifeless. Mir had almost forgotten how dangerous Boris was. The man could kill him any time he wanted.

Mir closed his eyes and saw Anton's face before him. "Fuck," he cursed, feeling guilty. He hadn't expected Anton's death to affect him so much. He felt like a coward, and this feeling was new. Even thinking about the divine datura and how close he was to his goal didn't take away this strange feeling. *I'm just exhausted,* Mir thought, falling asleep.

HE WOKE up a few days later in a panic, afraid that something had happened to Vesna while he was out. Looking out the window, he realized that the sun was already setting.

Mir quickly got ready, hoping Vesna was safe. An hour later, he was already knocking on Alex's door. He didn't want Vesna to see him like this, but Alex would surely know if she was okay.

"What happened?" Alex's eyes widened in horror as soon as he saw his friend. Mir was pale, his lips dry, and there were huge dark circles under his eyes.

"Boris happened," Mir muttered, but then fell silent when he saw Anna and Vesna sitting on Alex's sofa.

"You look like a fading blossom!" Anna said, clearly worried.

Mir turned his gaze to Vesna, who was silently looking at him, her eyes seeming to water. Mir didn't want anyone to feel sorry for him, so he quickly changed the subject. "You look better."

"Alex used his magic on me," Vesna said, then added quietly, "I was worried about you."

Mir held his breath, feeling disarmed. "I'm sorry, wicked flower."

"Well, you're not the only one who's gone missing. Anton hasn't shown up for work for a few days," Alex reported.

Images of Anton suffering rose before Mir's eyes again, and he closed his eyes briefly against the guilt. "Anton is gone." He cleared his throat. "Boris killed him right in front of me."

Everyone stared at him in shock.

"Anton had magic?" Vesna asked, breaking the silence.

"No, but he had some book that Boris desperately wanted."

Mir didn't miss the glance Anna and Vesna exchanged. His eyes narrowed slightly as he realized they knew what book he was talking about. Everything was slowly but surely falling into place, as if the Divine Blooms were revealing the future, throwing different petals into the wind. *They must be after this book too,* he realized. But perhaps Vesna wanted to destroy it, so that Boris would never get to the Veiled Wilds. Mir decided to find out as soon as possible where Boris had put the book and how difficult it would be to steal it.

"I hope Anton got to the eternal garden," Alex said softly, clearly saddened by the news.

"I don't feel like shopping anymore," Vesna said.

Anna looked at her reproachfully. "We're going!" she insisted.

"I'm free today. But then I'll be busy delivering invitations to that stupid spring ball," Mir sighed heavily.

At his words, both Anna and Vesna looked toward him, their gazes expectant. Vesna had mentioned the ball before, but for some reason, Mir didn't think it was that important to her. She had sounded too casual when she asked him about it. Plus, Mir didn't want Vesna anywhere near the rafflesia, and especially not near Boris. *Is this what they need?*

"You promised *me* an invitation," she said simply. But Mir noticed she was holding her breath.

"Vesna has always wanted to go to that ball!" Anna sang, a little unnaturally.

"Really?" Mir raised an eyebrow.

"Yes," Vesna quickly confirmed. "Life in the village is so boring. I want to feel what it's like to attend something grand."

She was obviously lying. "I can get you two invitations," he muttered.

"Yes!" Anna screamed excitedly.

"Thank you," Vesna said, lowering her face.

She's heading straight for the parasite's nest, Mir thought. "I'll bring them in a few days."

Anna seemed to be over the moon as she went to the

kitchen. "Let's say goodbye to Anton and continue living, in spite of everything," she said, pouring them all a drink. It was a custom to drink for the souls of those who had passed on to the eternal garden.

"Water for me," Vesna called after Anna.

"Mir, you look like shit. Come on, lie down here." Alex pointed to the couch.

Vesna continued to sit, saying nothing, and Mir came and sat down next to her. She was wearing a simple white top and a skirt, and her silhouette reminded him of a petal of fragrant jasmine.

"You're right, I think I should lie down." Mir couldn't help himself, and without warning, he laid his head in her lap.

"Excuse me?" Vesna bowed her head and stared at him in protest. Her soft hair fell across his face, touching his skin so gently that he almost closed his eyes in bliss. From this angle, her face looked like a flower framed by pink petals.

"Just for a second," Mir whispered.

"Fine." Vesna pouted her lips. "Maybe I should give you a head massage, too?" she said sarcastically.

"Oh, that would be perfect!" Mir sang, looking into her eyes and smiling widely. "Thank you."

"Unbelievable," Vesna murmured. But her slender fingers slowly touched his scalp, moving from the center, to his forehead, to the sides.

Every muscle in Mir's body tensed. Her touch was so gentle, so perfect. He breathed hard, wanting her fingers to touch his entire body.

"What did he do to you?" Vesna asked after a while.

Mir hid his smile. Somehow, it was nice that someone other than Alex cared about him. Or at least, he liked to think that Vesna cared. "His roots have penetrated my body. Nothing to worry about."

Vesna froze for a moment, her hands on his head, and Mir knew what she was thinking. She was the sacred one, and if Boris found out, he would drain all her magic.

"Why don't you just leave him?" she asked.

I want to, the thought flashed through Mir's mind. "I will, but not yet."

His gazed moved to her perfect mouth. *Hold yourself together,* Mir ordered himself, heated by her touch, by the sight of her slightly parted lips so close to him. *Fuck, I can't.* He couldn't help but want to grab her in his arms and kiss her. But it wasn't the time. Anna and Alex were right there, pouring drinks in the kitchen.

Mir stood up quickly, needing to get away from her before he did something he'd regret. "Thank you, I feel much better."

"Let's drink to Anton." Anna brought the drinks in on a tray. "May his spirit blossom."

Everyone raised their glasses and drank, and then they just sat in silence for a while.

Finally, Anna got up. "So, my friends, we need to remodel Vesna's room, so that it feels like an actual home." She paused. "I think Vesna needs an egg chair. It's all the rage right now."

Alex also expressed his opinion. "Anna is right, egg chairs are a statement. I'm thinking about getting one for my apartment, but I've found nothing that matches my interior color palette yet."

"Was there really no red chair with roses?!" Anna asked dramatically.

Vesna rolled her eyes. "Mir, please save me."

Mir laughed. "I will fight against the egg chair, wicked flower."

"I'm serious." She pouted her perfect lips.

"We'll decide later. Let's go while the stores are still open," Alex suggested, heading for the door.

Anna insisted that she knew the best shops, so she sat in the front seat next to Alex to show him the way. Mir and Vesna settled in the back seat. Vesna was distant, looking out the window the whole time, while Alex and Anna argued over some furniture designer. Mir had to admit that Anna could be a good match for his friend. They were so similar.

Going up a hill, the car suddenly made a strange noise and pulled slightly to the side. "What the hell?" Alex cursed, stopping the car.

All four of them got out and walked around the car, inspecting it. One tire was completely flat.

Alex turned to Anna with a glare and pointed a finger at her. "I'm never lending you my baby again!"

"What does this have to do with me?" Anna protested, but her voice wasn't very convincing.

Mir was certain Alex's jaw would drop to the ground if it could. "I know perfectly well how terrible you are at driving! Never missing an opportunity to crash into something."

"You've never seen me drive, so stop making up stories!"

Mir put his hand on Alex's shoulder to calm him down. He was afraid that Alex might reveal in his anger that they had followed Anna and Vesna to the herbalist. "I'm sure Anna is an excellent driver," he said, surprising everyone.

"Well, that's an exaggeration, of course," Vesna muttered, and Anna shot her an angry look.

"I can see that men with datura magic are proper gentlemen—not like guys with rose magic. Thank you, Mir," Anna said, holding her head high.

Alex's face turned rose red at that. "You know what…" He hesitated, clearly unsure of what to say. "Let's just walk. We're close."

Mir looked at Vesna. She had just gotten better. Who knew if her wound would reopen or not? He couldn't take any chances. "Vesna, jump on my back. Any physical activity is too dangerous for you right now."

"No way," Vesna protested.

"I'm waiting," Mir insisted. "You can't walk up the hill with your injury."

"Like I said, he's a gentleman," Anna couldn't help but chime in.

"Let me carry you too!" Alex volunteered. "Besides, you look light."

"Thank you, Alex, you gentleman," Anna teased, jumping on his back. "I've gained a few pounds in the last month, for your information."

"Wicked flower?" Mir narrowed his eyes on Vesna, as she kept rolling her eyes.

"No," Vesna mumbled, touching her stomach, clearly debating whether she could walk on her own. "Okay, fine." She finally agreed. "But we'll look ridiculous."

"Who cares?" Mir said, leaning down a little to make sure she could easily jump on his back.

"Wow, Vesna! I didn't know you were so athletic!" Anna said in surprise as Vesna landed on Mir's back on her first try.

"I grew up next to a forest. I can climb trees and all sorts of things," Vesna reported.

"All sorts of *things*?" Mir asked playfully. *You're an idiot,* he immediately scolded himself, angry at how childish he was around her.

"Pervert," Vesna muttered, wrapping her legs around him. Mir smirked and gripped her hips, making sure she was comfortable.

Alex kept complaining about the steepness of the hill, while Mir said little. He still felt weak. But Vesna was much more important than him. So, he hugged her tightly, carrying the most precious flower on earth. Her long hair fell on his face and tickled him gently. He was secretly enjoying this moment, her body pressed against his. Vesna's face was right next to his, and he felt the warmth of her breath.

"We'll take a taxi on the way back," Alex said, out of breath. "I'll pay."

"Proper gentleman," Anna teased, clearly enjoying the moment too much.

Mir cleared his throat, wanting to talk to Vesna, but not knowing where to start. "Are you comfortable?"

"Yes," Vesna said in his ear, and Mir felt goose bumps run across his skin. The desire to taste her from the very first day had not gone away. On the contrary, it grew stronger the more time they spent together.

"Mir, I have an idea," Alex sang. "Since you obviously like carrying Vesna in your arms, you could carry her on stage every time she performs."

"What a brilliant idea!" Anna enthusiastically supported him.

"Shut up," Vesna and Mir said in unison.

Mir didn't even notice how quickly, and most importantly, how pleasantly the evening passed. Anna and Alex walked around the shop as if they were in the eternal garden. And Vesna kept rolling her eyes at the furniture that the two enthusiasts were proposing for her room. Mir quietly laughed, looking at Vesna's suffering face.

✿

Vesna's tiny room was filled with boxes. Anna and Alex insisted on helping her arrange the furniture.

"At this rate, I'm getting claustrophobic," Alex complained. "Should Anna and I make dinner while you get everything set up?"

"Okay," Mir agreed immediately. He wanted to be left alone with Vesna.

"I'll make my signature dish," Alex decided, quickly leaving the room. Anna followed him.

"A little warning: don't eat Alex's cooking. He's a terrible cook, he just doesn't know it," Mir said playfully to Vesna.

She moved and sat down on a few boxes, her eyes indifferent and even sad. "Why am I doing all this?" she asked, clearly not expecting an answer.

Mir didn't know her story, but he felt her pain. He was sure of one thing: her life as a sacred one likely hadn't been easy.

"Life is hard, but that doesn't mean we can't enjoy it as best we can," Mir said quietly. "That's why I like being around Alex. He has a talent for making things lighter."

"So, are you enjoying your life?" she asked simply.

Mir was silent. If she had asked a month ago, he would have answered with the most brazen "no." But now everything had changed; everything suddenly made sense. Plus, the time spent with Vesna, Alex, and even Anna had made Mir forget his problems.

"Sometimes I do. When I'm with Alex, for example, away from Boris." He paused. "Alex was the same as a kid—funny, curious, unique. The truth is, he saved me from complete loneliness. After my parents left me, I decided I was better off alone. If you don't let people into your life, they don't have a chance to leave you," Mir said, realizing it was the first time he'd shared such thoughts with anyone. "But Alex is an exception."

Vesna was still sitting on the boxes, her face much softer than before. "I'm glad you have Alex. I only had my aunt when I was growing up, but now I have Anna too." She pursed her lips, as if she had decided she was talking too much, because she quickly stood up and began opening a box with her hands.

"I have scissors," Mir said.

"Ouch," Vesna groaned in pain.

Mir was next to her in a split second. "Let me see."

He gently sat her back down on the boxes and examined her hand. She had cut her finger, and a small drop of blood had appeared on her soft skin. The cut wasn't deep. Still, Mir knelt before her, and taking her finger, slowly brought it to his lips. He paused, as if expecting her to protest. To his surprise, she said nothing, instead staring into his eyes.

Mir licked the blood carefully—much longer and much more sensually than necessary. He never took his eyes off her. Vesna remained silent, her mouth parting slightly in pleasure, and her cheeks turned pink. This sight overwhelmed him. Unable to hold back, he touched her tender, passionate lips with his fingers. His whole body tensed with the desire to drink nectar from her petal-soft lips. His own lips parted in pleasure too, just from finally touching her. But he wanted more—so much more.

He leaned closer to taste her sweet mouth, when Vesna whispered, "Not my lips."

Mir didn't ask why. Maybe it was too personal. Or maybe she feared poison slipping into her precious body. Instead, he kissed her jaw, making his way down her neck. She tasted like the most delicate flower, which only made him want her more. When she moaned softly, something deep within him spiraled. He forced himself to go slowly, to give her a chance to stop him, though he prayed she wouldn't. Mir lowered his hand to her blouse and leisurely began to untie it. His breath hitched as her breasts became visible beneath the loosening fabric. He was panting, but she seemed to breathe even more heavily, her gaze still locked on his. He slid the blouse down, and one look at her bare skin was enough for the desire to overwhelm him. Leaning down, he ran his tongue along her collarbone, then moved slowly toward her nipple. Vesna gasped, and he felt his own cock jump in response. But Mir held back, afraid that if he gave in, he'd lose control and ruin everything.

Looking into her eyes, he flicked her nipples lightly with his tongue before gently sucking. With another moan, she grabbed his shoulders, leaning closer, pressing herself into him. *Wicked flower,* he thought with satisfaction. He wanted to give her everything she desired. With each pass of his tongue, her moans grew louder, driving him insane. His hands slid down her thighs, and when he squeezed her buttocks, she straightened and arched her back. He was burning with need, squeezing harder, drawing patterns of obsession with his tongue.

"Dinner is ready!" Alex called from the kitchen.

Vesna froze, and he cursed Alex's timing. She pulled away from him, quickly pulling her blouse back on.

Fuck Alex and his dinner, Mir cursed.

"This was a mistake. It can't happen again," Vesna said, not even looking at him.

THAT NIGHT, Mir tossed and turned in bed. He couldn't forget her face blushed from desire, her passionate sighs and moans. *She is a flower laced with salvation,* he thought, admitting that he wanted her madly.

Chapter Twelve

VESNA.

ANNA AND ALEX FINALLY AGREED THAT TOMORROW Vesna could come to work again. In the morning, she just walked around boxes, but Anna persuaded her to assemble the furniture together. Vesna had to admit that her room looked more like a home with a table, a chair, and a small shelf for books.

While Anna was getting ready for work in her room, Vesna secretly grabbed a book from Anna's shelf, and sitting in her new chair, dove into its world. *To kill time,* she told herself. The story captivated her. The heroes of the book were so alive, so passionate, they were ready to do anything for love and friendship. When Vesna came across a spicy scene in a book, she immediately thought of Mir, blushing.

When Mir had touched her yesterday, everything inside was ready to bloom in anticipation of more. She knew she should stop him, but instead she let him touch her as he wished. She had felt nothing like this before. She had ached with sweet languor, her body reaching for his lips like a dry flower in an approaching thunderstorm.

"One day, you will blossom under my poisonous touch." Vesna remembered his words, and frustration filled her. *I only need him to get to the book,* she thought decisively. *He's a means to an end—that's it!*

"Vesna, I'm going to work!" Anna shouted from the living room.

"Okay," she shouted back.

As soon as she heard the door close, she left the room, deciding to put the book back and never read Anna's books again. She tried not think about the fact that she was actually the sacred one, convincing herself that nothing had changed. She was simply following Anna's plan, because apparently, she couldn't kill Boris without the fern flower. She still thought about trying to do it once she bloomed, but she was afraid that she might lose her only chance to kill the man who had taken her mother away if she took that risk. *I need to focus on the ball,* she thought as the door opened.

"I forgot to give you something," Anna said as she walked in. She suddenly stopped, squinting at Vesna. "What do we have here?" Her gaze shifted curiously to the book.

"Nothing," Vesna said, quickly hiding the book behind her back.

A knowing look crossed Anna's face. "I know that book. It's as spicy as it gets," Anna teased.

Vesna blushed from head to toe and tried to shrug casually. "I'm bored."

Anna grinned at her. "Instead of just reading, you could try living it. Mir will most definitely volunteer."

"That's not what I need him for," Vesna said, feeling her cheeks burn even hotter.

"One doesn't interfere with the other." Anna winked.

"Of course it does!" Vesna fired too emotionally. "I've been using him since the beginning. I don't think he would like it if he knew. Nothing is possible between us!" She paused. "I'm lost. I've been waiting to fully bloom all my life to take revenge, but now it turns out that Boris is immortal!"

Anna was silent, clearly disarmed. Her eyes filled with tears as she took a deep breath, approaching Vesna. "You're still following the plan. Maybe the Divine Blooms planned all this so that you could take revenge and help them at the same time…" She paused. "But that doesn't mean you can't live and feel in the meantime. Maybe this is our only time to live."

Anna's voice was so tender and sincere that Vesna could no longer hold back, and tears gushed from her eyes.

"It's okay to cry. Flowers don't grow without rain." Anna hugged her.

"Mir hasn't come," Vesna finally said, wiping away her tears. "And he promised to bring invitations."

"Well, he said he might be busy. I'm sure he'll come tomorrow," Anna said hesitantly. "I'll let you know if I see him in the club." She paused. "If you care to know, of course."

"I don't," Vesna lied.

Anna narrowed her eyes. "Sure, you don't. I must go, but Sveta will come. Give her this." Anna pulled out some herb wrapped in cloth.

"Is this wormwood?" Vesna asked, taking the herb.

"Yes, I paid a fortune for it. Sveta needs it for your potion."

"Why don't we go to her place tomorrow instead?" Vesna asked, not looking forward to seeing Sveta.

"She told me she needs to talk to you about something," Anna muttered. "She should arrive soon. I'm going."

Vesna didn't like the idea of being alone with Sveta. The herbalist always stared at her, making her feel uncomfortable. Vesna stood up, deciding to put the herb somewhere close to the door, so she could just hand it to Sveta, preventing her from entering the house. Passing by the mirror, she realized her makeup was ruined and there were dark spots under her eyes. She quickly took a shower. She didn't want Sveta to notice that she had been crying.

She had just gotten out of the shower, still in her silk robe with a towel on her head, when the doorbell rang. *Sveta,* Vesna thought, dashing to the door.

Mir, dressed in a black as always, stood in front of her, his gaze immediately moving from her face to her chest, which was covered with slightly damp silk. Vesna blushed when his eyes sparkled hungrily. She was sure he had already mentally undressed her.

"Something urgent? I'm waiting for someone," Vesna said seriously.

He swallowed hard and cleared his throat. "I hope you're not waiting for a man."

"What difference does it make to you? You were gone all day," Vesna said, knowing she sounded pathetic. "Not that I cared," she said quickly.

Mir smiled smugly. "Sorry, wicked flower. Boris was pressuring me to find someone."

Vesna held her breath. *Is he looking for the sacred one?* The thought made her shudder. "Who?" She cleared her throat to hide her worry.

Mir didn't answer right away, still devouring her body. "The herbalist."

"Never heard of any herbalist," she lied quickly, her

heart pounding, silently praying that Sveta would be late.

"She helps people with magic hide from Boris," Mir added.

"She…" His words echoed in her mind. *So, they know the herbalist is a woman.* "She sounds like a good person," Vesna dared to say. "Why are you helping Boris, anyway? You have magic too." She couldn't help but ask, because part of her wanted to understand him.

"He was supposed to help me with something I desperately needed," Mir said, leaning closer again, towering over her like a mountain. "Are you going to invite me in?"

"No, the house is a mess," Vesna lied, apparently not very convincingly, because Mir laughed. "I'm serious." She crossed her arms in front of her.

"I thought you'd at least offer me a drink," Mir insisted.

"Are you thirsty?" she asked, looking up to meet his gaze.

"I'm thirstier than the flowers in the desert," he whispered, licking his lips.

"Not my problem."

"I brought you invitations to the ball," he said simply.

Everything inside Vesna tensed. She was so close. "Thank you. Give them to me." She held out her hand.

"It's bad luck to pass something over the threshold," Mir said seriously.

"I've never heard of that stupid superstition," she muttered, but stepped over the threshold. She was barefoot, and her toes curled as soon as she touched the cold floor.

Mir was watching her, and taking her by surprise, he

scooped her up in his arms. "The floor is cold and dirty," he sang.

His hair was slightly damp—it was raining outside—and his almond scent was even stronger than usual. There was no time to protest; she needed to get the invitations and get rid of Mir before Sveta arrived. "So, where are my invitations?" she asked, pursing her lips.

"In my pocket," Mir said and moved her quickly, wrapping her legs around himself. She felt the press of his hard cock against her, and heat pulsed low in her belly. Her thighs instinctively tensed, and she bit her lip, fighting back moans. The towel slid off her head, scattering her long, wet hair over the silk robe, making it wet and translucent.

Mir practically growled, looking at her body, inhaling her scent loudly and deeply. It was too erotic, and Vesna didn't even notice how she breathed heavily in unison with him.

"Maybe I should get them myself?" she finally whispered. *Maybe Anna is right. I should live while I can,* she thought, and staring at Mir, she licked her lips.

He growled darker this time, squeezing her hips. "Wicked flower," he whispered, pushing her toward the wall and pressing her back against the hard surface.

She wrapped herself around him, a pulsing sensation building at her core, her lips parting with a gasp. Mir didn't waste a second. His lips stole her kiss passionately, hungrily. He demanded obedience, and she obeyed, forgetting about everything in this fading reality. She felt like she was drinking his poison—and she desperately wanted more.

When Mir lowered his lips, exploring her neck, Vesna felt her whole body fill to the brim with lust.

"Mir," she moaned, writhing in his arms, wanting to feel him even closer.

Mir groaned, nibbling her neck. "I get hard every time you're near me." His hands lifted the thin robe, burning the skin of her thighs. He pressed himself against her, as if wanting to grow roots into her body. "Invite me in, Vesna, or I will fuck you right here."

Vesna moaned, dizzy from the way he tasted her, from his almond-honey scent, from the way her magic reached to him. She wanted him; she wanted to melt in his arms.

"I'm not sure we should," she whispered with a moan.

He kissed her face until he reached her ear and whispered, "Vesna, screw everything. Just let me in."

The way he said it made her shiver, as if he were talking not about the house, but about her very soul. And she wasn't sure if she was ready to let him in. There were too many secrets between them.

She took a deep breath, trying to stop the buds of desire from blooming in her blood. "I'm waiting for someone," she repeated, her voice shaking.

Mir froze, diving into her eyes. She had a feeling he was fighting himself. "Okay, wicked flower." He slowly lowered her to the floor, clearing his throat. "Here are the invitations."

Vesna wanted to cry. She didn't want to stop this, wanting to feel all of him. But it wouldn't be tonight. She silently looked at the two envelopes Mir took out of his pocket. "Thank you. This should be fun."

"I doubt it," Mir muttered, pulling away slightly.

It was cold and empty away from him. Vesna didn't want him to leave like this. "Mir," she whispered, and there was a pause in the air as they looked at each other in silence.

Vesna heard light footsteps and turned around, noticing someone's silhouette on the stairs. *Sveta!* she thought with panic. She looked at Mir and realized that it was too late; he had seen Sveta too.

"Vesna," Sveta said, stopping short when she noticed Mir. "I see you're not alone."

"He was just leaving," Vesna said nervously, pushing Mir away slightly.

Sveta narrowed her old green eyes at him. "Handsome." She laughed out of nowhere, as usual.

Mir looked at her, narrowing his eyes. "Thank you," he said. "I'm Mir."

If Sveta was afraid, she certainly didn't show it and simply looked at him while he looked at her. It was dangerous. Mir couldn't find out about Sveta.

"You should go, Mir. Thank you for the invitations."

"It's raining outside. Let him have coffee with us," Sveta suggested.

Vesna widened her eyes at her. *She is crazy!* The last thing Vesna needed was for Mir to investigate Sveta after this encounter.

"Your guest is right, it's raining hard," Mir said, heading for the door.

Great! Vesna thought helplessly. "Come in, I guess," she said, as if under duress.

They entered the apartment. Everyone was silent, and Vesna wanted to fall through the floor. Sveta sat down on the couch, and Mir followed her example.

"I'll get that coffee," Vesna offered, unsure of how to get out of this situation.

"Wonderful," Sveta sang. "Is he your boyfriend, Vesna?"

Vesna coughed, and Mir laughed. "Even the thought of me being her boyfriend makes her sick. But one day I will be, probably soon," he said, staring at Vesna.

How self-assured, Vesna thought sarcastically. "Unfortunately, we are from different worlds, so, no, he's not my boyfriend. We're just friends… Sort of."

"I see that you have magic," Sveta muttered, looking down at Mir's tattoo. "Datura?"

"Yes," Mir confirmed.

"Did your parents wield magic?" Sveta asked, seeming more interested in Mir than he was in her.

Vesna noticed the white mist dancing in Mir's eyes. After what she had heard about his childhood, she could imagine that he didn't like to talk about it. And Mir was no longer a stranger. "Let's not talk about the past," Vesna blurted out. "Here's your coffee." She sat the cups in front of the guests.

"So, what do you do for a living?" Sveta didn't give up, and Vesna threw her an angry look.

"I suppose you haven't heard of the rafflesia?" Mir looked at Sveta intently.

Sveta smiled, but there was dullness in her eyes. "When you're my age, you hear about many things."

"Well, I work for their leader, Boris," Mir said, shifting his gaze away.

Vesna only hoped that Mir hadn't noticed the change in Sveta's face, her eyes dancing strangely. Fortunately, Mir was looking at Vesna. He didn't seem to notice or suspect anything.

"I think the rain has stopped," Vesna said, rushing to the window.

"I heard he doesn't age," Sveta said, and Vesna turned to look at her, wishing to just show her the door. *Has she gone mad?!* she screamed inside.

"It's true," Mir said indifferently. "He looks thirty, thirty-three at the most. Someone stabbed him horribly several years ago, but he didn't even bleed."

Vesna clenched her fists. Mir's words confirmed that this bastard was immortal.

Sveta stared at a distant point, silent. Vesna had to do something. Sveta was playing a dangerous game.

"So, what should I wear to the ball?" Vesna asked Mir, trying to take his attention away from the herbalist.

"Whatever you want. You look beautiful in anything," Mir said eagerly, and quickly cleared his throat. "By the way, since you've finally bought some furniture, I thought a gift was in order." He took a small book out of his pocket.

Vesna lit up. Maybe it was all an act, but Mir was kind to her, and it was the first time a man had ever given her a gift. She excitedly grabbed the present. It was a book about the sacred magnolia.

"Thank you!" Vesna hugged him tightly, unable to stop the happy feeling that came over her.

"Why magnolia?" Sveta asked, looking at them.

Mir turned to her again. "Well, Vesna mentioned it's her favorite flower."

Suddenly Sveta laughed loudly, almost hysterically. Both Mir and Vesna looked at her in confusion. "A naïve girl like Vesna would fall for your tricks."

Vesna's jaw tightened as she stared at Sveta. She was definitely out of her mind. Anna had told Sveta about their plan, hoping she knew something useful. She knew they needed to get into Boris's building, and Mir was the key to that. *Why, then, is she trying to ruin everything?*

Mir's magic flashed in his eyes for a brief moment. "Sorry, but you don't know me at all."

"This story is as old as the Divine Blooms. A naïve

girl, a man with questionable magic… It's always the same story, always the same ending," Sveta said, without looking at Mir or Vesna, as if she were talking about something or someone else.

"She's a little crazy," Vesna whispered to Mir, hoping he could read her lips.

Mir smiled. "Can I have a word, Vesna?"

He headed for the door, and she followed him. He gently placed his hand on her shoulder. "Are you sure you want to stay with her?" he asked seriously. "She's a little weird."

"You should go. I'll be fine," she whispered, smiling.

"Or we could go for a walk or something," he said, leaning forward slightly.

Vesna wanted to go with him more than anything in the world. Besides, the prospect of being left here alone with Sveta didn't please her at all.

"I need to stay," Vesna stammered. "Anna asked me to take care of her," she lied.

Mir gently touched her ear before speaking, and Vesna wished Sveta wasn't there. She wanted so desperately to feel him again.

"Let me drive you to work tomorrow," he whispered, his voice honeyed. "And don't put the seat belt on this time."

Vesna stood on her tiptoes to reach his ear with her lips. "Don't be late. I don't want the boss to fire me." She couldn't help but smile.

As soon as the door closed behind Mir, Vesna turned around, staring at Sveta. "What the hell is wrong with you?!"

Sveta continued to sit on the couch, holding her mug of coffee. "I know you think you have it all figured out, but he could use you and break your heart along the way, at best. Or he could cost you your magic," she said under her breath. "The sacred one should be smarter than that."

"Look, I'm sorry if someone broke your heart in the past, but we need Mir!" Vesna said and took a deep breath, trying to calm down.

"I strongly recommend staying away from him," Sveta continued, and her voice was like a teacher scolding a student. "Think about it. What could a sacred magnolia have in common with poisonous magic? Do what you must, but don't fall for him."

Vesna remained silent throughout Sveta's speech. Sveta clearly didn't like Mir, and she had every reason not to. After all, he was looking for her at that very moment, hoping to bring the herbalist to Boris. But telling Vesna what to do was too much; even Nina didn't dare to talk to her like that.

"I can decide for myself," Vesna said coldly. "You must go." At that moment, she didn't care whether Sveta decided to never brew her a potion again.

"Wait." Sveta grabbed her hand. "Don't let him poison your mind. He is dangerous."

"Sveta, please leave," Vesna blurted out. After all, she didn't have to answer to Sveta. *She barely knows me,* she thought.

"I just don't want you to lose your magic because of an unworthy man," Sveta said quietly.

"Here's your wormwood," Vesna mumbled, grabbing the herb and handing it to Sveta.

Sveta looked at her, let out a deep breath, and left the apartment without saying another word.

Vesna sat on the couch for a while. She was angry at Sveta; she had no right to talk to her like that. Even if Vesna was the sacred one, it didn't mean everyone had a say in her life. But deep down, she was even angrier at herself, realizing that Mir had already poisoned her mind and heart with such toxic yet alluring magic. She couldn't deny her attraction to him. But also, she enjoyed just being around him, talking to him.

I need to find out what he needs from Boris, she decided, remembering his words about Boris and why he worked for him. *Maybe he's just a lost flower, blooming from old wounds.*

Chapter Thirteen

MIR.

MIR DIDN'T GO TO SEE VESNA DURING THE DAY BECAUSE Boris insisted that he and Ivan must search for the herbalist all day long. Boris was obviously desperate. Mir had to make up lies on the go, leading Ivan to people who had nothing to do with the herbalist.

Mir tried to get into Boris's library, but Boris had increased security. Mir also saw some workers bring a metal cage in. But from the angry look on Boris's face, Mir realized that Boris hadn't found out the location of Veiled Wilds yet.

As evening approached, Mir finally left the rafflesia, and his thoughts shifted to Vesna. Somehow, she managed to peer into his fading heart, past all the walls of thorns.

The need to possess Vesna had overcome him as soon as he saw her still wet and hot after the shower. This wicked flower was the only petal he wanted to pluck from a meadow full of myriad blooms. Her lips were soaked with charms. And when he finally tasted them, inhaling her moans, he had felt his heart unfolding.

But the evening didn't go as Mir expected. The herbalist had showed up, and she was strange, maybe even crazy. There was something suspicious in what she said.

Mir knew that he would soon have to visit Sveta. Ivan was now looking for the herbalist himself, and it was only a matter of time before he found her.

MIR WAS WALKING down the stairs when an alarm sounded throughout the building. Boris only used this alarm for emergencies. *What the hell is going on?*

People were running back and forth, and Mir barely made it to the lobby, pushing through the crowd. Boris and Ivan were already there, discussing something heatedly.

Boris raised an eyebrow at Mir. "Mir, it seems Ivan did your job for you."

Mir's heart was pounding, and he fought to keep a straight face. "What job?"

Ivan approached him tightly, and he had to hold his breath, enveloped in the smell of rotten flesh. Boris had probably just shared magic with him as a reward. "I spotted a strange woman on the outskirts of the city who smelled like herbs."

Mir's head was spinning. Sveta lived on the outskirts. It had to be her. "Great, let's go get her!" he said with false enthusiasm. He needed to get to her before they did.

"Finally!" Boris said, victory gleaming in his eyes. He turned to his men, raising his hand. "Brothers! I promised we would survive. Today, we are closer than ever. Let's find the herbalist and open the Veiled Wilds."

Mir still didn't know why Boris was so sure that the herbalist could take him to the Veiled Wilds. But it was obvious that he knew something that Mir didn't.

"What's the plan?" Mir asked Boris, trying to calculate how to get to Sveta first.

Boris raised his hand, heading for the exit. "Let's just get her!" Ivan and the others immediately followed.

Not on my watch, Mir decided, running after them. It was a good thing he knew exactly where Sveta lived.

Mir drove like crazy, following Boris's car closely. The other cars on the road parted at the sight of the cloud of brown rafflesia cars speeding along.

They arrived at the outskirts of the city in less than twenty minutes. Boris got out of the car, waiting for his men to gather around him.

"Let's check all the houses, and don't forget the basements. The herbalist is no fool. She knows how to hide," Boris said, his voice excited.

Mir had never seen Boris like this. His brown eyes burned with a white flame, and he constantly licked his lips, like a parasite who had spotted a victim on which he could feed.

"Yes, Boss," his men answered almost in unison and ran toward the nearest houses.

Boris looked at Ivan. "Take Mir. You should work together on this."

You've got to be kidding me! Mir screamed internally.

Ivan shook his head. "I'm faster on my own." He clearly hoped to be the one to find the herbalist for his beloved boss.

"As you wish." Mir looked away, trying to sound indifferent.

"Fine, but stay close to each other," Boris agreed, looking hopefully at the men who had finished inspecting the first house. They shook their heads in disappointment.

Boris growled. "Find her!" His angry voice echoed down the street.

Mir approached one house, and going around it, raced to Sveta's house as if his life depended on it.

He didn't have time to knock or somehow warn her; he just burst in like a mad man. Sveta froze with some herb in her hands, looking at him with wide eyes. Her quiet house was filled with the bittersweet smell of a potion brewing on the stove. Sveta's face went pale, but something told Mir she wasn't surprised to see him.

"Hello, Mir," she said, breaking the silence. "I knew it was only a matter of time before you found me. After all, everything is finally coming to an end."

"There's no time for philosophical discussions, Sveta," Mir said breathlessly. "Boris and his men will be here any minute."

A sick smile appeared on her face. "So be it," she whispered.

She's crazy! Mir thought, quickly approaching her. "Sveta, pull yourself together, for flower's sake! I need to get you out of here!"

She lifted her gaze at him. "It seems you really care about Vesna. But I can't go. I need to be next to Boris in case Vesna needs my help at the ball."

Mir's brows shot up. "And how can *you* help?"

"You don't understand," she whispered.

Time was running out. Sveta was either crazy or hiding something. Either way, now wasn't the time to find out. They had to leave as soon as possible, before it was too late.

Mir had to be smart. "I promise I will take you to him

before the ball, but not now." He paused, searching for words. "First, we need to prepare enough potions for Vesna and Anna. If you go to Boris now, he'll discover them."

It seemed his words had an effect, because Sveta looked at him with a limpid gaze and quickly straightened up. "You're right. But promise that you will take me to him."

"I promise. Let's just get out of here. Is there a back exit?"

"Yes, we can go out through the basement."

Sveta moved the carpet aside, and Mir opened a small door in the floor, while she quickly gathered her herb map and some herbs. At that moment, he heard voices outside the house. Mir practically pushed Sveta inside, quickly following her.

The space was small and dark. Mir had to bend down to walk. After a few seconds, he realized Sveta hadn't followed him, remaining in the same place.

"We need to move," he whispered, getting angry.

"I just want to hear his voice," Sveta whispered back, her voice shaking.

"This is her house! Look at all the herbs! Collect them!" Boris shouted, probably standing right above Mir's head.

"There, you heard his voice. Now let's move! I beg you," Mir pleaded.

Sveta didn't answer, but this time she followed Mir, and he sighed in relief.

After walking underground for a while, they came out into some forest. Mir looked around, trying to figure out how far they were from the city. It was not safe for Sveta to go back now.

She seemed to read his mind. "I know this forest; I

will stay here for the night. You can go. Come back for me tomorrow."

"Are you sure you'll be okay?" Mir asked, his voice suspicious. In truth, part of him was afraid that Sveta might go to Boris while he was gone.

"I'm the herbalist. I'm used to spending my days in the forest," Sveta assured him. "And don't worry, I'll not put Vesna at risk."

Mir hesitated for a moment. He didn't like the idea of leaving Sveta here, but he had to prepare to bring her somewhere safe. Plus, right now, Boris was probably patrolling the streets.

"Okay, but don't go anywhere," Mir said, but he still didn't move. "Is there something you want to tell me?" He dove into her eyes.

Sveta narrowed her eyes at him, as if deciding whether she could trust him. "Magnolia is a peaceful flower, though when it blooms, it can do extraordinary things."

"Great," Mir muttered. She was talking in riddles, and nothing made sense.

"But the sacred one was never meant to find the fern flower alone," Sveta continued. "She needs someone with powerful magic and a pure heart to be by her side to win this battle."

"Do you have someone in mind?" Mir asked, a little confused.

"I do," Sveta said thoughtfully.

"Anna?"

"Her heart is pure, but her magic is too peaceful for war," she muttered.

"You don't…" Mir's voice broke. He didn't even think she could be talking about him. Poisonous magic would be the last thing the Divine Blooms would choose for a big fight. "The Divine Blooms would never choose me. Plus, I have my own scores to settle."

"I knew it! You're using her! You're just like all men." Sveta's voice was crazed.

"Not again…" Mir rolled his eyes helplessly. Sveta was clearly not well; he decided that some ancient wound of hers had probably started bleeding again. "It's not about sacrificing Vesna, or anything of that sort," he assured her.

Sveta was by his side in seconds. "Don't betray her. History can't repeat itself."

"I won't," Mir said, pulling away from her. He silently clenched his teeth, filled with guilt. He was lying. He had planned to use Vesna, and she didn't deserve it.

Sveta let out a sigh of relief. "I will be somewhere nearby," she muttered.

"Okay, don't go anywhere, and try to rest," Mir said, hurrying away.

"She needs someone with powerful magic and a pure heart to be by her side to win this battle." Sveta's words swirled around in Mir's head as he returned to the city. This wasn't part of his plan. All he had ever wanted was to destroy the divine datura and not fight a war he felt had nothing to do with him.

HE HAD to lie to Boris again, saying that he had been following the herbalist's scent for a while before he lost it. Then Mir hurriedly got ready, knowing it was too late. He had promised to pick up Vesna to take her to work. Even if she had been waiting for him, she was probably already gone. He stepped on the gas, forgetting about the rafflesia for now, as all his thoughts returned to Vesna.

When he got to Alex's club, Vesna was just stepping onto the stage, looking divine in a weightless translucent dress. *She is made of petals, sweet fragrance, and alluring pollen,* he thought, licking his lips.

He wanted her to be his, wanted this flower to bloom just for him. He devoured her with his eyes throughout the song. And his mind flowered with the anticipation of being left alone with her. Mir knew he was already completely under her spell. His heart blossomed every time Vesna was near.

When the song was almost over, Mir did the most romantic thing he had ever done… He stood up and clapped his hands, whistling. Alex looked at Mir like he had gone crazy, rolling his eyes. But Mir didn't care. A barely noticeable smile touched Vesna's face, and that was enough for him.

"What was that?" Alex raised an eyebrow.

"Leave me alone, Alex," Mir said without even looking at him.

"I think you're knocking on closed doors."

Mir smirked. "You might be surprised," he said, thinking how perfectly Vesna was blooming for him yesterday.

"I know what I'm talking about. Some guy asked me if she was open to…" Alex trailed off. "A date. I asked Vesna before the show. Let me tell you, she wasn't in the mood, talking about how poisonous you are. Then she told me she would love to meet the guy after her performance."

Mir's eyes filled with jealousy. "She would *love* to?!" he seethed. "Tell me that guy is at least ugly."

"No." Alex shrugged. "He's quite handsome, and rich. He comes to the club almost every night."

"I'll show him a date!" Mir stood up angrily. "Where is he?"

"For flower's sake!" Alex grabbed his hand, stopping him. "Don't you think it's time to change tactics? Maybe you should make *her* a little jealous."

"You think so?" Mir frowned.

"So far, being all over her hasn't worked," Alex said pointedly.

"I don't want anyone else," Mir confessed.

"Well, Vesna doesn't know that. It's worth a try," Alex concluded.

"You sure?" Mir said, doubting whether it was a good move.

"Believe me, a real rose knows all about love."

Mir rolled his eyes, but leaned back on the couch. "You're an exception." He didn't know why Vesna would want to date another man after what had happened between them yesterday. His gaze darted back to her. She was walking gracefully toward the bar, dazzling everyone around her. "No, your plan is stupid," Mir decided.

He didn't want to be away from this wicked flower. He was about to approach her when a tall man with black hair walked up to Vesna and whispered something in her ear, kissing her hand gently. She smiled wildly at her date, then turned around for a split second, meeting Mir's gaze.

Mir's jaw tightened. *Don't play with poison.* His eyes, filled with fury, darted toward her. *I'll remind you that your eyes should be on me alone,* he thought, determined to teach her a lesson.

"Okay, let's try," Mir said to Alex, not taking his eyes off Vesna and her new man.

"So, should I bring the girls?" Alex asked, clearly believing in his plan.

"Fine," Mir muttered through clenched teeth, when the man whispered something in Vesna's ear again, and she laughed loudly, throwing her head back.

Alex returned, accompanied by two girls.

"Mir, do you remember Julia and Olga? You met before the…" Alex sang, introducing the girls, but Mir didn't care.

"She's smiling at him!" Mir fired, interrupting Alex and completely ignoring their new company. "She rarely smiles at me!"

Julia and Olga stared at Mir, and Alex laughed nervously. "Don't pay any attention to him."

"I can smile at you," Olga sang, sitting next to Mir, so close that her hip touched his. But Mir had no desire to talk to her, let alone look at her smile. He only wanted one flower.

Mir turned to Alex instead. "Should I go over there?"

"Don't even think about it!" Alex said. "Why don't you ask Olga to dance?" He winked at Mir.

"With pleasure," Olga sang, quickly standing up and heading to the center of the dance floor.

Fuck me, Mir cursed, but followed her.

He didn't even have to do anything, because Olga clearly saw this as an opportunity to seduce him. She took the initiative, and with every movement, she tried to touch him with her whole body, looking into his eyes and meaningfully biting her lip.

This is too much. He was about to leave when he saw

an angry spark in Vesna's eyes as she gawked at him, ignoring her date. Mir smirked with satisfaction; she seemed irritated, maybe even jealous. So, Mir continued this stupid charade. Yet he regretted everything…

When the song ended, Vesna no longer looked at Mir. She went back to talking to her date, laughing and looking happier than ever. Mir pressed his lips into a thin line in disappointment and glanced at Alex, who was giving him a thumbs-up.

I'm an idiot. Mir gave up. Vesna was so close, and Mir couldn't bring himself to just leave. Plus, the guy she was with needed to be taught a lesson. "Sorry, Olga, I'm not interested." Mir sent her away.

"The night is still young, poisonous one," Olga whispered seductively.

Whatever. Mir frowned.

When Mir approached the bar, Vesna acted as if he were invisible and continued to talk to her date.

Mir inhaled sharply. "Why the hell are you touching something that doesn't belong to you?" he asked, staring at the man.

"Leave him alone," Vesna fired.

Mir glanced at her. "Don't even think about defending him. I'll talk to you later." He turned his attention back to her date. "So?" He leaned toward the man.

"And who are you?" the man demanded.

"She's mine. No one speaks to her, no one looks at her, no one smiles at her, and certainly no one touches her," Mir declared.

The man looked him up and down, stopping his gaze at Mir's eyes, which were filled with poison. "But, Alex…" he whispered in horror, his face pale.

"*Mine*, got it?" Mir looked at him meaningfully. "Why are you still here?"

"I'm not." The guy got up from his chair and quickly disappeared.

Mir sat on the empty chair next to Vesna. "Hello, wicked flower," he sang, but Vesna didn't even glance at him.

"Can I get some water?" She looked at Anna instead.

Mir just sat there awkwardly, unsure of how to get Vesna's attention. "Smart choice, alcohol is bad news," he said—the first thing that came to his mind.

"Anna, make that a whiskey, double," Vesna said.

Wicked flower, Mir thought and licked his lips. This stubborn flower had burned his heart. "Have you ever even had whiskey?" He raised an eyebrow, looking at Vesna.

"No," she said simply, raising her glass. "Cheers."

So, you want to play? he thought with a smile, raising his glass in response. "How was your date? He seems to give in easily."

"It was good, he's very…" She paused, finishing her drink in a matter of seconds, and then gestured for Anna to pour her another, finishing it as well. "You know, he's very charming, very…" She paused again, looking for words. "Very charming, and…"

"Charming?" Anna giggled, watching her friend getting drunk at an incredible speed.

"Exactly, very charming." Vesna nodded her head.

Mir breathed wickedly; jealousy wasn't easy to control.

"Another double round, please," Vesna said, raising an empty glass.

Mir smirked. She was cute when she was drunk. It was odd; he usually hated girls when they were drunk—couldn't stand them, even. But the sight of Vesna's face flushed from alcohol made him smile. He wanted to pick her up and leave, wanted to be alone with her somewhere where she would blush only because of him.

"Maybe that's enough for the first time?" Anna suggested hesitantly.

"Don't be a bore." Vesna grabbed the glass, and throwing her head back, she drank it down.

"Are you celebrating something?" Mir asked tenderly.

"No." Vesna finally turned to face him, diving into his eyes. And Mir knew all too well that he couldn't stay away. He had already decided that tonight he would take her home, making sure that no one would disturb her.

"Is that your girlfriend?" Vesna asked and turned to look at Olga. She was staring at them, not even trying to hide her anger. "I saw you together the first night I performed here."

"Don't be ridiculous. I have my eyes on someone else," Mir whispered, moving a little closer.

"I want to dance!" Vesna suddenly declared.

Mir watched her with a faint smile. She tried to stand up, but the room must have been spinning, because she grabbed his shoulder, looking for support.

"I think it's time to take you home," Mir said tenderly, standing up too.

Vesna pointed her finger at Olga. "Go back to your date! Anna can take me home," she insisted.

"Well, I can't close the bar for at least two more hours," Anna said, looking from Vesna to Mir.

"Then I'll wait," Vesna slurred, sitting down again. "One more round!"

"Wicked flower," Mir sang.

"Mir," she sang his name back, and Mir couldn't help but smile at how nice his name sounded on her perfect lips.

"Time to go," he murmured.

"He's right, no need to wait for me," Anna quickly agreed with Mir.

"I'm not going with him anywhere." Vesna pouted her lips. "He already has a date. Goodbye, Mir."

Not a chance, Mir thought, and without warning, he scooped her up. "Bye, Anna." He nodded to her and walked toward the exit.

Vesna was shouting something over the loud music, and everyone stared at them, including Alex, who was giving Mir a thumbs-up again.

Mir walked slowly on purpose, enjoying this moment. *She's mine, and everyone should know better and stay away from my wicked flower,* he thought, smirking.

When they stepped outside, the piercing wind was blowing with all its might, and Vesna wrapped her arms around Mir's neck, trying to hide from the cold. He could have sworn he heard her slowly and deeply inhaling his scent. His lousy mood immediately transferred to a beautiful paradise.

She mumbled some song, and Mir smiled. *Like an idiot,* he scolded himself.

"Thanks," Vesna muttered when they'd reached the building. "Good night."

Mir didn't want to let her go just yet. "I'm not sure you can walk up the stairs."

She rolled her eyes. "I live on the first floor."

Mir smirked. "I'm not going anywhere until I know you're safe at home."

"Fine," she muttered. "But I will walk myself."

Mir walked behind her, watching her figure in her translucent dress, trying to contain his desire. He would have her, but not tonight. Not like this.

Vesna opened the door with the key on the third try, and then she turned to him with a smile. "You, see? Everything is fine. Plus, Anna showed me some moves," she said proudly.

"Did she?" Mir raised an eyebrow.

Vesna looked at him, her eyes trailing slowly to his lips. "Well, since I live in a big city now, I need to know how to stand up for myself."

"Show me what she taught you," he whispered, approaching.

Her eyes widened in surprise when Mir placed his hand on her waist. She tried to pull away, but Mir was already on fire. He grabbed her wrists, pinning her tightly to the door and trapping her hands with his on the top of her head. His lips moved slowly, almost touching hers. He said nothing, burning inside. She was so tiny under the weight of his body, and he could have sworn he heard her lips whispering a spell.

"Anna will be disappointed. I'm a terrible student," she whispered, and didn't even try to break away, touching his lips with hers as she spoke.

Mir wanted to kiss her like a hungry beast, like a parasite that needed those sacred lips to fulfill him. But Vesna was drunk, and it wasn't how he wanted to have her. He wanted her to bloom, to feel every cell of her perfect body as he entered her, killing her with every thrust.

"Good night, wicked flower," he muttered, and quickly left before he might change his mind.

She's a lustful torture, he thought, inhaling the air and trying to wake up from the love spell he knew was unbreakable. Mir returned to Fading Blossoms. He needed Alex's help to find a place where Sveta could hide, ideally near the club.

Chapter Fourteen

VESNA.

OH, GODS, WAS THE FIRST THING THAT CAME TO VESNA'S mind when she opened her eyes. The room was spinning, and her head was pounding.

"Rise and bloom!" Anna sang, apparently already sitting next to her on the bed, holding a glass of water.

"Shh, not so loud," Vesna begged, frowning. "I'm going to die," she muttered, grabbing the water and downing it in one gulp.

"Don't be so dramatic. We've all been there." Anna laughed.

Vesna closed her eyes helplessly. "I'm dying."

She collapsed back on the bed, wishing this awful feeling would go away. It had been stupid to drink so much last night. But Mir hadn't kept his promise to pick her up before work, and she'd waited for him, like a fool. She'd decided he didn't care about her, and that thought was tearing her heart apart.

When Alex had started talking about some guy who wanted to get to know her, she'd decided to teach Mir a lesson, hoping that he would become jealous… It was childish, and it was completely unlike her. Still, she went for it. She was a different person when it came to Mir. She could barely recognize her old calculating self. And then the sight of Mir dancing with another girl had driven her crazy.

Vesna remembered how she had almost kissed him yesterday and instantly blushed.

"Fuck…" She squeezed her eyes shut in embarrassment. "Why did you let me leave with Mir last night?!"

"Well, I knew you'd be safe with him," Anna sang, clearly enjoying this situation.

"And by 'safe,' you imagined him pushing me up against the door and almost kissing me?" She closed her eyes again, remembering that moment, and remembering the heat that had melted in her veins, like pollen under the scorching sun.

"'Almost' doesn't count." Anna grinned.

"I'll never drink again," Vesna said, touching her head. "I need more water, please."

Anna giggled, pouring her friend more water. "Mir likes you. He's different from Alex." She paused. "Alex told me once that he fears women are only attracted to his magic. The divine rose gave him the power of love spells. He enchants some girls, even without him ever using any spells. That's why he prefers to stay away from serious relationships—he's paranoid that women love not him, but his magic."

Even though Vesna was barely functioning, she could still detect a sad note in Anna's voice. "He doesn't know that you're immune because you have magic too," she dared to say.

"Maybe one day," Anna muttered. "Yesterday, he brought that Julia again… Stupid rose." She snorted. "Do we have a plan for the ball?" she asked, suddenly changing the topic.

"Partially." Vesna exhaled deeply, collapsing back onto the bed again. "We still need to find out which floor Boris's library is on."

"It's not that difficult. We can just casually ask Mir," Anna thought out loud. "Alex told me he would take care of dresses for us."

"I hope he doesn't dress us up like two lonely roses," Vesna said playfully.

"The odds are high." Anna laughed, lying down next to her. "When all this is over, I want to travel, maybe even live somewhere where it's always warm, under the blazing sun, like a real marigold flower," she said, clearly daydreaming.

"Why haven't you left before now?" Vesna asked in a whisper.

"I lost a lot of magic trying to keep my parents alive," Anna muttered. "They escaped from the rafflesia, with only a few drops of magic left. For years, I tried to keep them alive. Then, when they were gone, I was too weak and tired to ever dream again."

"I admire you, Anna," Vesna said gently, rolling over and facing her friend.

"You do?" Anna's face lit up. "Thanks to you, I can dream again."

"Thank you for not judging me for choosing revenge," Vesna whispered.

"That's what friends are for," Anna said, and started tickling her. "I remember when you were a child, you were very ticklish."

Vesna laughed, trying to get away from Anna. "Stop it!" she begged.

Anna was an actual sun that shone even in this fading reality, and Vesna was grateful. She couldn't imagine going through all of this without her.

"I'm hungry. Let's have breakfast at Alex's!" Anna suddenly stood up.

"I'm pretty sure he's still asleep," Vesna said, and then suddenly narrowed her eyes. "On second thought, let's go! He never invites us!"

When Alex opened his door a few minutes later, he looked at Anna and Vesna with half-closed eyes, yawning. "Have you and Mir agreed to take turns annoying me?"

"How inhospitable you are," Anna scolded him, stepping inside.

"Come in, I guess," Alex muttered, closing the door behind his uninvited guests.

"Are you alone?" Vesna asked, glancing at Anna. "I thought you were with that girl. What's her name?" She looked up, pretending she was trying to remember. "Julia, I think."

"No, Julia is out of the picture," Alex said indifferently. "It turns out she's obsessed with flowers and their magic. She keeps inviting me to some weird places, apparently very special, according to the books she's read." He sighed. "It's always about my magic and never about me."

"At this rate, you'll be alone forever," Anna said, already setting the table for breakfast.

"It's my curse. I can't know if a woman likes me naturally, or if it's just because of my magic." Alex's shoulders slumped, and his gaze was fixed on empty space.

"Then you need a girl who's a flower herself," Vesna suggested.

Alex glanced at her and then at Anna, lingering on her, clearly thinking about something. "Did you bring bacon?" he asked suddenly.

When they got back to the apartment, there was a small envelope lying near the door. Anna quickly opened it, scanning the text.

"I have bad news," she said, her voice strangely serious.

Vesna froze. "What is it?"

Anna looked at her, her gaze full of worry. "Boris found Sveta."

"What?!" Vesna gasped, pale as death.

"He only found her house, but she escaped," Anna quickly said. "She sent us a note with her new address."

"Let's go immediately!"

Vesna automatically changed into a simple cotton dress and a large cardigan, thinking about what would happen to Sveta and all of them if Boris succeeded in finding her. She couldn't help but wonder if it was Mir who had found Sveta's place. The thought made the pollen in her magical veins stop.

Sveta was hiding just a few streets down from the club.

"Thank you, Divine Blooms, you're safe!" Anna ran to her, hugging Sveta tightly.

Vesna glanced at the herbalist. She seemed tired, pale, and even older than before.

"You look tired. Did you rest?" Vesna asked timidly.

"Don't worry about me," Sveta said. "Come in."

They followed the herbalist, and Vesna froze, her chest tight with rage. All the herbs were gone, and Sveta had to live in this tiny apartment, leaving her actual home filled with bittersweet scent behind.

Sveta sat on a chair, constantly glancing at the door.

"Since they discovered my house, I've lost almost all the herbs. And without them, I'm useless."

"We'll think of something," Anna assured her.

"I still have some herbs hidden in another place," Sveta said almost indifferently. "I need to leave, but before I do, I will prepare as much potion as I can for you two."

"You can't leave now, it's too dangerous!" Vesna protested.

Sveta shook her head. "It's time for us to part ways."

"Are you going away for long?" Vesna asked, unable to shake the feeling that Sveta was going to leave forever, as if she were saying her goodbyes.

"Long enough." Sveta just smiled, clearly not wanting to talk about it. "I'm afraid that when you start the sacred bloom, my potion won't work. You'll need a more radical method."

Before Vesna could ask about this radical method, someone opened the door.

Vesna heard Mir's voice as he and Alex entered. "Sveta has lost all her herbs. She can't make a potion strong enough for Vesna," Mir said, falling silent when his gaze froze on Vesna.

He knows! Vesna thought in pure panic, and she deliberately moved toward Sveta, shielding her with her body. Vesna didn't care about anything anymore. She had avoided reality for too long.

"You're not taking her or me anywhere," Vesna said in an iron voice. Mir didn't answer, simply staring at her. "I don't know what you need from Boris, but you'll never have us," she warned him, raising her head high.

Mir was still silent, looking at her. He swallowed hard, his lips parting slightly, then pressing shut again.

Mir was much better at fighting than she was. But

she still quickly whispered a spell, and the creamy pink pollen left her body, spreading a sweet aroma throughout the room. "You will have to fight me first," she said, her voice trembling.

"You quickly marked me as an enemy," Mir muttered, his voice full of pain and disappointment. "Come on, go ahead!"

"Are you both out of your mind?!" Alex screamed, stepping between them.

"Alex, don't," Mir said, walking past him and stopping right in front of Vesna, almost touching her pollen. "Let's see what she has in store for me." He met her gaze. "Come on, what are you waiting for?" His face twisted into a pained smile.

"Mir, tell her!" Alex begged.

"Shut up, Alex. Let's see what the sacred one can do. Besides, no one will regret it if I lose my magic," Mir insisted.

He knew about me all this time! Vesna thought in a panic. She raised her pollen even higher, her hands trembling as her eyes welled with tears, blurring her vision.

"Vesna, don't!" Alex pleaded. "Mir helped Sveta escape!"

"What?!" Vesna froze. She wasn't sure who to trust anymore, afraid that maybe this was some kind of twisted game that Mir and Alex were playing.

"It's true, he did," Sveta whispered.

Vesna looked at her, completely lost, before looking back at Mir. She dove into his eyes and saw pain—pain like she'd never seen in him before. He was hurting, just standing there, not intending to fight.

A lump came into her throat, and she could barely hold back the tears. She moved toward him, surprising everyone, and emerged from her pollen, hugging Mir tightly.

"I'm sorry," she whispered, clinging to him even tighter.

"My wicked flower," Mir growled, hugging her back and lifting her off the floor.

Vesna couldn't think about anything right now. She felt relieved for the first time in a long time. She didn't have to lie to him anymore, and it felt like a blessing.

"How long have you known?" she whispered, wishing to stay in his arms forever, wanting to root herself in him.

"We knew almost from the start," Alex answered for Mir, walking right up to Sveta and bowing his head.

"And you are?" Sveta asked, looking him up and down.

"I'm Alex, a big fan of your work," Alex said admiringly.

"Thanks, I guess," Sveta mumbled. "But be careful who you admire. People are often not who they seem."

"Put me down," Vesna whispered to Mir, smiling.

"Okay, but when we're done here, you're coming with me," he sang into her ear.

"Can someone explain to me what the hell is going on here?" Anna, silent until now, stared at Mir and Alex.

"Marigold, try to keep up," Alex said. "We knew about you two almost from the beginning. We had no choice but to help you along the way."

"And how exactly did *you* help?" Anna raised an eyebrow.

"Well, if you must know, I was making sure Mir did nothing stupid," Alex said proudly.

"Oh, yes, you did a backbreaking job." Anna smirked.

"I want to know what happened," Vesna said, looking at Mir.

Mir spoke quickly. "I got Sveta out before Boris arrived. Then I brought her here." He paused, looking at everyone present and then again at Vesna. "I want to tell you everything, but in private."

Vesna tensed up, noticing that the fog was clouding his eyes. "Let's go." She turned toward the door.

"You might still need to hide your bloom until Ivan Kupala, if something goes wrong at the ball, and you end up staying in town longer than you planned," Sveta said quickly, before Vesna even moved.

"Ivan Kupala is the twenty-second of June," Mir muttered. "What date is your birthday?"

"Just over a week before," Vesna whispered.

"That's why I brought you all here. I realized Mir really wants to help, and he can," Sveta said. "He can poison Vesna in small doses to hide her bloom. I won't have time to gather the herbs for a potion strong enough to cover the sacred bloom."

"What?!" Alex said in shock.

"Are you crazy?!" Mir fired. "No one is going to poison Vesna!"

Vesna took a deep breath, looking at Mir's pale face. She wasn't afraid of his magic anymore. She knew he wouldn't hurt her. Not on purpose.

"Before the first herbalists, people used poison magic to hide from the rafflesia, almost putting their magic into a coma with the divine datura," Sveta explained.

"They did?" Mir asked, and Vesna saw the surprise in his eyes.

Vesna squeezed his hand, her gaze diving into his eyes. "I trust you."

"When the time comes, poison her, whispering this

spell." Sveta stood up and leaned toward Mir, whispering the spell in his ear. "This will mask her bloom, but only for a few days."

Mir frowned, staring at Sveta. "Are you sure it's safe?" he asked, concern in his voice.

"Yes," Sveta muttered, gazing between Mir and Vesna. "Looking at you, I want to believe that true love exists."

Vesna blushed. She and Mir had never talked about their feelings, and she felt awkward discussing it in front of everyone.

"Well, I think we're done here." She clapped her hands nervously. Mir immediately took her hand and headed toward the door.

They walked down the street to Mir's apartment in Fading Blossoms, and Vesna held her breath. She was afraid to hear what he couldn't say in front of everyone. But she finally wanted to know everything about him, even if the truth was ugly.

Mir's apartment was dark; only a single table lamp dimly illuminated the room. Vesna didn't move, hearing nothing but the thunder of her own heartbeat. As soon as they entered, Mir closed the door behind them.

"I want you to know the whole truth," he said, remaining near the door, as if he was sure that she would run away the moment she heard it.

Vesna nodded slowly, her eyes lifting to meet his.

"I knew you had the sacred magic," he said, his voice low. "And I decided to use you to get into the Veiled Wilds." He paused, swallowing hard and clenching his hand into a fist. "I need to get there to destroy the divine datura once and for all. But what's happened between us wasn't an act. The more time I've spent with you, the more I've cared. And then you put me under your spell completely."

Vesna didn't know how to react. Her lips parted, but she remained silent. She wasn't angry. If anything, Mir seemed purer than she was.

After a heavy silence, he spoke again. "Are you angry?"

"I used you too," she whispered, her gaze dropping to the floor. "To get to Boris." When she finally looked up, Mir's eyes seemed hollow. "Because he killed the sacred one. My mother…"

Shock crossed Mir's face. "The sacred one was your mother…?" he whispered, barely audible.

"Even now, I'm only going after the book that Boris will use to find the fern flower. I need power strong enough to kill him. I'm not a pure sacred one. Not even close." She sighed with sorrow. "You can come with me. Once I pick the fern flower, the Veiled Wilds will appear." She paused. "You can do whatever you want there."

She let out a deep breath. It felt good to finally have no secrets between them.

Mir stepped closer, his eyes locking with hers. "You're pure to me."

She reached for him, wrapping her arms around him, pulling him closer. He pressed her gently against the door. His breath brushed her ear as he whispered, "Last chance to escape … because I'll never let you go."

A shiver of desire slid down Vesna's spine. "I want to bloom for you," she murmured.

Mir's eyes danced with thunder, and he looked like he wanted to devour her. He pulled her closer, and his embrace burned sweetly and sharply. She wrapped herself around him without hesitation, reaching for this lustful storm.

Her lips touched his, and the sensation shattered the last seeds of her sanity. Magic thundered beneath her skin. She tangled her hands in his hair, soft moans escaping her lips as she breathed in his almond scent. They kissed for what seemed like an eternity, slow and savoring, like a flower sprouting from the ground with the whisper of spring. His fingers tightened around her, sending a shiver of goose bumps down her spine.

"Teach me how to bloom," Vesna begged breathlessly, still kissing him.

Mir growled low in his throat as he carried her to the couch. He swiftly lifted her dress and lowered her onto the cushions, pausing for just a moment to devour her with his gaze. His eyes traced every inch of her body with adoration. Then, slowly, his fingers touched her face, trailing down to her chest, leaving behind invisible marks of sweet, poisonous imprints blooming on her skin. She bit her lip, soft moans escaping her as his touch deepened.

"Fuck, you drive me crazy," he whispered huskily, kissing her neck for a while. Then his mouth moved lower, trickling sensual kisses across her body and causing a hurricane in her veins.

Her body writhed under his mouth, until she felt his hot breath above her core. His tongue dipped into her, and she arched her back and cried out at the pleasure filling her. Her body screamed with a need she didn't understand, and she whimpered. Mir looked up at her, a delicious glint in his eyes.

"I want you," she whispered.

Mir growled, replacing his mouth with his fingers.

He moved up, quickly stripping off his clothes.

Vesna devoured him with her eyes. His muscles were carved to near perfection. Her gaze slowly slid down to his aroused cock, and she swallowed hard. Her hand moved unconsciously down her body, to where she ached for him. His eyes flashed as he watched her touch herself.

When their bare bodies met, she felt his smooth skin against hers, and her lips parted in satisfaction.

"This might hurt a little," he murmured, sucking gently on her earlobe.

Vesna didn't care. She was already on the edge, breathless and burning with the need for him. She laced her arms around his neck, pulling him closer.

"Let me taste your poison."

Mir growled again, darker this time, and demandingly spread her thighs. His cock pressed against her core, and she froze in silent anticipation.

Bracing himself on his hands, he met her gaze and slowly entered her, the feeling a strange mix of pleasure and satisfaction.

"Aah," Vesna cried out.

He moved slowly, letting her adjust to the feel of him. When her cries softened into moans and her body began to move instinctively with his, Mir growled and deepened his thrusts.

Soon he was moving without restraint, taking complete possession of her. They met each other thrust for thrust, again and again… A cry escaped her lips every time he entered her, the sensation overwhelming. Beads of sweat ran down their bodies like dew on flower petals at dawn.

"You're perfect," he groaned, his voice strained, clearly on the edge.

She was breathing into his ear, her hands wrapped

around his powerful back, clinging to him as tightly as she could. It seemed he felt her need for more, and he quickened his thrusts with a low growl. Vesna cried out loudly as pressure built deep in her core.

With the next thrust, Vesna felt the bloom—millions of flowers erupted inside her, flooding her with a blissful storm of petals. Her body shook, and her cry rang out so loud, it felt like even wilted flowers would awaken to blossom at the sound of her euphoria. Mir growled with his own release. The air thickened with the scent of their passion—a lush mix of sweet magnolia and earthy datura.

<h1 style="text-align:center">Chapter Fifteen</h1>

MIR.

MY WICKED FLOWER, YOU GROW IN MY HEART NOW, MIR thought, studying Vesna's soft face in the rays of the morning sun. He had finally taken the risk of letting someone into his life, and he didn't regret his decision for a second. He had never been so obsessed with anyone in his entire life. She burned and blossomed under his touch eternally, and it was an unearthly sensation.

He didn't judge Vesna for choosing revenge on Boris. She accepted his decision to destroy the divine datura without any judgment, and he was going to do the same for her.

Vesna opened her eyes and smiled softly at him. "Good morning."

"Good morning," Mir sang, getting closer and kissing her soft lips.

He had dreamed of Vesna so many times, and now that it had become a reality, he didn't want to spend a second away from her. She gently wrapped her arms around him, pressing herself against his body, awakening the hunger in him in a matter of seconds. His hand slid down her back, gently stroking her hips. Vesna moaned, ready to give him all the tenderness and all the passion again.

"I will never let you go," Mir growled—but a knock on the door made him freeze. No one knew about this place.

"Wait here, and don't come out," he said, quickly standing up and getting dressed.

"Okay." Vesna stood up too, putting on her dress.

Even before Mir opened the door, he knew it was bad news. The smell of rotting flesh permeated the apartment, taking with it the blissful atmosphere that had just reigned in his heart.

It was Boris. He entered the apartment without waiting for an invitation, sniffing and squinting.

"How did you find me?" Mir asked boldly. He couldn't hide his anger right now.

"You've been disappearing a lot lately," Boris said without meeting Mir's gaze, studying the place instead. "I'm beginning to think you're plotting something behind my back."

Before Mir could decide how to get rid of Boris, he heard light footsteps, and his heart sank with fear. He spun around, staring at Vesna.

Has she gone mad?! he screamed internally, staring at her. She didn't even look at Mir, her eyes boring into Boris. Her downcast face showed silent shock as she held her breath. She was clearly studying her enemy, her eyes sharp and unblinking. Boris stared at her as well. Two sworn enemies, determined by the Divine Blooms themselves, had finally met.

Mir wasn't sure what Vesna felt right now, but she took a deep breath, and her face blossomed into a smile.

"Good morning," she said to Boris, and Mir noticed she was breathing through her mouth.

Boris laughed theatrically. "Now I understand where you disappear to all day long."

"I'm afraid it's my fault," Vesna said playfully.

Boris moved closer, clearly studying her, and Mir clenched his fists. He didn't want this parasite anywhere near his wicked flower. He remained alert. If necessary, he would use every drop of poison that flowed through his veins.

"No need for apologies," Boris sang charmingly. "Even I was in love once."

Mir saw how Vesna's eyes widened in surprise. "I admit, I've read a lot about the magic of flowers, and I never thought that the rafflesia gave meaning to such a feeling as love."

Boris laughed again, but this time a little sadly. "You're right. It was tragic for her, of course."

"Would you like some coffee?" Vesna offered, and Mir was ready to sink into the floor.

Why the hell is she playing with fire? He felt his breath catch in his chest. Yet he realized Vesna was probably trying to get to know her enemy. It made sense. But Mir didn't like it. The game she was playing was too dangerous. Mir knew Boris too well; he was a parasite who would stop at nothing to get what he wanted.

"What a charming girlfriend you have," Boris said and sat down on the sofa, watching Vesna go to the kitchen. "So, this is the singer you were talking about?" He turned to Mir.

This parasite forgets nothing, Mir thought, sitting in the chair in front of his boss. "Yes, Vesna works at Fading Blossoms."

Boris's eyes widened. "Vesna?" He asked, clearly surprised. "Your name is Vesna?" He looked at her.

She tensed, though her response stayed calm. "Yep."

"Interesting." Boris touched his beard. "Vesna means 'spring' in the old language. Did you know that?"

Even if Vesna knew, she didn't show it. "No," she said simply, walking over to the coffee table and sitting down next to Mir. He immediately grabbed her hand, hoping that his touch would soothe her.

"Many have forgotten the old language," Boris said, glancing at their intertwined hands. "You two remind me of a time I've almost forgotten."

"What time?" Vesna asked, the tone of her voice higher than usual.

"I can tell you, but only if you agree to do me a small favor in return," Boris said, narrowing his eyes. Mir noticed how they flashed.

"Vesna is a simple human. I doubt she can do anything for you."

"So protective," Boris murmured, turning his gaze back to Vesna. "I'm throwing a ball, and it would be wonderful if you could come. After all, maybe it's not a coincidence that I met a girl whose name means spring itself right before this."

"Why would you want me there?" Vesna asked quietly.

"Just so you can bless us with your youth—as a talisman, so to speak." Boris smiled, touching his beard again.

Mir had noticed before that Boris was always touching his beard when he was planning something. This conversation was becoming too dangerous. The more time Boris spent with Vesna, the more likely he was to sense her magic. Mir was afraid that he was already suspicious.

"Shouldn't we go? The herbalist is still missing," Mir said, breaking the silence.

"Yes," Boris said, getting up. "Come to the ball, Vesna, and I promise to tell you a story of tragic love."

"I will." Vesna smiled charmingly.

"Wonderful!" Boris clapped his hands. "Mir, be in the building in an hour. We'll start a search party. I know she's somewhere nearby." He sniffed the air again.

After Boris left, Vesna and Mir sat in silence, still holding hands. "Why didn't you stay in the room?" he asked, with no judgment.

"I wanted to see him…" Vesna muttered. "I wanted to see the face of the man I'm going to kill."

An icy shiver ran down Mir's spine. It wasn't just her words; it was the way she said it. She sounded determined, even absolute. And Mir was afraid she would sacrifice everything to get to Boris. Mir stared at her, and her face resembled a flower blooming from the thirst for revenge.

"He's surprisingly charming," she thought out loud.

"Vesna, he didn't become so powerful out of thin air. He's smart and calculating. Don't underestimate him," Mir begged.

"Believe me, I know," Vesna sighed heavily. "It seems he values you."

"I suppose." Mir smirked. "My magic is only useful to parasites."

"That's not true," Vesna said. "I'm slowly beginning to understand that it has a place in this world."

Mir made a stern face, staring at off into the distance. "I'm not." He fell silent, and his face twisted in pain.

After Mir had taken Vesna home, he returned to Sveta. The thought that she was hiding something wouldn't leave him. It seemed that she had a personal score to settle with Boris. In any case, he had promised her that he would bring her to Boris before the ball. Mir wasn't sure how she would be able to help Vesna if she needed it, but deep down, he thought they might need all the help they could get. Boris's library was heavily guarded, and he couldn't get in without Vesna using her magic.

"I hope you didn't poison Vesna," Sveta muttered, sitting in her chair and drinking coffee.

"She's safe with me," Mir said almost defensively. "She met Boris today."

Sveta jumped up from her chair and screamed hysterically, *"What?!"*

"Don't panic, he didn't suspect anything," Mir assured her, afraid that Sveta would have a heart attack. After all, she was old—older than anyone he had ever met. "He invited Vesna to the ball. Something about her name."

"It means 'spring,'" Sveta said, deep in thought as she calmed down. "The time has come. Take me to Boris. I've made as much potion as I could for Anna and Vesna."

"If you go to him, he will never let you go," Mir warned her.

"I have nowhere to go but to the eternal garden." She signed sadly.

THEY TOOK the elevator up to Boris's floor, and Mir couldn't hide his anxiety. His heart was pounding, and he was sweating. He was afraid that Sveta would do something stupid, somehow exposing Vesna or him.

Sveta was looking at the changing numbers on the elevator display, her gaze empty.

"Don't tell him anything about Vesna. You're just an herbalist; you don't know her."

She raised her green eyes to him. "I won't. I hate Boris as much as you do." She paused. "Even more."

Boris was lying on the couch and feeding on the magic of some girls when they came in. His gaze immediately darted to Sveta, and he jumped up, calling his roots away.

"You?" His voice broke as he stared at her. "Finally!"

She held her head high, glancing briefly at the girls lying on the couch. "Still hungry?" She grinned, but her voice shook, as if she were fighting back tears.

Mir just stood there silently, secretly studying Boris.

Boris's eyes danced as he quickly ran to Sveta, inhaling her scent. "Still using the potion?" Then his gaze moved to Mir. "Everyone out!" he shouted, and the girls hurried away.

Mir followed them. He heard Boris's door being locked. It was obvious that he didn't want anyone to know what business he really had with the herbalist.

Chapter Sixteen

VESNA.

VESNA SAT IN HER ROOM FOR MOST OF THE DAY, thinking about Boris. The way he seemed so normal and civilized in real life surprised her. *Parasites must adapt to get what they want,* she reminded herself.

Anna poked her head in the door, smiling widely. "How was your night?"

Vesna blushed, feeling how Mir's beautifully poisonous touch still burned sensually on her skin. "Good."

"Just good?" Anna asked with a raised eyebrow, entering the room.

"Fine—it was perfect," Vesna admitted, smiling to herself.

"Yes!" Anna jumped with excitement and smiled widely.

"I met Boris," Vesna muttered.

"What?!" Anna stared at her, her mouth dropping open. "How? Why?"

"Don't worry, he suspected nothing."

"What's he like?" Anna quickly sat down next to Vesna, looking at her expectantly.

"Dangerous," Vesna said after a moment. "And smart. He was in a good mood."

"Don't worry about him now," Anna said, squeezing Vesna's hand. "First we need to steal the book, and then head to the location of the Veiled Wilds."

"When this is over, we can travel together somewhere nice," Vesna dared to dream.

Anna's eyes sparked with enthusiasm. "We need to go somewhere where there's plenty of sun!" she said, clearly dreaming out loud, and Vesna smiled, looking at her friend's face illuminated with inner hope. Anna deserved happiness; they all did.

Vesna's heart was filled with pain and fear as the day of the ball finally approached. But somehow, everything was becoming clearer. The winter of her life was finally ending, bringing with it spring and the promise of a new beginning. *Or the end,* she thought.

She was in her room, trying to button up the dress Alex had insisted on ordering especially for the ball. He kept saying his sense of style was impeccable. The invitation had said that the dress code had to be spring-themed. Alex had wanted to find something special, and now, as Vesna tried it on, she realized that her dress was too much. It was puffy, like a cake, embroidered with many flowers. First off, it wasn't her style. And second, she needed to get into Boris's library, and something so bright and puffy would just attract too much attention.

"Anna!" Vesna shouted, making sure her friend could hear her in the other room.

"What is it?" Anna came in wearing a dress as green as the earth itself, with some birds embroidered on it.

"Oh my, we look ridiculous!" Vesna laughed hysterically.

"Wait!" Anna quickly ran to her room. She came back with a hat; a fake bird was attached to it. "It comes with a hat," she said, putting it on, her words slurred with laughter. "A masterpiece!"

"I can't…!" Vesna put her hand on her stomach, which was hurting from laughing so much.

"We're going to be unforgettable," Anna said sarcastically.

"Are you kidding? I can't wear this!"

"Yeah, Alex went too far this time," Anna agreed.

"I'll wear one of the dresses I have for the club," Vesna decided. "Anything is better than this flower explosion."

A knock on the door interrupted their conversation.

"It must be Alex. He'll be heartbroken," Anna said playfully and left the room.

Vesna was taking off her dress when Anna returned with two boxes in her hands.

"Did Alex bring new dresses?" Vesna asked, staring at the boxes with dread. What if these were even worse than the first ones he'd chosen?

"No. This is from Mir. He sent it with some boy," Anna reported with a smile. "One for you, and one for me."

Vesna's eyes brightened. "Seriously?"

Mir poisoned her heart with lust and desire, but she didn't regret it, because it was the sweetest poison out there. He was probably the most real thing that had ever happened to her.

"He attends the ball every year. I'm sure he knows what's best," Anna said excitedly, opening the box with her name on it. "Wow!" She jumped, holding up a gown made of a glittering material that looked like liquid gold.

"Beautiful," Vesna murmured. Mir thought of everything. And Vesna was grateful that he was next to her, that he was hers.

"Let's open yours!" Anna said, already opening the second box. She took out a white dress studded with diamonds. A waxy polish, reminiscent of magnolia petals, coated the fabric.

VESNA WAS silent the entire way to the ball. Alex had offered to give them a ride, and he kept talking, but Vesna wasn't listening. She was too nervous to follow the conversation.

They stepped out of the car, and the air, filled with the promise of coming change, played with her loose hair. Vesna shivered; her thin dress left her bare shoulders exposed. Although it was nothing compared to the chill that crept into her heart with every step as she approached the brown building that reached the sky.

"Boris lives on the top floor. The library is on the same floor. His security is top-notch," Alex reported.

"And where is the ball?" Vesna asked, trying to calculate how difficult it would be to get into his library.

"One floor down," Alex said. "See the room with the light on the first floor?" He pointed to the window. "That's Mir's apartment. He still keeps it, just in case."

Vesna sighed heavily. Mir didn't belong in this place with these parasites. He was nothing like them.

"Who is invited tonight?" Anna asked seriously.

"Rafflesia, politicians, people like me with magic,

some rich humans." Alex fell silent as they stopped next to the security guards.

"Invitations," the guard requested, studying the three of them. He smelled of rotten flesh, but his scent was barely noticeable. No wonder Boris desperately needed more magic to feed them all.

Parasites, Vesna thought, gritting her teeth. She still remembered the day Nina had taken her away. She remembered her mother's last gentle kiss on the cheek and her warning to stay away from the parasites. *So much for staying away,* Vesna thought, studying the guard. She felt Anna squeeze her hand, as if to remind her that she wasn't alone.

"Thank you. Take the elevator to the thirty-second floor," the guard said, stepping out of the way.

Anna leaned toward Vesna as they walked, whispering in her ear. "Remain calm. Boris must not see the hatred in your eyes."

Vesna knew she was right; the stakes were too high to let her emotions get the better of her. She tried to remind herself why she was doing all this. This was bigger than her; it was for her mother … and she knew she would do anything to finally get justice.

"I'll be fine, I promise," Vesna whispered back, trying to put her friend at ease.

But when Vesna stepped out of the elevator, she froze, her head spinning and her heart pounding. Rafflesia paintings were everywhere. They depicted the parasite as a god, with a crown over it. A colossal statue of a rafflesia flower stood right in the middle of the room.

"Breathe," Anna whispered, squeezing her hand.

"It smells awful," Vesna said, wrinkling her nose in disgust.

"Would a drink help?" Alex asked, giving her a smile full of encouragement.

"Great idea," Anna agreed immediately.

"I'll be back." Alex headed for the bar.

"Anna, I want to destroy this ugly place right now," Vesna whispered, but she fell silent the moment she noticed Boris standing next to the statue, clearly studying her. She met his gaze, and holding her head high, took a deep breath. He looked good in his orange suit, strong and young. *Living on my mother's magic,* Vesna thought bitterly, clenching her fists so hard that her nails slightly pierced the skin.

Boris moved toward her, touching his beard. "Vesna," he said, stopping right next to her. At that moment, Vesna wished her magic were lethal. The desire to finish Boris off right next to his stupid statue was all-consuming. "I'm so glad you came."

"I wouldn't have missed this for the world. I'm fascinated by magic," she said, smiling charmingly.

"If the Divine Blooms had the courage to face me and were still among us, I'm sure they would have blessed you with magic."

"You're too kind." Vesna lowered her eyes, glad he couldn't hear her heart pounding.

Boris narrowed his eyes at Anna. "And who is your stunning friend?"

"I'm Anna." She smiled.

"Shining flower," Boris sang, kissing her hand.

A tart voice from behind brought relief to Vesna's heart. "Boris, don't you have more important guests to entertain than my girlfriend and her friend?" Mir asked, walking up to them and grabbing Vesna by the waist, pulling her close to his body.

She was grateful that Mir was here. The Divine

Blooms had intertwined their lives, for better or for worse.

"I'd like to get to know the girl who's caused you so much trouble," Boris said, shifting his gaze to Vesna again. "You know I had to punish Mir after he killed some of my people to protect you. When the rafflesia roots enter the body, it hurts like hell, but he didn't even scream."

Vesna stared at Mir with a frown. He'd made it sound as if what Boris did wasn't a big deal. She realized now that she hadn't understood how much Mir had suffered under Boris's command. Yet he had been doing it for years. *All because of his hatred for his divine flower,* Vesna thought.

"Boris, I don't want to talk about it," Mir brushed him off.

"So modest," Boris said, though Vesna sensed he was displeased that Mir dared to speak to him like that. He turned back to her. "I must admit, if I didn't know you were only human, I would have sworn I could almost feel your magic." Boris narrowed his eyes, studying Vesna's face.

She held her breath as fear crept into her soul.

"You must be starving to imagine such things." Anna laughed unnaturally, obviously trying to take Boris's attention from her friend.

Boris looked Anna up and down for just a second, his eyes flashing furiously. "Enjoy the ball," he said, moving on to the other guests.

All three watched him leave. Mir still held Vesna by the waist, and brushing a lock of hair from her face, he whispered, "You're not alone."

His words meant everything to her. Mir was there for her, no matter what. Vesna didn't answer, because she might cry. Mir touched her heart, even if his touch was poisonous.

Alex finally returned with drinks, stealing glances at Boris. "Sorry to dump you, but I can't stand Boris," he said, taking a sip from his drink. "He always looks at me like he's going to suck all my magic out."

"I'm pretty sure that's exactly what he's thinking." Anna smirked.

"Flowers forbid." Alex shuddered. "I plan to keep a low profile. At the ball last year, he invited me to spend some time alone. Of course, I declined." Obviously, even the thought of being alone with Boris alone made Alex feel sick.

Vesna looked around the room, wondering what to do now. Yes, she had finally made it to the ball, but getting to the library and finding the book seemed impossible. She had no idea how to get there undetected, especially with the ball filled with the rafflesia and everyone who supported them. It felt like everyone was watching her, or maybe she was just being paranoid. She looked at Mir, hoping to find strength in him. Only now did Vesna notice the white flowers embroidered on his black shirt.

"Have you become a believer?" Vesna asked, leaning into him.

"I'm obsessed with one wicked flower that makes me do many things," he whispered softly in her ear. "And I want to help this flower blossom."

"I'm already blooming brighter than any other flower, because I have you," she whispered.

Mir smiled and looked around, scanning the room. He took her hand, turning to Alex and Anna. "Follow me," he blurted out.

Vesna wasn't sure of his plan, but she trusted him.

Chapter Seventeen

MIR.

MIR SQUEEZED VESNA'S HAND, WISHING TO PROTECT HER from every parasite that was present at the ball. She didn't belong here. And Mir knew he would stop at nothing to protect her. This perfect wicked flower had illuminated his reality from the moment she entered his life that grey night at the club. He was ready to become a believer, worshipping only her.

Mir entered the small empty room, making sure no one was there, his friends following him inside. "The library is on the thirty-third floor. It's guarded." He cleared his throat. "I can distract the guards, and Anna can put them to sleep. Once they're out, we can look for the book."

Mir had only been to the library once, a long time ago, but that was enough for him to notice that all the books were arranged on stands encased in glass, like in a museum. Breaking the glass would make too much noise. He had to think of something.

"Let's go back inside," he decided. "When Boris starts his speech, we can slip out one by one and meet back here."

They returned to the ballroom. Fortunately, no one had noticed their absence. Mir was looking around, waiting for Boris's speech, when Ivan caught his gaze.

"Fucking parasite," Mir cursed, tightening his hand around Vesna's waist as Ivan approached. "What do you want, Ivan?" Mir asked, taking a deep breath, trying to remain calm.

"Let's put our differences aside for such a special evening," Ivan said coolly, staring at Vesna. "Oh—how did you survive?"

Mir felt Vesna tense up at Ivan's words. "Hating you gave me strength," Vesna said, her eyes flashing with fire.

"Fuck off. Tonight I'm spending time with my girl-friend," Mir said through clenched teeth.

"Adorable." Ivan laughed theatrically, walking away.

"What a jerk!" Alex said loudly, making sure Ivan could hear him.

"He's not worth it," Anna muttered.

At that moment, Boris walked to the center of the room, standing next to the rafflesia statue. He raised his glass, expecting everyone's attention.

"Dear friends, I'm glad to see so many of you supporting my precious flower. I would like to raise a glass for this blooming season. Let us drink to finding the Veiled Wilds. It will be beneficial for my human friends too, I promise."

Everyone raised their drinks, and Mir wished to turn it into poison in their hands. He shifted his gaze to Vesna.

She raised her glass too. "To your end," she whis-pered, finishing her drink in one gulp.

Boris continued speaking, and Mir decided it was time to make a move. "Anna, you first," he whispered.

Anna's face didn't even flinch, and Mir thought she was a true representative of her divine flower. Marigolds were known for their calm wits, even in the most stressful situations.

Before Vesna could escape, Boris spoke again, looking directly at her. "We're lucky to have a guest here tonight whose name literally means 'spring'!" he exclaimed. "I thought it would bring me good luck if my first dance of this blooming season was with spring itself."

Vesna stiffened, looking at Mir in panic, and he was seriously considering saying no to Boris. It was suspicious how much Boris was focusing on Vesna, despite so many important guests. Vesna was about to approach Boris, but Mir squeezed her hand, stopping her. His movement didn't go unnoticed by his boss.

"Mir, I didn't know you were the jealous type," Boris said in an unnaturally friendly tone, coming closer.

Vesna looked at Mir softly, all traces of panic gone, and squeezed his hand back. "One dance."

"Only because my wicked flower wishes it," Mir said, letting go of her hand.

While Vesna danced with Boris, Alex slipped out next. Mir watched his precious flower dance with the most dangerous parasite in the world. He couldn't hear what they were saying, but at some point, he noticed how Vesna's eyes widened, and her face turned pale. She took a deep breath, her chest heaving, without moving for a few seconds.

Mir could hear his own heartbeat; whatever Boris had told Vesna, it affected her, and Mir was afraid that she wouldn't be able to calm down. But the next second, Vesna smiled, looking down. *That's my wicked flower,* Mir thought, taking a deep breath.

When the song ended and everyone clapped, Boris took Vesna's hand and led her to Mir. "You have a charming girlfriend, Mir. I return her safe and sound. No need to be so gloomy."

"Thank you for the dance." Vesna smiled at Boris. "If you'll excuse me, I need to go to the ladies' room," she lied. Mir knew she would wait for him with Anna and Alex.

Mir was about to follow her, but Boris clearly wanted to chat. "I admit, I'm jealous. I'm not sure what she sees in you," he said, watching Vesna leave.

"Neither am I. Maybe I just got lucky," Mir muttered, mostly to himself. "Excuse me." He walked away quickly, but Boris called after him.

"I don't see Alex and that golden woman." He raised an eyebrow, looking around the room.

"I'll find them," Mir said, trying to sound calm.

His friends were waiting for him, nervously glancing at the enormous clock on the wall in the shape of a rafflesia flower.

Vesna's eyes lit up when Mir walked in. "How are we going to get there?" she asked impatiently.

"Alex and Anna must go back. Boris is looking for them," Mir said. "We can't risk it."

"Screw him. I'm not leaving you two alone," Alex said. "Let's get the book and leave town."

"Exactly!" Anna agreed. "I'm the only one who's actually seen the book."

"No, Mir is right. We can't risk it," Vesna said. "Anna, distract Boris while we're gone."

Anna pouted. "Fine. Don't forget, the book is white, as if woven from magnolia petals."

"Alex, Ivan is on you." Mir patted his friend on the shoulder.

Alex nodded immediately. Mir knew he was lucky to have such a friend.

"Come on, Anna. Time to use your charm," Alex said, trying to force a smile.

"I wish I could just put him to eternal sleep," Anna muttered and turned to Vesna. "Good luck!"

Vesna gave Anna and Alex a quick hug before they headed back to the ball again.

"Let's use the stairs." Mir thought quickly. "I'll distract the guards somehow, or just put them in a coma."

Mir didn't want to waste any time. He took Vesna's hand in his and walked toward the stairs. His wicked flower followed him without asking questions. Suddenly, they heard voices from above. Mir had to think fast. He grabbed Vesna, pushing her against the wall. His hands touched her waist, and her body immediately arched. His magic stirred excitedly at the same second. As the voices got closer, Mir lowered his head, slowly touching her lips. He kissed her passionately, and Vesna leaned toward him like a flower seeking the touch of spring.

"Someone is having fun," a man said, passing by them. Mir recognized the voice; it was the guard.

Vesna tensed up, and her lips froze. Fortunately, no one suspected anything, quickly descending the stairs. Mir wanted to hold Vesna in his arms forever, forgetting about the book, about Boris, and even about the divine datura. But reality always haunted him.

"Let's move. We can't waste any time," Mir said, clearing his throat.

Vesna hid behind a column while Mir walked confidently into the library. At least, he tried to look like that. His heart was beating fast, echoing in his ears. His life wasn't that important. But tonight, for the first time in his life, he had something to lose: Vesna.

"Who's there?" the guard immediately asked.

"Oleg, security seems very light for a night with so many strangers in the building," Mir said, walking up to him. "You know how Boris loves his library."

"The other guys will be back soon," Oleg reported. "They took a brief break."

Perfect, Mir thought. And without wasting a second, he released his magic, immediately enveloping Oleg. The datura pollen didn't paralyze him completely; Boris must have shared a lot of magic with him, because he should have been out already. Instead, his roots were slowly growing from his hands. Mir was about to move closer, but Vesna walked in.

"Wait." She stopped him, her bright voice filling the room. "We don't want to make a mess."

She whispered a spell. The creamy pink pollen left her body, and a sweet, all-consuming scent immediately hit Mir. He wanted to inhale that scent for the rest of his life.

Even Oleg no longer tried to move, and just stared at Vesna, his mouth ajar. The scent was a problem—someone might smell it—but Mir didn't have time to think about it now.

Vesna walked slowly toward Mir, looking like a goddess descending from the eternal garden. "Give me your hand." She touched Mir, and her pollen surged through his veins, strengthening his magic in an instant. Raw, unconditional power rose in him. It felt absolute. It felt like infinity, like complete oblivion.

Mir finally came to his senses after a few moments, sending hallucinations into Oleg's mind. Oleg slowly stood up, talking to himself, and left the room.

"Let's find the book." Mir strung together the few words, although he felt intoxicated by the power that Vesna had given him. He couldn't imagine what she must feel, living with such magic all this time. A part of him now understood why Boris was so obsessed with sacred magic. It brought euphoria.

Without waiting for Mir, Vesna ran from one stand to another, focused on finding the book, while Mir released his pollen into the air as much as he could. He needed to mask Vesna's fragrance.

"Mir!" Vesna called, her voice shaking slightly. She was standing next to a stand in the far corner. A white book made of magnolia petals, just as Anna had described, was placed under the glass and dim light. An ancient lock bound it; there was no way to open the book now.

Mir hurried to Vesna, but she didn't even wait for him… She broke the glass, and the loud sound echoed through the hall.

"We need to hide it," Mir blurted out in a panic. "They could have heard the sound."

"Where? It's too big," Vesna said nervously, her eyes darting around the room.

"We can hide it in my apartment for now," Mir decided.

It was risky, because as soon as Boris realized the book was missing, he would search the entire building. But they had no other choice. At least Mir would have time to come up with a plan.

"Here's my key, just in case. I have a second copy." He handed her the key. "Follow me."

Before they even moved, Anna's loud voice filled the room. "Boris, what a wonderful collection!" she said admiringly, though Mir could hear the worry in her voice.

At that moment, Mir heard a strange sound, and looking up, he saw a metal cage falling from the ceiling —right where Vesna was standing. He didn't even breathe; he ran up to her and pushed her away. The cage fell right on his foot, and Mir growled in pain. He tried to move and push the cage to free himself, but there was no way to shift something so heavy.

Vesna didn't move. She just stood there, storms dancing in her eyes as she looked at him, colder than the harshest winter. Her gaze shifted to the book.

"Vesna," Mir whispered, though his heart had almost stopped beating, meeting her cold gaze.

"I need to get my revenge," she whispered, so quietly that Mir had to read her lips.

The lips that had led him to a blooming paradise just moments ago now led him to a fading hell with a few words. She quickly ran away, hiding behind the columns.

She's choosing the damn book! he thought. *Of course she's choosing the fucking book.*

Mir had been so stupid to think that someone as holy and sacred as her would choose him, a vile poisonous flower. He felt empty—dead, even, as if his magic had poisoned him from the inside. He should have known better than to let someone into his heart.

Chapter Eighteen

VESNA.

Vesna felt as if the Veiled Wilds had exploded on her, covering her in wilted blossoms, burying her alive. She had made her choice. She realized she couldn't risk losing her chance to get her revenge, even for Mir.

Her eyes welled with tears. She felt like a traitor. She *was* a traitor.

As she made her way to the exit, she kept stopping and hiding behind the columns, when suddenly she heard Boris's screams.

She decided taking the elevator would be faster, and she pressed the button hysterically. She hid, afraid that when it opened, there might be someone inside. But the divine magnolia was probably helping her; the elevator was empty. Vesna quickly entered, and pressing the first floor button, she waited impatiently for the door to close.

"Divine magnolia, no one should enter this elevator," she prayed under her breath, her heart pounding.

Fuck, Vesna cursed internally as soon as the elevator opened. Ivan was standing a few meters away, locking a door with a key. *Probably his apartment,* Vesna thought, running out of the elevator and quickly placing the book on the windowsill in the hallway.

Ivan turned around at the noise.

"What a surprise!" His gaze focused on Vesna as she stood in front of the window, trying to block the book with her body. "What the hell are you doing here?"

"Waiting for Mir," Vesna lied, without even thinking. "We want some privacy."

A nasty smile played across Ivan's face. "I assure you, I'm much more cheerful than the eternally gloomy Mir," he sang, coming closer, licking his lips.

She clenched her fists. "I like gloomy men," she said coldly. She couldn't let this parasite touch her. She would rather die than feel his hands and his scent on her body.

"You won't know until you try," Ivan sang, dangerously close.

The next second, a siren wailed. It was so loud that both Vesna and Ivan slapped their hands over their ears.

"Next time, human!" he shouted and ran to the elevator.

Vesna had no time to waste. The siren could mean only one thing: Boris was now looking for the book. She pulled out Mir's key; number sixteen was written on it. In a few moments, she reached his apartment.

She went inside and froze for a second, studying his place. Sadness overcame her, looking at his grey, lonely apartment with empty walls. The place smelled like Mir, and Vesna burst into tears.

She opened the vast window, looking down at the ground. Even though it was only the first floor, the ground seemed rather far away. She was about to climb out, but noticed a bunch of people running outside and circling the building. It was too late…

I need to go underground, she decided, recalling the faded plans of the building she had studied at the library.

She descended the stairs to the level below, hiding in the shadows. The space was dark, lit only by the flickering of fading wall sconces. She paused, holding her breath, listening. It seemed everyone had run upstairs the moment the siren sounded. This was her chance.

The air was dense, and Vesna barely resisted the instinct to use her magic. She couldn't risk filling the air with her sweet scent. She tightened her grip around the precious book and moved forward carefully, afraid to make a sound.

This place was worse than she'd imagined. Her eyes widened in horror as she saw chains scattered on the stone floor and smelled the faint scent of different flowers still present in some rooms. Boris obviously used this place for holding and draining magical people.

The labyrinth twisted the deeper she went, and she began to worry she'd never find her way out. Eventually, she came back to the room of chains she knew she had passed almost half an hour ago, and she let out a hopeless sob. Sitting on the floor, she tried to remember the plans she had skimmed in the library. If she couldn't find the exit, someone would come down here eventually and discover her.

Tears of fear and pain over her betrayal of Mir took over, and she soundlessly cried, sitting on the cold stone floor. But the thought of her poor mother, who had probably been kept in this very labyrinth, gave her courage. *Boris will die,* she promised herself, standing up abruptly.

Mentally recalling the plans, she moved again, and after some time, she finally stumbled into a spacious round chamber. It was different from the rest of the rooms, with more light and an earthen floor instead of a stone floor.

Vesna's veins froze to ice. A huge rafflesia flower grew right from the ground, its reddish-brown bud closed. Orange spots covered the huge petals.

That's why Boris needs so much magic! To feed that nasty flower, she thought with a hatred she had never felt before. It was even bigger than the hatred she felt for Boris. After all, it all had begun with this flower.

She clenched her jaw, suppressing the desire to destroy this ugly flower. Her gaze moved to a narrow corridor in the wall that looked like a tunnel. But it seemed the flower sensed her sacred magic. A loud sound pierced the space, and long roots appeared suddenly from under the flower, charging toward Vesna with frightening speed. With a gasp, she sprinted for the tunnel, but the roots were faster. She screamed as one pierced her leg and immediately began growing inside her bones. It felt as though a million knives had stabbed her and exploded inside her. The pain was unbearable. She struggled to escape, but the root was stronger, pulling her back.

Grabbing a huge stone from the ground, she pounded the root. "I will cut my leg off if I have to!" she screamed at the parasite with hatred.

When the stone didn't work, she bit the root, hard, until it finally backed off, leaving her body. Her leg was turning blue and almost numb, but she didn't care. She needed to get away. Vesna, constantly looking back, crawled along the dark tunnel, her skin scratching against the rough walls.

When she finally made it out, she laughed hysterically, scared, tired, and heartbroken.

VESNA DIDN'T QUITE REMEMBER how she made it home. She vividly recalled that people on the streets were staring at her, but she didn't care, just walking slowly, cradling the book, barely holding the screams of pain back.

She was now sitting on the windowsill, no emotion in her eyes. In horror, she thought that even when she was in Mir's embrace, blossoming under his touch, she had still known deep down that she was going to choose her revenge over him if needed. Vesna was afraid she was a monster. Ultimately, she was no better than Boris. He was also only focused on his plan, without caring about anyone else.

Hours had passed, and Vesna used almost all the spells she knew, but the book remained locked. The Divine Blooms wouldn't let just anyone to open it. *There must be some trick to it*, she thought, as the door of the apartment opened and Anna came in.

"Vesna!" she screamed, running toward her with open arms.

"I'm safe," Vesna whispered, continuing to sit. Tears rolled down her face, like water on the window on a rainy day. A scary thought ran through her mind: if she had to sacrifice Anna, she would probably do that as well. "I'm a broken flower," Vesna muttered, her voice reflecting a feeling of doom.

"Why do you say that?" Anna asked, her brows drawing together.

"I abandoned Mir there for Boris to find him," she said with an empty voice. "I grabbed the book and ran, leaving him behind."

Anna was speechless for a moment. "Why the fuck did you leave him?!"

"I had no time," Vesna muttered. "I had to make a choice."

"He's our friend!" Anna fired. "I thought you'd changed, but your heart is locked, just like the Veiled Wilds!"

"I know it was a mistake!" Vesna tried to fight the tears, her lips trembling. "Please, tell me he's safe! After that, you don't have to talk to me," she begged with bated breath. She couldn't live with herself if Boris had killed Mir.

Anna hesitated for a second before she spoke. "We did see Mir in the library, but he screamed that the book was missing. Boris was ready to kill him right there."

Anna told her the rest, and Vesna could clearly imagine everything that had happened after she left. She saw Boris releasing his roots toward Mir. She saw the guard Mir had brainwashed rush in and vouch that Mir had only followed someone suspicious into the library. Vesna had to admit that Mir was smart to think ahead like that. He must have inserted those fake memories when they first ran into the guard.

"Boris was looking for you, but luckily Ivan came in. He reported that you were waiting for Mir outside his apartment, and you didn't have the book. I didn't see the rest, but they didn't let anyone leave until they searched the entire building. How did you escape?" Anna stared at her coldly.

"I went underground," Vesna whispered, inhaling a deep breath of relief. Mir was safe, she had the book, and no one suspected her. But somehow, Vesna didn't feel happy. She had left part of her soul in that library.

"I found the last flower that remains on earth down

there," she said, lowering her gaze to her leg, which was still blue.

Anna gasped in shock as her gaze followed Vesna's. "It attached itself to you?!"

"Yes, but I managed to escape." Vesna tried to smile.

Anna was about to attend to the wound when her gaze froze on the book. "Oh! Have you opened it?"

"No," Vesna whispered. "I can't. We need to go to Sveta. She might know how to open it."

Anna shook her head. "You can't walk like this."

"I don't fucking care! I'll crawl if I have to!" Vesna snapped, all the emotions of the night finally catching up with her.

THEY WALKED IN SILENCE. During their dance, Boris had told Vesna something so outrageous that she didn't know if she should laugh or cry. They spoke about his immortality, and his words would stay in Vesna's mind forever.

"She loved me. She gave it to me willingly," he said with some sadness in his voice.

Vesna couldn't and wouldn't believe it. Her mother would never give up her magic, sacrificing herself to offer it to a nasty parasite like Boris. Still, the seed of doubt had entered her soul.

It's all a lie, Vesna thought with a heavy heart as she limped along, holding onto Anna's shoulder. She didn't want to believe Boris; she knew how tricky parasites were. They would take a piece of truth and twist it into a perfect lie.

When they arrived, Sveta wasn't there. The apartment seemed empty, as if no one had ever lived there. Instead, bottles of potion filled the space.

"Vesna," Anna muttered, staring at something on the table.

A sealed envelope with Vesna's name on it lay there. She opened it with trembling hands and skimmed it, reading it aloud.

"'Vesna, Mir took me to Boris. Don't blame him; I insisted on it myself. There is something I need to finish with Boris. Stay strong, and be a better sacred one than your mother was.'"

Vesna turned pale. *Sveta left... Why?* She couldn't help but wonder. She took a deep breath and tore up the letter. She refused to believe her mother was unworthy.

Chapter Nineteen

VESNA.

VESNA SAT ON THE WINDOWSILL, WATCHING THE SUN SET over the horizon. Yesterday, she had turned twenty-five, but she still hadn't bloomed. *Maybe the Divine Blooms decided that I'm unworthy,* she thought with an empty heart. *After what I did, I don't blame them.*

She deeply regretted leaving Mir behind—not because she feared losing her ability to bloom, but because she had changed. And back in the library, she had acted like the girl she used to be. Her mind was capable of holding that illusion, but her heart was no longer the same—and it had broken in the process.

She stood up, took the book from under the bed, and whispered different spells. Nothing worked, just like all her previous attempts. Biting her lip in frustration, she went to the kitchen and grabbed a knife. Standing over the book, her hair falling over its cover, she tried to pick the lock. But the blade didn't leave so much as a scratch, as if the book were protected by powerful magic.

She returned to the window, narrowing her eyes at Boris's men who were patrolling the streets. Vesna couldn't leave town; Boris was desperately searching for the book, and his men not only roamed the streets, but also guarded every exit from the city.

Vesna and Anna had decided to lay low, living their normal lives and going to work. If Vesna bloomed, she could escape the city by simply cursing Boris's men. She hoped the book would open once it sensed the sacred bloom. After that, Vesna would make her way to the Veiled Wilds.

She took a deep breath, trying not to give in to the tears of hopelessness that overwhelmed her, and went to get ready for work.

ALEX DIDN'T SHOW up at the club, same as Mir. Something told Vesna that Mir would never come back if she was still working there.

Vesna went on stage, and as soon as she began singing, she picked up the fragrance of fresh roses. *Alex is here!* She couldn't wait to finish her song. There were so many questions she wanted to ask him. Mostly about Mir, of course; she just wanted to make sure he was safe.

But suddenly, the smell of rotten flesh filled the space, and she noticed at least ten figures walking into the club. The smell was so bad that some customers began to complain. Vesna felt her face get red with worry and fear as she wondered if they were here for her.

As soon as the last notes of her song melted into silence, someone clapped loudly—Boris. He stood in the middle of the club, staring at her with a wicked smile. His men surrounded him. Mir was one of them. Vesna couldn't help but stare at his face. Shame and regret filled her heart again. She missed him terribly. She knew she would never forget him, even if they could never be together.

"Bravo. I didn't know you have such a lovely voice," Boris said, ignoring everyone, as if he were the owner of this place and could do anything he wanted.

"Boris, what the fuck?" Alex demanded, walking toward him. "I thought we had a deal."

"No need to be alarmed. My guys will take a quick look. I've been looking for my book everywhere, and your club should be no exception," Boris said before he turned to Vesna again. "Mir told me you two broke up?"

Vesna glanced at Mir for a second, but he didn't look at her. His face showed no emotions, as if he were a dead man walking. "We did," Vesna said with an empty heart.

"It's for the best. Such a sweet girl should stay away from poison," Boris said, then turned to address the club. "Let the night of vanished petals begin! The sacred one has appeared again!" he exclaimed, making sure everyone present could hear him.

Vesna barely kept from gasping, as his men moved immediately, checking under every piece of furniture, behind every picture on the wall, tearing everything apart. They also approached every person in the club, checking their eyes and inhaling their scent.

A noise in the far corner caught everyone's attention. Ivan was holding some guy; his eyes were as pink as a gentle tulip.

"Got one!" Ivan reported with victory in his voice.

Vesna was looking at the poor guy, who didn't even try to escape. She knew everything was coming to an end, as if a flower were closing its petals as the winter was approaching.

Her gaze shot to Boris as he stalked closer to her. *He knows,* she thought helplessly, unable to move from her spot.

"Sorry, no exceptions," he said and stared into her eyes, licking his lips hungrily.

Vesna could swear she felt his parasitic roots trying to enter her soul. She had drunk the potion right before work, hoping it would work.

Boris took his time. Clearly, he was desperate to find the sacred one. His hand reached to her hair.

"Boris, don't you dare *touch* her!" Mir fired, breaking the silence. "I don't want your parasite hands on her!"

Vesna stood in shock. It was too dangerous for him to confront Boris like this. "Mir, it's okay," she said hurriedly, trying to calm him down.

Mir clenched his firsts. "He will not *touch* you!" he hissed, coming closer to them and pushing Boris aside.

"Quiet!" Boris growled, glaring at Mir. "By the way, I've been craving roses for far too long," he threatened and shifted his gaze to Ivan.

Ivan ran to Alex, releasing his nasty roots on the go. The silence that covered Fading Blossoms was broken by Anna's scream.

Then, as if in a dream, Vesna saw Mir release his poison, plunging everything into a dangerous mist.

"Touch him, and your men will die," he hissed to Boris.

The rest of the rafflesia moved, ready to take Mir, but Boris put his hand up, stopping them. "Years of working with me, down the drain over minor magic?"

"No," Mir said through clenched teeth. "Not only over Alex, but because you are a nasty parasite that plagues this world."

Is he trying to get himself killed?! Vesna thought in a

panic. She ran down from the stage, stopping close to Mir. She was ready to reveal herself and empower Mir's magic. *I will not leave you again,* she thought.

Boris locked his raging eyes with Mir before his gaze moved briefly to Ivan. "We can't lose men when we're so close to the final battle." He paused. "Suit yourself, Mir. Leave. But remember, you never know when a parasite might creep up your petals. I'm closer to the sacred one than you think."

Mir spat on the floor. "Till never," he muttered, his voice like ice.

Everyone was silent, even after Boris and his men left, like frozen blooms under the first snow.

"Come with me." Mir took Vesna's hand and moved to the exit, filling her with hope that he'd forgiven her.

He walked in silence into the alley behind the club, then stopped, releasing Vesna's hand. "Leave the city tonight," he demanded.

Vesna stopped close to him, trying to look into his eyes, and the hope she'd felt faded. "You have nothing else to say?" she asked, wishing he would blame her, wishing he would scream. Anything but this coldness.

"No," Mir muttered, still avoiding her gaze. He leaned on the wall, his arms crossed in front of him.

"Nothing at all?!" Vesna said, feeling helpless.

His white eyes shot to her. "You chose the fucking *book*, Vesna. You chose your revenge." His voice was full of pain and silent disappointment.

"Please forgive me," she said, tears streaming down her face.

His mouth twisted. "No need to be sorry. We've just used each other, that's all." His voice echoed in the empty alley.

Vesna was quiet, diving into his eyes. He was right.

She had chosen her revenge, even though her heart wanted to choose him. She moved closer, stopping a few centimeters away from him, her lips almost touching his. "I'm sorry," she whispered. She didn't want to be that person; she didn't want to scarify her soul on the way to avenging her mother. "Please forgive me."

Mir tensed. She noticed how his mouth twisted again, and she could see he was in pain. "Leave the city, Vesna."

She held her breath as he brought his hands to her waist, but he only moved her aside, his touch scorching, then quickly disappeared from the alley.

Vesna stood there all alone for quite some time. No thoughts in her mind, just emptiness.

"Here you are!" Anna's worried voice snapped her back to reality.

Alex stood next to her. "That was close," he whispered.

"Mir was reckless," Anna scolded, taking a deep breath. "Did he say anything?"

"Nothing, he said *nothing*! He doesn't want anything to do with me!" Vesna blurted out, trying to hold the tears inside.

"You broke his heart," Alex said, crossing his arms. "Mir hasn't let anyone into his life for so many years. And now that he finally has, you showed him he was right all those years."

"Alex, I made a mistake!" Vesna said, looking at him pleadingly. "Please help me."

"I barely see him these days. He told me he doesn't care about the Divine Blooms, or even about the divine datura anymore." Alex paused, shaking his head. "You have to forget him."

Vesna's heart exploded. She didn't think she could

ever forget him. Pain and guilt wracked her body, and she burst into tears.

Her heart exploded again, but something was literally happening this time… She felt a painful heat on her cheek, as if something were being carved into her skin. A tattoo began to appear, sparkling and blinding her. Pollen rushed through her veins and spilled out through her skin, plunging everything around them into a sweet aroma capable of hypnotizing anyone who would inhale it with harmony.

She was blooming.

Chapter Twenty

MIR.

Everything was much easier than had Mir thought. Even Ivan, without realizing it, had vouched for Vesna, clearing her from suspicion. Mir kept away from the club, not wanting to see her. The fact that Vesna had left him without even much hesitation hit him much harder than he had expected. He had been alone all his life, but for the first time with Vesna, he felt like he could be happy. Obviously, it had just been a twisted mirage. She had left his life like a flower that suddenly withered on a chilly autumn morning. He still craved her, dreamed about her, but everything had changed. Now he knew that being with Vesna could only be real in his dreams. Happiness had faded away.

But the worst part was that Mir didn't know what to do. He had given up on everything, even his plans to destroy the divine datura. Doing so would mean he would have to see Vesna again.

He continued to work for Boris, even though he could have just disappeared. *I will stay until Vesna finally leaves the city, watching her from afar,* Mir decided. After that, he planned to leave himself and live alone somewhere in the wilderness.

But working for Boris became even more difficult than before. Mir could barely keep his hatred and disgust from showing on his face whenever Boris was near.

The visit to the club had been worse than Mir expected. The moment he saw Vesna on the stage, his heart betrayed him. It seemed it didn't belong to him anymore. And when Boris touched her and threatened to kill Alex, his only family, Mir couldn't pretend anymore. He didn't hold back, finally speaking his mind, and it felt like relief. Mir knew Boris could kill him, but he wasn't afraid. *At least I can die with some dignity,* he thought. He didn't expect Boris to just let him go.

When Mir had stood with Vesna in the alley, he couldn't make himself move. Her eyes showed regret and even devotion. But Mir had learned his lesson. She had looked at him almost the same way at the ball, but it hadn't stopped her from leaving him behind.

Hold yourself together, Mir. You're used to being alone, he thought, trying to cheer himself up, walking aimlessly on the streets before he went back to his apartment at the Fading Blossoms. All these years, he had been right to not let anyone into his life. Vesna was a mistake—and that mistake would haunt him forever.

When Mir finally made his way home, he found Alex pounding on his door.

"Alex?" Mir froze, staring at him.

Alex whirled around, his eyes covered in a red haze. "We need to go. Now!" he demanded, already running down the stairs.

"Okay," Mir muttered, following him with a frown.

"Get out of town and straight into the forest!" Alex

said, his words rushing out in a hurry. He was already getting into Mir's car.

"What the hell is going on?" Mir asked, pushing the gas to the fullest. It was clear that Alex was on edge.

"She's blooming… So strong that it seems like magic will soon cover the Earth again!"

"Fuck," Mir muttered, pressing the gas pedal harder.

When they approached the screening point, Mir realized the guards were sleeping, and the scent of marigold filled the air. "Anna," he said, realizing her magic was probably amplified by Vesna's.

"You were too harsh with her," Alex dared to say. "She truly loves you."

"I doubt it's actually love." Mir smirked, but he couldn't hide the pain in his voice.

"Cut her some slack," Alex said. "I'm sure it's not that easy to be the sacred one."

"Whose side are you on, anyway?" Mir asked, glancing at him in irritation.

"I'm on your side, of course. But without her, you look like a ghost. I'm afraid you're poisoning yourself from the inside." Alex paused. "Don't argue with her when we arrive. It's hard enough for her now," he muttered.

"Don't worry. I'll do my job and leave." Vesna had finally bloomed, and now he could leave this city. But his heart ached, and a lump rose in his throat at the thought of leaving her forever. He wanted to be near her, just as he realized he still wanted to destroy his divine flower. He tightened his grasp on the steering wheel, trying to pull himself together.

They wandered through the forest for a while, following the sweet scent, but Anna and Vesna were nowhere to be found.

"I hope Anna didn't get into an accident," Alex said, worry in his voice.

"I hope not too," Mir muttered—when the overpowering scent of magnolia hit him. He pressed the brake pedal sharply. "They're here."

Mir narrowed his eyes, trying to see anything in the darkness. He noticed Alex's car. It was camouflaged, covered with tree branches.

"Mir is here. Come out!" Alex shouted, getting out of the car.

Anna and Vesna came out from behind a tree, and Mir couldn't believe his eyes. Vesna's skin was sparkling, and glowing tattoos of blossoming magnolias covered her entire body. Flowers were blossoming even in her eyes. This was not how magical people usually bloomed. Their powers grew stronger, but it didn't manifest in actual *blooming*. She truly was the sacred one…

"You came!" she said, as if not believing her own eyes.

A lump came into Mir's throat. She looked so lost… He fought the urge to run up to her and wrap her in his arms, shielding her blossoming from the entire world. "I promised Sveta I'd help you," he said, trying to sound indifferent.

"Thank you," she whispered, and Mir's heart stopped again.

"This reunion is lovely, but her scent will soon reach the city," Anna said with a raised eyebrow.

"Right." Mir cleared his throat, coming closer to Vesna. *What if I miscalculate the dosage?* The moment the thought ran thought his mind, fear gripped him.

"I trust you," Vesna whispered, as if reading his thoughts.

"Close your eyes," Mir said.

"No, I'm not afraid of your magic," Vesna insisted.

Stubborn flower, Mir thought, calling on his pollen. He whispered the spell Sveta had taught him, making sure to pronounce everything correctly.

His poisonous pollen touched Vesna's blossoming skin, and she shivered. Mir dove into her eyes immediately. "Is it too much?" he asked, ready to call his magic away.

"No, it's nice," she said, her voice distant. "It's peaceful."

"Is it working?" Alex couldn't help but come closer, stopping right next to Mir.

White streams of poison, visible on the skin, flowed through Vesna's veins. Soon, the glow of the blooming flowers faded, and a bright, blinding flash from her body illuminated everything around. Mir and his friends had to close their eyes against it. When they opened them, the forest had fallen into darkness again, and Vesna stood in front of them, back to normal.

"Thank you, Divine Blooms!" Anna squeezed Vesna in a fierce embrace.

Alex raised an eyebrow. "I think it had nothing to do with the Divine Blooms."

"You're right. Thank you, Mir," Anna corrected herself.

"Are you all right?" Mir couldn't help but ask Vesna. She seemed unnaturally pale, and he was afraid he had done something wrong. "Do you feel numb?"

Vesna looked at him and smiled gently. "No, I feel great. Your magic is beautiful."

Mir took a deep breath, feeling as if a weight had been lifted from his shoulders. "Sveta said it only works for a few days. You need to get away right now," he insisted.

"First, we need to get the book," Anna said. "We couldn't risk going for it with Vesna blooming."

"She's right. We get the book, and I'll leave the city and try to open it somewhere safe," Vesna said.

"I can go to get the book alone," Anna suggested.

Vesna shook her head. "If someone tries to catch you, you need my magic. Now that more rafflesia are feeding again, they'll be too difficult to deceive."

"I thought you didn't care who gets caught when it comes to your revenge," Mir fired, knowing very well that his words would hurt her. But he had to bring her back to reality, no matter the cost.

"Is it what you think of me?" Vesna shot back. Her eyes shone, and he could see a creamy pink color appearing.

"That's exactly what I think of you," Mir said, crossing his arms against the pain he felt. "When did you suddenly become so noble?"

Vesna bit her lip. She was obviously hurt. Mir hated to do this to her, but it was the truth. She had abandoned him, but now suddenly she was going to risk everything, when Anna and Alex could simply get the book on their own.

Vesna's eyes filled with tears. "Everyone makes mistakes, Mir," she whispered.

The desire to scoop her into his embrace took hold of Mir again. He took a step closer, but stopped himself. "Leave the city tonight," he almost begged.

They were diving into each other's eyes, completely forgetting about Anna and Alex. Mir still cared for her, still wanted her like no one else before. Part of him wanted to forget about everything and just be with her. But it came from his heart, and his head knew this was for the best. He hadn't known he could be so naïve, believing that his poison could ever enter the blossoming garden.

Mir finally broke his gaze from her and turned to Alex. "Are you coming?"

"I'm going to stay here," Alex said, his gaze shuttered. "I'm going to follow Vesna, Mir."

Mir tensed, somehow feeling jealous and sad. Alex had been the only good thing in his life since his parents left him. He wasn't just a friend; he was the family Mir had never had. Plus, Mir had to admit he was jealous that Alex would stay with Anna and Vesna. The times when Mir was with the three of them were the happiest moments of his life.

Mir turned around, not sure how to force himself to leave.

"Mir!" Alex called after him. "I love you, man." He came to Mir and hugged him tightly. Mir froze for a second, but almost immediately hugged him in return.

"Take care of them," Mir said to Alex, briefly glancing at Anna and Vesna. He walked to his car quickly, almost running. He didn't want to stay even a second longer, because he knew if he did, he wouldn't be able to leave.

He looked at Vesna one last time as his car was driving past her. She was crying, whispering something to herself. Mir pushed on the gas, trying to convince himself it was for the best. The blooming season of the sacred datura was about to start too. He could feel it. He was already barely fighting his desire for her, but when he bloomed, it would be practically impossible. He couldn't risk being near her. She was a flower he could never have.

Chapter Twenty-One
VESNA.

Vesna had hoped Mir would stay with them. But it seemed he had already decided everything; his lips talked of nothing but rejection. She refused to accept it. She wasn't a cold flower driven only by revenge anymore, because Mir had given her a promise of a new life filled with love and bliss.

Her heart seemed to leave her body when he drove away. Helplessness fell upon her like a night shadow after the amber dusk. Of course, Mir was right; she had to get out of the city before Boris could find her. And now, with her sacred bloom, he would surely find her if she waited. Mir's magic could help only for a few days, maybe even less. She needed to open the book some-where else and find the fern flower.

"What's the plan?" Alex asked, finally breaking the silence.

"I think you and I go for the book, and Vesna should wait for us here," Anna suggested.

Vesna knew it was the best plan, but her heart was protesting. *I should have never let him go,* she thought, unable to fight her tears any longer. She couldn't leave town.

"Actually," Vesna whispered, raising her wet eyes to Alex, "can you take me to Mir?"

"Are you out of your mind?!" Anna fired.

"Vesna, he made his choice," Alex said hesitantly.

"Please, I need to talk to him," Vesna begged. "In private. Let's leave in the morning."

"Oh, man." Alex rolled his eyes.

They didn't talk during the ride. And Vesna was grateful her friends didn't try to talk her out of it.

Vesna had knocked on the door a few times when she finally heard Mir mumbling. "Alex?" he asked, opening the door.

His eyes froze on Vesna immediately. Mir was obviously getting ready to go to bed. He was wearing only sweatpants. Her eyes slid over his shoulders, his muscular chest.

He moved his disheveled hair from his face, staring at her silently. Vesna didn't know where to start, and tears came unbidden to her eyes.

"Can I come in?" she asked nervously. "Please."

"Come in," Mir said simply, letting her pass inside.

He leaned on the wall, watching her like a hunter in a dark forest. She nervously turned to face him.

"What is it, Vesna?" he asked, his snowy eyes illuminating the dark space around them.

"You can't decide for us both," she breathed.

"You decided first," Mir snapped, his brows slamming together.

"I made a mistake! Don't be so cruel!" she said, much louder than she intended to.

Mir growled, dragging his hands through his hair in frustration. "What do you want from me?!"

"I want *you*," she whispered, getting closer to Mir.

He put out his hand. "Vesna, don't," he muttered. "You need to leave town."

"I'm not leaving! Not without you."

He finally said what was on his mind. "You've never chosen me. And it's all right. Now go. I might bloom any minute now."

No, Vesna thought. She was missing him desperately—missing his company, missing his scent. "I'm not going anywhere." She moved closer, and felt the fragrance of his body enveloping her. "I'll stay here until you bloom, and then you won't be able to say no to me. I know it." She paused. "Please forgive me. I choose you forever," she whispered, and she dared to move closer until their lips met.

His lips were so hot, burning her entire body just with one touch. Mir growled, his eyes sparkling. His hand laced around her waist, pulling her body against his. He felt so strong and so tempting. Her mouth opened immediately, and she moaned with satisfaction when he put his hand in her hair and kissed her back hungrily. She laced her hands around his neck, and Mir moved his hands down, seamlessly lifting her dress and searing her hips with his touch. Goose bumps covered her body, and she could already feel pleasure building within her just from his touch. He paused, taking off his pants quickly, and Vesna's mouth watered at the sight of his strong manhood.

She slowly slid her dress down, freeing her breasts, then her hips, and finally her legs, feeling desire pool at her core as Mir devoured every inch of her exposed flesh with his eyes. He stepped closer, brushing her neck with his mouth, and she gasped, needing him in a way she'd never felt before.

Just when she thought she couldn't take it anymore, he lowered his hand to her center.

"Good flower," he growled with satisfaction at how wet she was for him, then he claimed her mouth hungrily.

He lifted her up, and without taking his mouth from hers, walked to the kitchen. He laid her on the counter, putting her legs on his shoulders and slowly kissing them, coming to her center. She was aching with anticipation, her nipples so hard they almost hurt. Arching her back, she buried her fingers in his hair, pulling him in, needing him closer.

"You're driving me crazy," Mir growled before diving between her legs.

She moaned with every swirl of his tongue on her clit. Flowers bloomed in every cell of her body. Desire was building up, taking the last fragments of reality away. But she needed him closer; she couldn't wait.

"Fuck me," she begged.

Mir grabbed her immediately, moving to the windowsill and sitting Vesna on top of him. She was running her nails down his back, moving against his hard flesh. When he lowered his kisses and circled her nipples, she arched her back immediately, throwing her head back in pleasure.

"Ride me." He sounded drunk.

Vesna sank onto him slowly, until he filled her completely, making her shudder with need. They both moaned at the exquisite feeling. His hand landed on her hips, helping her to move the way she wanted. It felt unearthly, every cell in her body, every seed of her magic ready to bloom for him. His growls grew, encouraging her to move even deeper. Needing more, Vesna braced her hands on the window and moved her hips down on him faster, feeling the pressure inside her building.

"Bloom for me," Mir sang into her ear, and his tattoo sparkled, dazzling her eyes. His blooming season had begun too.

His voice washed over her like the rays of the sun, just as he grabbed her hips tightly and thrust deeper, harder and faster, until the pressure inside her burst into a violently sweet release.

His growls drowned her moans out as he came together with her. Her skin burst with millions of flowers. When her body gave its last shudder, she felt as if part of her magic had left her, transporting into him.

"The rarest flower on earth blooms just for me," Mir whispered, tracing his fingers over her breast.

They sat silently in each other's arms, as if becoming one.

"Don't leave me…" She paused. "Never leave me. I can't bloom without you."

She didn't know why she felt like crying. She had never surrendered to anyone like this. Not just with her body, but also with her magic, with her soul. It was overwhelming, it was beautiful, and it felt perfect.

Mir scooped her in his arms, squeezing her tightly. "I won't leave you even if your magic is lost somewhere in a withered garden, and you are only a whisper, carried away by the howling wind."

Chapter Twenty-Two

MIR.

FINALLY AND FOREVER MINE, MIR THOUGHT AS HE GENTLY lowered her dress. He clearly realized how obsessed he was with this sacred flower. It was pure madness. He was lost in her bottomless eyes, in her scent, in every inch of her body, in every inch of her soul. Her eyes transported him to another reality, where the sun burned and endless fields of blossoms beckoned. She bent like a flower stem in the wind under his touch, under his every hungry kiss.

He couldn't stay away from his wicked flower any longer, knowing that his love was stronger than any fear of being abandoned again. His heart forgave her long before his mind finally could.

Mir had never bloomed for anyone. In fact, he always avoided sex during his bloom. It seemed too special to share this moment with someone. But with Vesna—for Vesna—he wanted to bloom all year round.

After she surrendered to him unconditionally, a strange feeling got hold of him. He felt that her magic had entered his veins, but never left, as if Vesna had left a part of her within him.

Afterward, Mir poisoned Vesna again, making sure no one would pick up her fragrance. They fell asleep melting into each other's embrace.

VESNA PEACEFULLY SLEPT with her leg on top of him. She smiled in a dream, and Mir couldn't help but smile back. He slid her messy hair from her face and gently kissed her. He knew he could never let her go. Even the grey morning didn't seem so depressing when she was in his life. She was shining brighter than the fern flower in the Veiled Wilds. She looked unworldly.

She is *unworldly,* Mir thought.

Vesna slowly opened her eyes, looking so perfect, so gentle, and so tempting. "Good morning," she mumbled, still half asleep.

Instead of answering, Mir kissed her again, slowly savoring each second. He was constantly hard around her. He wanted to possess her as she possessed his soul, ready to taste her in every way his imagination had ever dared to dream. But they had to move. Staying here was too dangerous.

Mir looked at the window. "The sun is coming up; we need to hurry. Let me poison you a little more."

They got dressed quickly, and Mir was watching Vesna the whole time. She was his, and it felt like the divine datura had finally blessed him.

Something shifted in the air, and Vesna froze, her face pale and still. "Rotten flesh," she whispered in a trembling voice.

"We'll fight. Empower my magic, and I'll do the—"

But he didn't even have time to finish his sentence—

he suddenly felt roots digging into his body from behind, piercing deep, reaching for his heart. He turned around just before collapsing to the floor.

Boris stood at the door, surrounded by his men, Ivan on his right. A smug smile played on his lips. Mir couldn't move, and the thought of leaving Vesna alone echoed painfully in his heart. In the blink of an eye, Boris's men surrounded her.

Mir growled loudly, trying to summon magic from the most hidden parts of his veins. He shouted the spell, gritting his teeth from the pain in his body, and from the even more unbearable pain in his soul. He called upon the rarest part of his magic, and datura petals with thorns as sharp as the ache in his heart rushed toward Boris.

Ivan leapt in front of him, thorns slicing through him.

Ivan's face twisted in pain as he collapsed to the floor, clutching his bloody stomach. He narrowed his eyes at Mir, lips trembling as they pressed into a thin line. "Fucking poison," he growled, then coughed, spitting blood. He began to crawl toward Mir, trying to call upon his roots. Nothing came. Clinging to the floor and leaving a trail of red behind him, Ivan finally managed to reach Mir.

Mir growled like an animal, and with the last of his strength, he clenched his fist so hard that he felt the bones crack. "Die," he whispered through gritted teeth.

Only a few specks of his magic appeared, sinking into Ivan's skin and dissolving. Ivan met Mir's gaze for a brief moment, and then his body went still.

Boris had been silently watching the entire time. He didn't even flinch. "I must admit, hiding her in plain sight all this time was smart. So was sending me the herbalist to distract me. But did you really think I'm that stupid?" he said, his voice dripping with sarcasm.

"How did you find out?" Mir asked, his voice a growl, thick with hatred and pain.

"Your luck was that I'd been searching for the wrong sacred one all along. That's the only reason I didn't question whether someone else could be the real one." Boris smirked. "Fucking Divine Blooms always play their little tricks. But the book disappeared, and no matter how hard the herbalist tried to convince me that she stole it, things just didn't line up. That's when I suspected that the Divine Blooms were trying to fool me. And everything clicked into place. My men checked Vesna's room this morning. Of course, the book was there." He paused, his tone shifting to cold indifference. "Well, then. Till never, my poisonous friend."

Boris drove his roots deeper, reaching into Mir's heart. Mir's blurred gaze found Vesna. She was cursing the men restraining her, slowly breaking free. He saw her as if in slow motion, time melting into darkness. She was crying, tears as big as petals rolling down her perfect face. When she looked at him, it felt as though she were staring into his very soul.

He couldn't move, but with all his strength, he took a deep breath, inhaling her sweet fragrance, willing himself to remember it in every life he might ever live.

She's the only flower I worship, Mir thought, as life and magic had almost left him. "I love you, wicked flower," he whispered, before falling into darkness.

He felt his soul shudder into millions of petals, carried away by destiny. It was peaceful. He could see a blooming meadow ahead of him. *The eternal garden,* the thought crossed his mind. The swaying flowers sang a melody, inviting him to enter.

Suddenly, he felt a tug; the sturdy branches of the magnolia wrapped around him and pulled him back into darkness.

255

Chapter Twenty-Three

VESNA.

Pollen uncontrollably left Vesna's body, and tears showered her like rain would shower petals during a thunderstorm. Her body trembled as she watched how Mir's magic left him, and his bewitching eyes closed forever. He was gone in a matter of seconds; this flower closed its petals, going to the eternal garden.

Silent hatred consumed Vesna as she shifted her gaze to Boris. Her eyes blazed with fury, and she clenched her jaw so tightly it made her teeth ache. Life didn't make sense anymore; only revenge did.

I will be the first flower that plunges everything into veiled obscurity, she promised herself.

Her magic rushed through her veins, the sacred bloom releasing sparkling pollen to the point of suffocation. Boris stared at her, admiration and thirst in his ugly eyes. He was obviously drawn to her magic, like bees to a blooming flower. Vesna realized how difficult it probably was for him to contain himself next to her magic. After all, he was nothing more than a thirsty parasite.

"I curse you to death!" she roared, not even sure what she was doing.

In that moment, her magic enveloped everyone. Boris's men, who had been restraining her all this time, fell lifeless in the same instant. But not Boris. He stood unharmed, smiling maliciously.

"I became immortal the second I drank the sacred magnolia magic. No one has ever reached immortality before. Now I only wish the same for my divine rafflesia flower."

"Die!" Vesna screamed, closing her eyes helplessly for a brief moment. Then, taking a deep breath, she stared at Boris again. She was ready to attack, until the last of her magic was gone.

"I have your mother. She's alive," Boris blurted out.

Vesna and her glorious magic froze immediately. "You're lying!" she screamed, gasping for breath.

"She's outside," Boris sang smugly. "Nadia!" he yelled, still staring at Vesna, licking his lips.

Vesna's gaze went to the door, her stomach a mix of hopeful elation and panic.

The door opened, and Sveta entered the room, lowering her head.

Vesna looked at Boris and then again at Sveta in confusion.

"Hello, daughter," Sveta whispered, before Vesna could say anything. "I'm sorry for everything."

Vesna felt as though her world had shattered into pieces. *"You?!"* She clenched her fists, anger covering her like a cold mist crawling through a forest before midnight. "So, everything is true? You *gave* him your magic?!"

"I'm sorry," Nadia whispered again, lowering her eyes.

"I might be a parasite, but I'm not a liar. Everything I told you before is true," Boris said, slowly coming closer to Vesna. "If you want her to live, you must find the fern flower for me. Then the Veiled Wilds will reveal themselves."

Vesna felt utterly defeated. She had always thought there was only one monster: Boris. But her mother wasn't the noble sacred one, as Vesna had always thought she was. Nadia had left her—for *him*.

Nadia stood soundlessly; she looked like a flower that had stopped blooming ages ago.

Vesna's jaw clenched tight. "What did you do to her?!" she demanded, shifting her gaze to Boris. There had to be a reason. Her mother would never betray the Divine Blooms. *My mother would never betray me.*

"I did nothing to her. As I told you at the ball, the sacred one gave me her magic willingly," Boris remarked flatly. "After I captured Nadia, she was glued to my side. First, she wouldn't even look at me. But slowly she saw things the way I did. She realized how unfair the Divine Blooms were to my flower. After that, we became lovers."

"Shut up!" Vesna snapped, her skin glowing, her eyes blinding everything around with such light that Boris and Nadia had to close their eyes.

Boris opened his eyes, his face twisting into a smug smile, as if he were enjoying torturing Vesna like this. "When we couldn't find the Veiled Wilds, I was starving. So, Nadia gave me her magic. The amount of power knocked me out. But when I woke up, she was gone. All these years, I have searched for her, believing she was still the sacred one … only to find out she's just a shadow of the flower that once bloomed the brightest."

Vesna bit her trembling lip, diving into Nadia's eyes, hoping beyond hope that it was all a lie. But Nadia only lowered her head, her silence louder than words.

"I *loved* you!" Vesna screamed. "I lived only to avenge you!"

Boris smirked. "You can still try. Maybe your destiny will differ from the destiny of your mother. But I doubt you can win on your own."

Maybe he was right. But Vesna wouldn't give up. She owed it to Mir.

All or nothing, she decided silently. If she found the fern flower, she would be able to perform a miracle: kill the immortal Boris. "Let's find the fern flower and finish you and your nasty flower once and for all!"

Boris just laughed. "Your daughter reminds me of you, Nadia, when I first met you."

Vesna's face twisted in pain. It was hard to see how close he was to her mother. Vesna was still in denial, trying to find some reasonable explanation. *Maybe she's planning something*, she thought, unable to admit that her mother had indeed chosen Boris over the Divine Blooms and over her own daughter.

More men barged in, lowering their heads before their boss, but secretly staring at Vesna. One of them held the sacred book and handed it to Boris.

"Take the bodies away!" Boris commanded.

His men moved immediately, carrying Ivan and the rest out of the room. One man grabbed Mir's lifeless body, and Vesna screamed, falling to her knees, unable to endure the pain that filled her heart.

"You will wither into oblivion, parasite!" she vowed through helpless tears.

"What a temper you have." Boris smirked, laying the book on the table. "Open it, or I will finish your mother, just as I did my poisonous friend."

The weight of loss hit Vesna again. She couldn't catch her breath, clutching her chest as tears streamed down her face. Mir was gone… He would never bloom for her again. *Still, I will bloom only for you, Mir…*

"Open it!" Boris screamed, his voice echoing through every corner of the room.

"I tried! I can't open it!" Vesna cried, shaking her head helplessly.

"It only opens for the sacred one. You weren't until you bloomed," Boris said knowingly.

I will make the rafflesia rot, Mir, she promised, still seeing Mir's lifeless face before her eyes.

Vesna moved to the table, looking like raw power that could bring destruction even to the eternal garden. Her long hair was tangled, her skin covered with pollen, her tattoo blooming, releasing enchanted magic into the air.

She put her hand next to the book, gently touching it with her long fingers. The petals on the book moved slowly, like a flower opening to the sunrise. Her magic streamed into the book, and the lock opened by itself with a loud click.

Vesna took a deep breath, feeling scared of what was waiting for her on Ivan Kupala Night. She carefully opened the book, and pollen of all colors poured out of it, mixing with her own magic. The room seemed to plunge into timeless space. No one made a sound or even breathed.

Vesna lifted the first page as carefully as she could. The paper looked ancient, and she was afraid she might tear it just by touching it. The next page was blank, but an image was appearing, as if someone were painting it with golden paint at this very moment. Vesna narrowed her eyes. The more details that appeared, the more familiar the place looked. The Veiled Wilds revealed themselves within minutes—and

Vesna recognized it. Her mother had painted this place! The picture was still hanging in her old house right above her table.

Frowning, she glanced at Nadia. *Did she know that it's the Veiled Wilds?*

"Let me see!" Boris stepped closer, pushing Vesna aside. His eyes sparkled with triumph. "The cursed lands," he announced.

Vesna had read about the cursed lands before—the land where magic was gone forever, stripping everything, even the earth, even the air, of life. Nothing grew there now, and fearing being cursed as well, people had abandoned the lands. Vesna couldn't help but wonder if the Divine Blooms had killed that place on purpose.

"Nadia, the Veiled Wilds are in the cursed lands! We finally did it!" Boris looked at Nadia, and for a moment, he seemed different.

Maybe he truly loved my mother at some point. Vesna couldn't help but wonder.

"It's a long journey; we should move right away to make it in time for Ivan Kupala Night. Time to feast on the Divine Blooms."

VESNA AND NADIA silently sat next to the gigantic rafflesia statue at Boris's building while he was getting ready to leave this fading city. Nadia soundlessly moved her hand, trying to touch Vesna's hair.

Vesna jerked away from her. "Don't."

"I wish you hadn't found out," Nadia muttered. "After all, your mother really died many years ago."

Tears welled in Vesna's eyes, and she tried to fight them back. "Did Boris tell the truth?"

"Parasites know how to take a piece of truth and twist it into the perfect lie," Nadia said.

Vesna held her breath, her eyes fixed on Nadia, clinging to a thread of hope.

"Time to go!" Boris yelled, hurrying down the stairs. "Don't even think about running, or Nadia is dead." He stared at Vesna.

"Divine magic would never run from someone so unworthy as a parasite," Vesna spat.

"You're just as ignorant as all the Divine Blooms." Boris smirked. "If the rafflesia flower had the divine magic too, not just roots to drain others, we wouldn't have to live like parasites."

"Glad you can justify all the death you've meted out," Vesna hissed through clenched teeth.

"You were born with privilege. You would never understand," Boris said, almost indifferently.

"You're right. I will never understand," she muttered, getting up.

The rafflesia left the building all at once. They stood waiting for Boris, a street filled with parasites. Vesna saw how they looked at Boris with devotion and respect. They had their own truth. Still, there was no truth that could justify killing innocent people.

Vesna understood that the cursed lands were far. There was still almost a week left before Ivan Kupala Night, but Boris was afraid they wouldn't make it on time.

They arrived at some port next to the forest. A wide, fast river flowed there. A few ships were already waiting for them.

Vesna sat on the ship's deck, watching endless forest melt into one green mass, listening to the calming song of the river. The sound lulled her, somehow bringing stillness into her broken heart. She was the chosen one. She had to believe she could find the fern flower and kill Boris.

The boat sailed silently along the river that had many offshoots and twisted constantly, and Vesna was surprised that Boris knew which turns to take. The sun was about to go down, coloring everything in a golden glow. It looked like Anna's magic. Tears fell silently down her cheeks. She missed her friends, but most of all, she grieved Mir.

Nadia approached her, soundlessly sitting next to her daughter. Vesna just glanced at her. She looked a little better than she had in the city. Maybe the fresh air did her good, or maybe being next to Boris gave her a reason to live.

"Is it okay if I sit with you?" she asked nervously.

Vesna didn't answer, holding her breath. She was both thirsting for the truth and afraid to hear it.

Nadia took a deep breath, looking into the distance. "I know you are disappointed in me, but this was my life and my story." She paused. "It was my choice to make."

"Maybe," Vesna said, looking at her point blank. "But your choice made this world a living hell!" She tried to fight the tears that came. "Remember Mir? Well, he's dead."

She couldn't hold back and started sobbing. She knew she would never accept his death. Now she was sure of only one thing: Boris would pay for everything.

Pain flashed across Nadia's face. "Let me tell you my story. After that, I promise to leave you in peace." She paused, but without waiting for Vesna's answer, spoke again. "When I realized I held the sacred magic, I was so grateful to the Divine Blooms for such a gift. I was a young woman who wanted to live life to the fullest. I met some guy who left me even before you were born. I knew immediately that you had the same magic as I did. Your cute baby eyes were so pink, so perfect. But then the rumors about the prophecy spread, and my life became hell. I had to hide all the time, fearing being captured at any moment. Fearing *you'd* be captured. So, I went to my sister, your aunt, asking her to take you away. The Divine Blooms had blessed me, and I had to stand up to the rafflesia.

"Long story short, after some time, Boris captured me. At first, I hated him. I decided I would rather die than find the fern flower for him. But the more time I spent with him, the more I saw how unfair the Divine Blooms have been to him and his people. He assured me he only wanted to find the Veiled Wilds so he could beg the Divine Blooms that reside there to grant the rafflesia flower its own magic. Obviously, he lied.

"I didn't forget you. I found my sister, telling her I was safe with Boris. Nina called me crazy, and she sent me away, telling me to never come back. By the time the night of Ivan Kupala approached, Boris and I were in love." She paused, and a sad smiled crossed her face. "At least, *I* was in love. But my magic wasn't enough, apparently. When I failed to find the fern flower, Boris was starving. We'd searched for so long, and he couldn't feed for all that time. So, I offered him my magic, trying to save the man I loved. He agreed. But once he tasted it, he couldn't stop. When he passed out from the power he now held, just a few sacred drops remained in me. But I aged immediately, with my magic mostly gone. So, I ran, deciding I'd try to make up at least a little for what I'd done."

"So, you became the herbalist," Vesna whispered, feeling hollow.

"Yes. I knew Boris possessed a rare map showing the distant lands where herbs still grew. And I stole it from him." She smirked. "I didn't go to see you. After all, I was a traitor, a whisper of a flower that had once bloomed." She paused. "But when you suddenly showed up in the city recently, I tried to help in every way I could. I went to Boris willingly, hoping to make him believe I was still the sacred one, to distract him."

Vesna fell silent again. She had grown up worshiping her mother almost like goddess, only to realize she was just human.

Vesna didn't say anything, just slowly reached out and touched Nadia's hand. The two of them sat in silence, staring at the horizon.

Chapter Twenty-Four

MIR.

MIR OPENED HIS EYES, LOOKING AT THE CEILING covered in roses. For a second, he thought he might be in the beautiful eternal garden of the afterlife. But soon he frowned, realizing the roses were just a mural.

Sitting up and looking around, he realized he was lying on the couch in Alex's apartment. He immediately examined his wounds, but his body looked and felt like new.

He remembered the strange feeling he'd had yesterday—the feeling that Vesna's magic was still in his veins after they'd blossomed together.

Vesna's magic must have saved me… he mused.

"He's awake!" Anna shouted, coming from the other room, and Mir's head rang.

"Mir!" Alex ran in too. He hugged his friend tightly.

"Where is Vesna?!" Mir asked, finally coming to his senses, and stood up abruptly.

"Boris took her," Alex said, and Mir's heart stopped.

He rushed to the window. It was night already. "Fuck," Mir cursed. He had been out for too long; Boris had probably fled already. Mir ran to the door. "Let's move!"

"Where are we going?" Alex asked, following his friend.

"I need to check if Vesna is still in the city," Mir explained on the go.

"They've already left. The book is also missing," Anna said with a worried look. "We hid, and then it was too late. Boris and every single one of his men left the building. It was empty when we entered and found you underground."

"Maybe they left some clues," Mir insisted.

They went to the rafflesia's building. As Anna said, it was empty—abandoned, even. As if in the matter of a few minutes, all the rafflesia had vanished from this world. Mir was breathing shallowly, thinking about the years of torture that he'd spent here. Still, his choice had led him to Vesna, and he wouldn't have it any other way. He would endure all of it all over again just to meet his wicked flower.

Mir walked around the entire building looking for any clues. "Nothing," he said, cracking his knuckles before striking the rafflesia statue and knocking it over in anger. It fell loudly, breaking into pieces.

Mir was silent, trying to think of how he could possibly find Vesna. Boris might think he had won, but there was still time before Ivan Kupala Night. The prophecy clearly referenced the magical fern flower. Without the flower, Boris couldn't find the Veiled Wilds.

Boris would not hurt Vesna until it's over. She's too important, Mir thought hopefully. Though the thought that Boris had drained the last sacred one made him growl. After all, Boris was a parasite, maybe not strong enough to resist feeding on sacred magic.

"What should we do?" Anna asked, silent until now, and Mir turned to face her.

He had never seen her like this, so magical, so different. Her eyes shone like gold under the midday sun, her citrusy aroma filling the room with warmth. *She probably has no more potions left,* Mir thought. *She doesn't need it anymore, anyway. It's the end of the tale.*

"We need to use your gift," Mir thought out loud.

She looked at him like he'd grown two heads. "You think I can dream something useful?" she asked.

"No. Enter Vesna's dream and ask her where Boris is taking her."

Anna stared at him, blinking in surprise. "I've never used my magic like that…"

"Your magic is powerful," Alex encouraged her, squeezing her hand. "You can do it. You should pray to the divine marigold, Anna."

Anna kneeled and plunged herself into golden pollen, silently praying. Then she lay down on the couch right in the hall, staring at Alex and Mir as they sat in chairs right next to her. She told them that the dreams were hard to remember, so she had to tell it to them as soon as she would wake up, which might be in the middle of the night.

"I guess good night, then…" Alex muttered, smiling sweetly at her.

"Hear my prayer, divine marigold," Anna whispered, closing her eyes, putting herself into a profound sleep using her magic.

"Sweet dreams," Alex said, and carefully adjusted the pillow.

Mir sat right next to Anna, without taking his eyes off her, hoping she would wake up soon with some news.

Alex giggled, and Mir stared at him in bewilderment.

"Sorry, but it's an awkward moment, watching Anna like this," Alex explained.

"Shut up." Mir rolled his eyes. "When it's over, ask her on a date finally."

Alex made coffee countless times, as he and Mir were trying to stay awake, hoping the divine marigold would speak to Anna.

"She's quite pretty," Alex whispered, watching Anna's face and touching her hair.

"You're a creep," Mir whispered back.

He didn't feel like talking. All his thoughts were with Vesna. He knew Boris needed her. Still, the idea of his wicked flower in the hands of that parasite made him growl.

"Are you turning into an animal?" Alex complained, having listened to his growls for quite some time. "She'll be fine." He paused. "She has to be."

"Anna is pale. Check if she's breathing." Mir tried to change the subject. Talking wouldn't help Vesna; they needed to act.

"Fine," Alex agreed, coming closer to Anna's lips, trying to feel her breath. At that moment, she suddenly opened her eyes, staring at Alex.

"Is this how you've imagined our first kiss?" Anna blurted out, clearly caught by surprise, pushing Alex away. "While I'm unconscious?"

Alex's cheeks burned as red as his rose. "I was checking if you were breathing!" he said defensively.

"A deep state of sleep makes your heart slow down, you creep," Anna said, sitting up on the couch.

Mir didn't even hear them, his heart racing in anticipation. "Did you see something useful?"

"Yes." Anna took a deep breath, telling them she'd seen Vesna.

Mir made a silent promise. *I will find you, wherever the wind carries you, my wicked flower.*

MIR was a little nervous about going to the place where Vesna grew up, and he was even more nervous about meeting her aunt. He didn't know what she thought about poisonous flowers and their magic. But he had to find the painting that Anna had talked about after her dream. Mir hoped it would help them find the Veiled Wilds. There was still time to find Vesna, and he was ready to do anything.

Rain pounded the car, and it was the perfect weather to match the mood that filled Mir's heart. *I should have protected her better…*

Mir glanced in the rearview mirror, looking at Alex, who was dozing in the back passenger seat. Anna was sleeping peacefully next to him, her head on his shoulder.

Alex opened his red eyes as if feeling Mir's gaze. "Are we there yet? I'm starving."

Mir rolled his eyes and looked back to the road. He couldn't help but be drawn to the veil of the sleeping forest. It was beautiful. It reminded him of Vesna. She was mysterious, but gentle, like this place.

"I'm hungry," Alex complained again.

"You already said that," Anna said, sitting up and looking around. "Their house should be around here somewhere, if I remember correctly… I'm sure her aunt Nina is still waiting for Vesna to return."

"While we're here, you can ask Nina's blessing for you and Vesna," Alex suggested.

"Shut up, Alex," Mir muttered.

"I think I see their house!" Anna said, straitening up and pointing her finger.

Alex squinted. "More like a hut."

Mir glanced in the direction Anna was pointing. He saw the flickering of flames in a tiny window and pulled over.

"Let's check it out, but be on guard," Mir whispered, getting out of the car quietly. "Boris could have sent his men here."

The closer Mir came to the hut, the more convinced he was that this was the right place. A familiar but barely noticeable scent entered his veins and brought his heart back to life. The place still smelled of his wicked flower, softly, but all-consuming.

The three of them approached the window without making a sound. An older woman sat by the fire, humming a song to herself.

"I know that song! Vesna sang it one night in the club," Alex whispered behind Mir's back.

"But let's make sure she's alone. It could be a trap," Mir said cautiously—without even realizing that Alex had already left.

Still looking through the window, Mir and Anna saw a small door open, and Alex stumbled into the room.

"Auntie!" he shouted, opening his arms for a hug.

Nina quickly stood up, clearly frightened.

"Idiot!" Mir shouted, unable to control himself.

Vesna's aunt turned her head to the window, peering into the darkness outside. Shock registered on her pale face.

Damn, so much for a good first impression, Mir cursed, coming to the door.

Anna followed him, not even trying to hold back her laughter. They entered, and Mir threw an angry look at Alex, who was still standing with his arms outstretched, waiting for a hug.

"Put your hands down," Mir said quietly through clenched teeth.

It took Nina a moment to come to her senses. She was staring at Mir, Alex, and Anna in turns. Everyone was silent, and Mir wanted to sink into the floor. He had never felt so lost and out of place.

"Are you of the datura flower?" Nina finally asked, looking into Mir's eyes.

"He is," Alex answered for Mir. "But don't worry, he's Vesna's boyfriend. She turned him from devil's trumpet into heaven's bell."

Mir looked at Alex, wanting to shut him up once and for all. "For your own sake, shut *up*," he hissed through clenched teeth.

A faint smile touched Nina's lips. "Well, you must be hungry," she said, inviting them to sit by the fire.

"Thank you," Mir said, meeting Nina's eyes. They were grey, ordinary human eyes. There was no magic in her. "I'm Mir. That annoying guy is…"

"I'm Alex, and I'm starving!" Alex interrupted, and Mir rolled his eyes, giving up.

Nina couldn't help but laugh. "Nice to meet you. I'm Nina. Let me bring you some soup." She disappeared into the tiny kitchen.

"Soup?" Alex whispered, grimacing.

"You will eat until the last spoonful," Mir whispered back in warning.

"I miss the city!" Alex cried out dramatically.

Mir looked around. This was the place where his wicked flower had grown up. It was small and isolated, but it felt like home. A variety of paintings covered the tiny house. Mir stood up, squinting at a painting of the divine datura.

"Vesna's mother loved to paint. She believed every flower is sacred," Nina muttered, returning with food. "Even the rafflesia." She put the soup on the table. "Please, eat."

"Thank you." Alex frowned, but catching Mir's threatening look, he quickly grabbed his spoon.

"Where is Vesna?" Nina asked timidly.

"It's a long story." Mir took a deep breath and told Nina everything, ending with the fact that Vesna's magic had somehow brought him back to life.

"So, it finally comes to the last bloom," Nina muttered, but her face suddenly seemed older, as if the news had made her age in a matter of minutes.

"Vesna talked about a painting when Anna entered her dream," Mir said, changing the subject. "It's very important." He stared at Nina hopefully.

"We have a lot of paintings," Nina said, looking around. "Which one?"

"Can I see Vesna's room?" Mir asked, his heart pounding. How was he to know which one? They were so close, yet still seemed so far from her. He was afraid they would never find the Veiled Wilds.

"This is her room." Nina pointed to a small door adorned with a flower pattern. "I haven't touched anything since Vesna left. I've been waiting for her to come back…" Her voice broke.

Mir walked into the room and just stood there for a few minutes. An open book was still lying on the bed.

Mir could clearly imagine Vesna sitting in that very spot, reading it.

He took a deep breath, trying to concentrate. He didn't have any time to waste. His gaze moved to the walls. They were covered in drawings, all of them flower-themed. Then his eyes landed on a small, depressing painting that was unlike the others. Rather than flowers, it was some grey ashy forest. It looked lifeless, but there was still some hidden magic emanating from it. Mir didn't recognize this place. He grabbed the painting from the wall and returned to the main room.

"This must be it. It's the only painting that shows a place, other than just flowers. But I have no idea where it could be," Mir said, unable to keep frustration and worry from his voice.

Nina and Anna stepped closer. Even Alex stopped eating, staring at the painting.

"This place looks forsaken," Anna muttered.

"Let me see." Alex took the painting into his hands. "I might know where this is," he said, surprising everyone.

"How do you know?!" Mir shouted. It was too important. He had to make sure Alex knew what he was talking about.

"Remember that girl I dated briefly—the one with the cute freckled face?" Alex said, rubbing the back of his neck. "Julia!"

"Seriously? You want to talk about girls right now?" Mir rolled his eyes helplessly.

"Actually, I do. Since she was a believer, she tried to drag me to visit this very place with her, and showed me this picture in a book," Alex said defensively. "These are the cursed lands, if I'm not mistaken."

Mir's eyes lit up. He had heard of the cursed lands;

he even vaguely knew where they were. Although it seemed strange that the Veiled Wilds would be in such a dark place. But Mir had no choice but to follow their only lead.

"I love the fact that you dated Julia!" Mir said enthusiastically, placing a hand on Alex's shoulder.

"All for a good cause," Alex said playfully, and quickly turned to Anna. "But I didn't like Julia that much."

Anna crossed her arms in front of herself. "What do I care?" she snorted.

"The cursed lands are far," Mir said seriously. "We need to leave right now."

He caught Nina's dim gaze. He wanted to promise her that they would return her niece, but Mir didn't like to make promises he wasn't sure he could keep. Of course, he would do everything possible—or impossible —to save Vesna.

Some patterns of fate are drawn without our control, he thought.

"May the Divine Blooms hear our prayers again," Nina whispered, forcing a smile.

As far as Mir remembered, the only way to get to the cursed lands was by water. "Where can we find a boat?"

"I hate boats. They make me sick," Alex immediately complained.

Nina, like the others, pretended not to even hear Alex. "Cross the forest to the east, then follow the current. The guy who lives there has a few boats. Or at least, he used to." Nina paused. "It's been a while since I left home."

"Thank you," Mir said, unsure of how to say goodbye.

But Nina walked up to him, and without warning, hugged him tightly. "She deserves love," she muttered.

They left immediately, but none of them knew the forest. After they wandered around for a few hours, Mir feared they were lost.

"I miss the city," Alex complained.

Mir smiled to himself. Alex liked to complain, but when it was something important, Mir knew Alex would always have his back.

"We get it: you're a city boy," Anna said. "Julia and the other girls are waiting!"

Mir noticed how Anna's eyes flickered with fury at Alex.

"Don't be jealous, Marigold," Alex sang, smiling.

Mir noticed that Anna and Alex were getting closer. *They'll be a good couple*, he thought, then halted.

"Listen! I think I hear water," Mir said, trying to figure out from which side the noise came.

They pursued the sound, and after a few minutes, they found themselves next to a vast river with a strong current.

"Okay, let's follow the river, like Nina said." Mir moved immediately, almost running.

They found the boats by the river less than an hour later. The owner was away.

"Alex, leave him some money," Mir said, already pushing a boat out into the water.

"What a noble thief you are." Alex smirked.

The current picked up their boat, and they quickly floated down the river. Although strong, the wind wasn't cold. Spring was already coming into its own.

Mir stared around. It was strange to suddenly find himself surrounded by nature. But it felt natural, like coming home.

Alex was shifting his gaze from one side to the other. "It's peaceful. I wonder what it looked like when flowers covered the Earth."

"Save that romantic talk for your next date," Mir teased, but his imagination was already picturing colorful trees with fresh flowers. Ultimately, Mir and every person with magic were part of this nature. They were fading blossoms that walked the Earth.

Chapter Twenty-Five

VESNA.

The journey dragged on like a vast meadow with no end. Vesna spent most of her time alone or with Nadia. They weren't close yet, but they were slowly getting to know each other after so many years apart.

Vesna was avoiding Boris, and especially his people. With each passing day, they gazed at her with a wilder, hungrier look.

She was now sitting at the prow of the ship, looking at the dim moon rising in the sky. Stiff wind played with her hair, bringing memories with its whisper. Her thoughts drifted to Mir, as they always did. He had thought of himself as nothing more than poison, but he had found a way to bloom with purity.

She closed her eyes, imagining his face before her, hoping that she would never forget even the smallest detail about him. Her magic swirled, strengthened by these thoughts, and the pollen left her body, permeating every crevice of the ship.

Time to sleep, Vesna thought, standing. But she froze immediately. Several men stood near her, their brown eyes full of hunger.

"Get away from me!" Vesna cried, her body tensing.

"Your magic is as sweet as flower nectar," one man said, licking his lips. "We only need a few drops."

"Get away from me!" she hissed again, quickly running toward the back of the ship.

They chased after her, like a pack of wolves after prey. Glancing over her shoulder with wide eyes, she caught her foot on some rope and fell sharply to the deck, hitting her face. Blood gushed from her nose.

She turned over quickly, her heart pounding wildly as they approached. She began to panic until she realized: Boris's people didn't have the same magic as he did. She could curse them, and it would work.

She opened her mouth to do just that.

"Stop!" Boris shouted, appearing in front of Vesna and shielding her. "How dare you?!" he yelled, glowering at his men.

The men turned to him, heads down. "Just a few drops… We're hungry," one of them dared to say.

"Idiot!" Boris snapped. But from the way his eyes gleamed at Vesna, she knew he desperately wanted to drain her himself.

She stood up, wiping the blood from her face. "Disgusting parasites," she spat, hoping they could feel her hatred for them in her gaze. The rest of the rafflesia had clearly heard the screams, because the deck was now filled with parasites, watching them.

"No one will touch her!" Boris said loudly for all to hear. His disgusting roots left his body and rushed toward the men who had dared to disobey him. They were dead in seconds.

"I will kill anyone who touches her!" he proclaimed.

MINUTES FLOWED INTO HOURS, then into days, and Vesna no longer knew how long they lasted. But one morning suddenly brought reality back. She looked out the tiny window in her cabin, and her heart sank at the sight before her. They were sailing through a forest that seemed to be made of ash. Everything was covered with some dark pollen; even the river was shrouded in this fog, which colored the water into nothingness. And the sound all around was fascinating and terrifying at the same time… The wind was whispering spells, warning everyone who dared to enter the cursed lands.

"Finally! The cursed lands!" Boris cried, bursting into her room.

She turned to look at him. His eyes were shining. She could see how long he had waited for this moment. *So have I,* Vesna thought, taking a deep breath.

"I'll take Nadia with us, just to make sure you don't do anything stupid," Boris said, tilting his head and locking eyes with Vesna knowingly.

They left the ship, and Vesna stepped carefully into the cursed lands. The rustling of the withered leaves above sounded like the muffled voices of damned souls. Ashy leaves covered the ground, creating a faint grey glow. Lost magic filled the air, making it hard to breathe. Vesna, with her sacred bloom, was like life itself that had stepped into the realm of death, illuminating everything with the promise of rebirth.

"No time to stand around." Boris nudged her. "Ivan Kupala is tonight. We need to find the right place. You will find the fern flower for me, sacred one. It's supposed to appear to you right at midnight."

"I will … but you'll regret it," Vesna promised, mostly to herself.

They went deeper into the forest, and with every

step, the cursed magic became thicker and thicker. Vesna was on guard, afraid that at any moment, something evil could attack them. But everything was relatively quiet, and closer to sunset, Boris stopped abruptly, touching his beard.

Vesna felt relieved; she could barely move her legs anymore. She looked around, trying to understand why Boris had chosen this place. A silent ash-black lake flowed lifelessly nearby.

"The Divine Blooms need water," Boris said, looking out at the lake, triumph and anticipation in his voice. "You will search for the fern flower here."

"Even I know it has to be done in private," Vesna muttered. She needed to be alone, to make sure she had time to figure out how to use the power of the mystical flower to kill Boris.

"Don't worry, sacred one." Boris grinned. "We will wait somewhere nearby. Once you have the fern flower, I will find you. The old text says that when the fern flower blooms, you can see it for many miles. Still, we'll make a fire, to make sure I can see where you are."

Nadia squeezed Vesna's hand silently. Vesna looked at her, and a needle pricked her soul. She felt heartbroken every time she thought about how Boris had used her mother.

"Get to work!" Boris commanded his men.

His men moved immediately. They gathered fallen tree branches and built the makings of a fire so gigantic, it would be taller than any tree in the cursed forest. Vesna didn't want to just to sit around and do nothing, so she picked up the withered leaves and wove them into a wreath.

The closer the night came, the stronger Vesna's heart pounded. Of course she was afraid, but she also felt excited that all this would finally come to an end one way or another. Even death didn't frighten her so much anymore. She'd felt death's touch when Mir poisoned her to hide her blooming, and it had been peaceful.

As the night approached, Boris lit the bonfire himself. It reached to the sky, illuminating everything around.

Nadia quickly approached Vesna. She hugged her, whispering into her ear, "I'm the flower that desperately wants to wither."

Vesna's eyes widened. The thought that her mother wanted to leave her, just after she'd found her, made her heart stop. But Nadia's old face shone with hope, and Vesna realized how broken and tired her mother truly was.

"Let's go," Boris said, pushing Nadia forward and signaling to his men. "We'll be close by, sacred one."

Alone, Vesna stared at the bonfire for a while, a dark wreath of ashy leaves on her head. It was a sad picture… Once, hundreds of people had celebrated Ivan Kupala. Now she was alone. Magic had faded away, after all.

The flames flickered in Vesna's eyes as she sat, quietly singing, waiting for midnight. She was thinking about the Divine Blooms, about Mir, and about her friends.

Raising her head to the moon, she realized midnight had finally come. She felt there was time to stretch, as if the hour would last for eternity. Then she stood up quickly, scanning her surroundings, hoping to see the mystical glow of the fern flower. But she saw nothing.

Her heart exploded with panic, and she ran, peering into the darkness, her own heartbeat echoing in her ears.

Please, appear, she begged silently, every inch of her being aching with hope.

Eventually, she froze, completely exhausted. She leaned helplessly against a tree near the lake.

Just then, she noticed a faint glow shimmering beneath the water, and she held her breath. She stepped closer, peering into the depths. She could have sworn that the lake was filled with dark petals. It looked cursed, or even poisoned. She dared to touch the water with her foot. To her surprise, it felt soft, velvety, like cream.

Vesna took a deep breath and slowly walked in. The dark petals enveloped her, as if creating a waxy barrier on her skin, like the petals of a magnolia flower. She felt the urge to surrender completely to this magic. She inhaled deeply and slipped beneath the surface.

The murmur of the current filled her ears, lulling her into a state where past and present merged into one endless moment. She reached for the glow that was calling to her. But as her fingers touched it, it vanished. It was just a mirage…

She emerged from the water, gasping, when she heard someone's deep breathing behind her. And then came the tart scent of almonds, lifting her soul higher than the most distant star in the moonlit sky.

Chapter Twenty-Six

MIR.

MIR HELD THOUGHTS OF VESNA IN HIS HEART throughout the journey down the river, and it was helping him not lose hope. He followed her like a believer would follow the Divine Blooms he worshiped. Mir was blooming, and the need to be with Vesna clouded his thoughts to the point of suffering.

I knew I was obsessed with her even before the blooming season came, Mir thought to himself, recalling every second he had spent with his wicked flower.

Mir couldn't help but think that he might encounter the divine datura if they got inside the Veiled Wilds. He still hated the fact that his poisonous magic had cursed his life from the start. And he was determined to destroy the divine datura, making sure no one would ever suffer like he did.

He stood now at the prow of their small boat, trying to make out something in the darkness, which was dispelled only by the dim light of the moon. He had lost track of time, but he knew that the night of Ivan Kupala was approaching. And they still hadn't found the cursed lands.

I can't let my wicked flower down, he thought helplessly.

"Dinner's ready!" Anna said, tearing Mir out of his thoughts.

"Dried fish again." Alex frowned.

Fish was their only food, because Mir didn't want to stop anywhere. He couldn't afford to waste a minute.

"It's not so bad," Anna said, trying to cheer Alex up.

"When we're back in the city, I'll take you to a fancy restaurant." Alex winked at her.

"I'll think about it," Anna teased, beaming. During this week of travel, the two of them had gotten closer than ever, and they were always next to each other. Mir hoped they would have a chance to become something more than just friends when this was all over.

They sat in the stern of the boat, eating in silence, looking out over the dark, still expanse of the river.

"We should be close," Alex said, his eyes lifting to the moon. "I think Ivan Kupala is tomorrow, or maybe even tonight."

"I pray every day, but it seems the divine marigold has gone silent on me," Anna murmured.

"We will be there on—"

The unnaturally strong wind that suddenly blew drowned out Mir's words. It gusted so hard that he could barely stand up. But that wasn't the strangest part. He also heard whispers that tried to squeeze into his mind. It reminded him of the hallucinations he inflicted on other people. Mir closed his eyes and shook his head, trying to fight this strange magic.

"Let's get inside!" he shouted to his friends.

With horror, he realized Alex and Anna were already moving toward the bow of the boat, as if reaching for the whisper of the wind. Mir immediately rushed toward them, trying to move as fast as possible against the wind.

"Divine Blooms!" Alex shouted, gazing dreamily at the water.

He's hallucinating, Mir thought with dread. Anna was probably seeing the same things, but she was moving slower than Alex.

Shielding his face from the gust of wind, Mir approached Anna and hugged her tightly.

"Let me go! We found the Divine Blooms!" she screamed, trying to break free from his embrace.

Holding her with one hand, Mir grabbed a rope that was fluttering in the wind. "This is a hallucination!" he screamed, and then he tied Anna to the mast. She struggled as if she had gone mad. But Mir had no time to bring her to her senses, watching in horror as Alex dove into the water and disappeared in the inky darkness.

Mir took a deep breath, gathering all his strength, and jumped overboard after his friend. The water was cold, and he was shaking, trying to find Alex. But it was so dark all around, and enormous waves from the gusting wind slapped Mir in the face. He could hardly see anything.

Suddenly, he noticed a red flash under the water, and his heart stopped.

"Alex," he muttered, swimming against the current as hard as he could.

He took a deep breath and dove under. Alex's body, his shining rose pollen pouring out uncontrollably, was sinking slowly to the bottom. Mir swam quickly after him, never taking his eyes off his friend.

When he emerged with Alex in his arms, the wind had died down, as if it had all been just his imagination. He spotted their boat in the distance and quickly swam toward it. Exhausted, he silently hoped that Alex was still alive. But the boat was quickly drifting with the current, moving farther and farther away from them.

He spotted Anna's figure with a lantern in her hands, and a seed of hope sprouted in his heart. Anna had probably come to her senses when the wind died down and somehow managed to untie herself. She dropped the anchor, and the boat stopped drifting. When Mir finally reached it, Anna helped him drag Alex aboard.

"Alex!" she screamed, seeing his pallid face.

"Anna, move," Mir said, kneeling over his friend. "He's not breathing," he whispered in horror, then quickly laid Alex on his side. Water poured out of his mouth. Mir checked his breathing again before pressing hard on his chest. *Not you,* Mir thought. Anna cried silently as she watched Mir fight for Alex's life.

Just when Mir thought he had lost his friend forever, Alex jerked and sputtered, more water spilling out of his mouth.

"Alex!" Kneeling next to him, Anna hugged Alex as tightly as she could.

THE THREE OF them lay on the deck, almost in one another's arms, trying to keep warm. Their gaze was fixed on the sky as the stars appeared one by one.

"I love your magic," Alex muttered, turning to Mir.

"Don't be silly," Mir said, frowning. But thoughts of the few times he'd used his magic for something good crept into his mind. He had numbed Vesna's wound and hidden her bloom, and now he'd saved Alex and Anna.

"I'm serious. We only survived because that crazy hallucination wind didn't affect you," Alex insisted.

"It's probably a trap the Divine Blooms set to keep people from reaching the cursed lands. Which means we're close."

"Do you think Boris fell into it?" Anna asked hopefully.

"Maybe not," Mir said thoughtfully. "The river has many branches and turns. Who knows which route Boris took?"

"I thought you were gone," Anna said, hugging Alex tightly.

"Not until I take you out on an actual date, Marigold," he said, smiling tenderly.

Suddenly, Mir smelled burning wood. He sat up quickly and noticed a fire in the distance. It seemed to reach to the sky. Mir's magic rose, swirling inside. There was still a chance to find Vesna.

The wind was barely blowing now, and it would take some time for the boat to reach the shore. "See you there," Mir said. He immediately stood up and dove into the water, swimming to shore like his life depended on it.

When he entered the cursed lands, a shudder ran through him. It seemed like his magic was trapped under the dark air of this place. But he didn't care, sprinting toward the fire like a madman. Soon he found himself next to an enchanted dark lake. Something was glowing in the water like a lost treasure.

"My wicked flower!" Mir whispered.

Vesna emerged from the water without noticing Mir. His gaze slid over her pink hair, decorated with a withered wreath. She looked like an ancient flower that had blossomed on a magical night to bring wonders to the world. She stood still, and he saw her shoulders rise and fall as she took a deep breath and turned around. Her eyes sparkled in the night like a moonflower under the stars. Another second, and they moved toward each other, as if they saw nothing around them. Mir entered the water and swam quickly toward her.

"Mir!" she whispered in disbelief, falling into his arms.

Her lips burned him with heat, and he kissed her hungrily, pulling them both under the water, still kissing her. The lake enveloped them like a liquid veil. The current rushed over their bodies, washing away all their troubles. When they emerged from the water, they gasped, as if it were the first breath of their lives. Streams of water flowed down Vesna's hair and her delicate face. Mir hugged her tighter and carried her to the riverbank.

"You're alive! You're my home, Mir," Vesna whispered, her eyes welling with silent tears.

He looked into her eyes, and something shifted in his heart. He realized he wanted to truly live, free from the weight that had poisoned his soul for so long. He no longer wanted to destroy the divine datura. Because of Vesna, he finally understood that his magic had a place in the world. His wicked flower didn't mind his poisonous bloom, and he was willing to live his life blooming only for her.

"I want to help the gods bring the magic back," he whispered.

Vesna stared at him in silent shock. "But the divine datura…"

"My magic was a curse," he murmured, "and you lifted it."

Chapter Twenty-Seven

VESNA.

Vesna didn't question how Mir was still alive. She just felt eternally grateful to the Divine Blooms who had brought him back to her.

Suddenly, she sensed a shift in reality. The cursed veil that covered this forest fell, and a stream of unknown magic hovered in the air. Near the lake, a glittering red light caught her eye. She held her breath, afraid she was mistaken. But it wasn't a mistake; the prophecy was coming to life.

Holding hands, they walked toward the mystical flower. Red sparks played on their faces as they slowly approached the rarest bloom in this fading world.

The fern flower blooms only for a fleeting moment, Vesna thought, afraid it might disappear as suddenly as it had appeared.

A tiny flower, red as the most precious ruby, radiated eternal light. It looked mesmerizing and unreal. She leaned down and dared to touch it with one finger. She cried out and jerked away as it burned her hand. Steeling herself, she tried again, but this time the fern flower scorched her skin even more.

She frowned. It was clear that the fern flower didn't want her. She didn't understand why it had revealed itself to her in the first place.

Her gaze drifted slowly to Mir, and then the realization hit her. She wasn't pure; *he* was.

"Mir," she whispered. "Pick the flower."

His brows shot up. "What?"

"You're the pure one."

Mir shook his head, and she noticed that his chest had stilled. "Me…?" he muttered.

Hesitantly, he reached for the fern flower—and picked it, unharmed. He closed his eyes, as if afraid that when he opened them, all the magic might be gone.

But Vesna smiled as she looked at him. The flower began to glow, shining with every color of the rainbow, filled with the magic of every Divine Bloom that had ever existed.

"Take it," he said, carefully handing her the fern flower.

"You did it," she whispered, gazing at him with admiration as she gently took the flower from his hands.

The silence of the moment was broken by distant voices, harsh as reality.

Vesna felt her magic ice through her veins. The moment she had been waiting for had finally come. "Boris is coming," she said, taking a deep breath.

Boris bolted toward the colorful glow. "The fern flower is real!" he muttered, staring at the bloom in Vesna's hand. Only after a few moments did his gaze shift to Mir, and Boris's mouth twisted into a false smile. "Well, well. Poisonous flowers are always the most tenacious."

"I finally have something to live for," Mir said through clenched teeth.

Nadia stood behind Boris, surrounded by his men. "You found it, Vesna! You are worthy, unlike me," she muttered.

"No time for sorrow," Boris cut her off. "Where are the Veiled Wilds?!" He spun around, frantic, waiting for the mystical realm to appear.

The time has come, the thought raced through Vesna's mind. She raised her hand, holding the fern flower high, and whispered a spell. Her pollen filled the air in an instant.

"I curse you to death!" she screamed.

Boris just laughed, standing before her untouched. "What a stubborn flower," he hissed.

Vesna didn't have a moment to react or even think. A strange pull stirred her chest as light suddenly burst from the fern flower, illuminating the dark forest with its magical glow. A stream of shimmering petals unfurled into the air, rushing ahead toward a hidden realm.

Breath caught in Vesna's throat. She hadn't killed Boris, but there was still hope. Maybe the Divine Blooms would finally intervene.

Boris broke the silence. "Move!"

Vesna stepped forward, following the trail of petals. Magic flowed through the air, slipping into her heart. They hadn't walked far when towering doors made from millions of living flowers suddenly appeared right in front of them.

The Veiled Wilds!

Slowly, Vesna approached, raising the fern flower toward the door. Streams of magic surged through the petals, and they shook, awakening from a long sleep, releasing ancient magic into the air. She felt the pull again, and the fern flower burst from her hands, taking its place among the other flowers that were guarding the hidden realm.

Then, with a thunderous creak, the doors began to open on their own, revealing the mystical realm beyond where the Divine Blooms resided.

It was pure magic. Everything around was blooming, captivating their eyes with the glow of blossoming reality. Vesna had never known that there could be so many different flowers in the world. And the fragrance in the air… It was the rarest mixture that could ever cover the earth. A breeze played with the infinite petals, humming a peaceful melody. Rivers filled with myriad flowers flowed everywhere, as if each Divine Bloom had its own river and role in the Veiled Wilds.

Vesna noticed a giant tree in the middle of the meadow. "The sacred magnolia," she whispered, tears welling up in her eyes.

The tree reached for the sky, as if connecting different realities. It bloomed eternally, and magic flowed from each petal, mixing in the air with the magic of other Divine Blooms.

No one moved. Even Boris seemed to have forgotten why he came here, looking around, enchanted.

Just then, Alex and Anna appeared out of nowhere and ran inside, attracting everyone's attention. Their arrival seemed to snap Boris back to reality.

"Kill them!" Boris shouted to his men.

They immediately released their roots, which surged toward Alex and Anna.

Red pollen, full of sharp rose thorns, immediately surrounded the rafflesia, cutting their roots out as Alex whispered a spell. Anna also acted quickly, trying to put as many of the men to sleep as possible.

Boris hissed as he watched his men fall to the ground

one by one. With a frustrated roar, he released a parasitic root that reached out and stopped right at Nadia's heart. "Don't you dare try to stop me!" he warned Vesna, moving closer to the divine magnolia tree and dragging Nadia with him.

Nadia's eyes didn't show horror, or even disappointment.

She's just a flower that wants to be laid to rest in the eternal garden, Vesna thought. Still, she wasn't ready to sacrifice her mother like this.

"Time to take your power back, Divine Blooms!" Vesna shouted, hoping that her gods would intervene. But nothing happened—not a single leaf fell at the sound of her voice.

Her heart shattered into pieces. She had failed. Boris didn't die, and now he would only grow more powerful, with enough magic to feed the vile flower hidden beneath his building for eternity.

"The game is over," Boris said, reaching the flowering magnolia tree and sending out a hundred roots that attached themselves to it.

Vesna watched in horror as this horrible parasite fed on the world's first divine flower, at a loss for what to do.

She hadn't even noticed when Mir disappeared. Without warning, he jumped out from behind the tree, cutting off the root threatening Nadia's heart.

"Vesna, empower me!" Anna screamed, snapping her out of her stupor.

Boris looked at Anna with furious hatred and shot one of his roots at her heart before Vesna could even blink. She didn't have time to react; none of them did. Her friend's beautiful, freckled face instantly lost all color, and her hair turned white.

"Anna!" Vesna screamed so loudly that the Veiled

Wilds shuddered. "No! Anna!" She ran to her friend as quickly as possible. "You can't leave me! I love you," she managed to say, choking on tears.

Anna didn't have the strength to say anything. She only smiled, as sweetly as always. And she illuminated everything around her with her golden magic one last time before her eyes closed forever.

Vesna screamed, her voice filled with the pain that had taken hold of her heart. "I will *kill* you! Even if you're immortal—even if I must die along with you!" she swore, turning on Boris with eyes full of fire.

Her magic left her body in a rush, rising like a tsunami in the sea.

Alex roared, his eyes red not from magic, but from tears. He and Mir ran to Vesna and stood on either side of her. Vesna wasn't the only one who was ready to fight to the death. Pollen infused with rose and datura thorns filled the air, amplified by the magic of the sacred magnolia. A beautiful and deadly cloud rushed toward Boris. He looked at the approaching magic with fear, but still didn't move, draining the power of the divine magnolia tree. After all, he was a parasite to his core, drunk on the sacred magic, unable to stop.

As the deadly storm approached Boris, cutting through his roots, slicing through his skin, he still did nothing, reveling in the magic that filled his veins. Vesna, Mir, and Alex ran toward him, closing in on Boris. More and more of his parasitic roots were cut away, and fear twisted his face.

All the muscles in Boris's body tensed as he screamed, and a few giant thick roots, empowered by the magic he was drinking, rushed toward Vesna, entering her body in a split second.

The pain struck instantly as the roots reached

straight for her heart. She struggled to breathe, but choked on blood surging up her throat, falling to her knees before collapsing entirely. She screamed internally, gasping for air.

Silence followed, with a gentle voice that stirred the air. *"You've tried,"* the voice murmured.

The divine magnolia had finally spoken to Vesna, but it was too late. Her glow flickered before fading completely.

She heard screams as Mir kneeled beside her, scooping her up in his strong arms. "Vesna, don't leave me!" he begged. "Please!"

Vesna smiled, Mir's magic wrapping around her, numbing the pain. "I love you, Mir." She paused. "Let me dive into your peaceful eyes as I wither."

"No!" Mir pleaded, not even trying to stop his tears. Vesna saw him as if in slow motion. Taking a deep breath, he plunged himself into his magical pollen and looked up at the sky. "I pray to the divine datura that blessed me with its magic. You bring death, but now I ask you to bring life!"

The air suddenly rustled, and lightning lit up the sky. The almond scent of poisonous datura enveloped the Veiled Wilds.

"Only a pure heart can perform a miracle." The low voice seemed to come from everywhere.

Divine datura. The thought flashed through Vesna's head as she closed her eyes powerlessly.

When she was sure she was taking her last breath, it suddenly became cold, and she shivered. Her body went numb, and she froze, suffocating, unable to do anything, not even breathe. This wasn't a peaceful death; it was torture. Hallucinations followed, and she saw a million snow-white datura petals falling on her, burying her alive. She sank into a deathly silence; even Mir's cries were muffled.

The next moment, she took a deep breath that was louder than the thunder. Her magic quickly returned to her body, soaking into her veins from the million petals that covered her.

"Thank you!" Mir whispered, clearly not believing his own eyes.

Vesna didn't look at him, because her attention was caught by a single glowing petal that slowly flew straight to her from the entrance of the Veiled Wilds. The petal was whispering spells of ancient power, landing right in her palm.

A petal from a fern flower, Vesna thought hopefully. It melted into her skin, silently singing a long-forgotten spell to her.

Suddenly, she felt endless, and new magic coursed through her veins. It felt like power unbound by any rules.

She shifted her gaze to Boris, whose roots were still entwined around the magnolia tree. But when their gazes met, fear filled his face.

She didn't wait, sending her pollen toward him that very moment. It covered his entire body, seeping into his skin, as deep as his very heart. "Be locked here forever, unable to drain others for the rest of eternity," she commanded, meaning every word.

"Stupid girl!" Boris hissed. "You're even more stupid than your mother…"

But he couldn't finish the sentence; in a matter of seconds, all his roots had fallen off the sacred magnolia tree. Boris screamed, clawing at his skin. Flower petals grew all over him at an incredible speed, covering his face, his neck, and spreading downwards. The flowers were burying him alive.

Nadia looked at Vesna and smiled softly, her eyes turning pink, just as Vesna remembered them from childhood. A moment later, Nadia ran up to Boris, hugging him tightly. "Take me with you," she whispered —and the flowers began to spread across her body, infecting her too. "This is the perfect ending," she murmured, looking at Vesna one last time.

When flowers had covered their bodies completely, a wind blew, tearing off petals and scattering them in the air. A small flower with white waxy petals and brown dots grew from the ground, right on the spot where Boris and Nadia had stood a few moments ago.

"Your wish has been granted, Mother," Vesna whispered, hoping her mother had finally found peace.

She took a deep breath, afraid to look back. Anna's lifeless body lay on the ground. Alex sat next to her, crying soundlessly. Vesna slowly moved closer, pale as death. She took Anna's cold hand and cried out, unable to endure the pain that squeezed her heart. Her screams broke the eternal peaceful silence of the Veiled Wilds.

Vesna fell to her knees, looking at Anna's withered face. Happy memories with her sunny friend flashed before her eyes. She saw Anna's playful, warm smile when she had come to Vesna's isolated home and changed her destiny forever. She saw Anna's sparkling eyes that day when they lay on the bed and laughed, as if there were no problems in their fading reality. Anna had come into her life as a sacred light, illuminating Vesna's path and walking it with her. And Vesna knew that she would never have succeeded without her gracious friend.

But now Anna's light had left her. She was a dead flower.

Overcome with regret and sadness, Vesna took Anna's cold hand and released her pollen, enveloping Anna's body. "Bloom here forever under the everlasting sun, my friend." She whispered a spell, barely audible, choking on tears, hoping Anna's spirit could hear her.

Anna's body began to bloom, reaching the earth, sprouting and returning to life as an eternal flower. A meadow of marigolds, bright and elusive, like Anna, now bloomed where her body had just been…

"She'll like it here," Alex whispered.

Epilogue

Vesna walked soundlessly toward the gates, with Mir and Alex following close behind. As they stepped out of the Veiled Wilds, Vesna paused and turned around.

The flowered gates remained open, streams of petals drifting out and flowing into the world, whispering blessings—until the gates slowly began to fade. Vesna smiled and breathed in deeply. The air no longer smelled lifeless; it was full of magic.

As they crossed the cursed lands, the wind stirred the ashy leaves, sweeping them from the ground and the trees. Vesna stopped when she noticed a small flower sprouting beside her foot. She knew the world wouldn't bloom overnight, but magic was seeping back into nature, gently preparing it for a new flowering season.

She took another deep breath just as a stream of marigold petals fluttered past. Her eyes shimmered with tears, and she looked at Alex and Mir. Their gazes followed the petals until they vanished into the air.

"I think my club needs an upgrade," Alex said,

glancing at Vesna. "How about a new name: Marigold Garden?"

Vesna smiled, a soft warmth glowing in her eyes. "It's perfect."

"Picture it—marigold skies for the ceiling, a menu written on golden…" Alex rambled on, and Vesna let his voice fade into the background.

She was still smiling, thinking of Anna. Her friend had never gotten the chance to see the distant lands where the sun burned bright above the flowering meadows, as she'd always dreamed. So, Vesna would go for her. And maybe, just maybe, Anna's spirit would have a vivid dream and see them too.

About the Author

Anastasiya Serada is an indie author of immersive fantasy romance, weaving stories filled with magic, desire, and eternal devotion. This is Anastasiya's second published novel.

For more information, please visit:

www.anastasiyaserada.com

instagram.com/authoranastasiyaserada